TANK

VALLEY OF THE WOLVES

By

Rob Burnett

ISBN-13: 978-1523377725
ISBN-10: 1523377720

In loving memory of Mum.
Georgina, a woman of courage.

CONTENTS

CHAPTER 1 1
CHAPTER 2 14
CHAPTER 3 27
CHAPTER 4 37
CHAPTER 5 51
CHAPTER 6 66
CHAPTER 7 81
CHAPTER 8 92
CHAPTER 9 114
CHAPTER 10 124
CHAPTER 11 140
CHAPTER 12 154
CHAPTER 13 168
CHAPTER 14 206
CHAPTER 15 220
CHAPTER 16 225
CHAPTER 17 235
CHAPTER 18 242
CHAPTER 19 250
CHAPTER 20 261
CHAPTER 21 269

Personal note from the author

I believe the wolf to be a beautiful and intelligent animal, contrary to the historic view held in folklore, of an evil manhunter. The wolf is a highly social animal destined to survive in very harsh environments, where it hunts to feed itself and its family. It has a big part to play in the delicate balance of the natural world. I believe passionately in the restoration of this balance, by the reintroduction of the wolf to former territories when possible.

Inspired by 'Watership Down', I have written an adventure with wolves as the main characters, set in the wild wood which covered Britain after the last ice age.

I am a member of the UK Wolf Conservation Trust (working to keep wolves in the wild).

CHAPTER 1

The wolf pack loped along the trail at an easy pace. It had patiently followed Leaf who had tracked the elk skilfully. Excitement gripped the younger wolves as the scent of their quarry grew stronger. Several youngsters dashed past Leaf in their haste to make the kill. Swift, a more experienced wolf, watched from the rear of the pack with growing alarm. He shook his head in frustration at the inclusion of mere cubs in the hunting pack. The elk was a bull with an injured hind leg and needed to be treated with caution.

Around the next bend in the trail the pack stopped abruptly. The elk was ready to take them on. It faced them, head lowered, displaying its huge antlers menacingly. Steam rose from its glistening, sweat-soaked hide and the pack smelt its fear. It wasn't decrepit or riddled with disease but in its prime, making it dangerous quarry. The pack hung back, barking their triumph at having cornered the animal but unsure of what to do next.

Swift moved up next to Leaf. "This is madness, Leaf, we should let it go."

"I know, somebody's going to get hurt."

Thorn, acting alpha wolf, in charge of the hunting

pack, pushed his way through. "What are you waiting for? Lost our nerve have we? Root! Stag! Who wants first blood?"

Root, a yearling, emerged from the pack. He glanced at Swift but ignored the silent plea in his eyes. The craving for glory had blinded him to everything but the elk. He broke from the pack and charged towards the cornered animal. The elk's eyes rolled in terror as Root leapt at its snout. Instinctively it pulled its head back out of range and kicked out with its forelegs. Root took the full force of the kick on his temple and the crack of bone was audible as he spun in the air on impact with the elk's hoof. The pack was silent, open-mouthed, as though it too had been struck. Root lay still on the track.

The elk was momentarily frozen with surprise. Then it saw its advantage. Temporarily ignoring its injured leg, it powered towards the shocked wolves in a daring attempt to save itself. This rapidly restored the pack's presence of mind and wolves scattered in all directions, opening up the escape route the elk had been looking for. No one gave chase. Swift ran to where Root lay but saw instantly there was nothing he could do. Root's blood flowed freely from a jagged gash to form a crimson pool on the frost-hardened earth.

Swift turned to confront Thorn, his voice trembling with emotion. "He was only a cub and you killed him."

"He was doing his duty," Thorn answered coldly.

Swift drew back his lips in a snarl, exposing long canines, his tail erect and ears pitched forward aggressively. Thorn matched his stance and growled threateningly. Swift had never faced another wolf in real combat and suddenly he was afraid. He braced himself, expecting an attack but instead Thorn turned away.

"I'll deal with you later," he snarled, "we've an elk to catch."

By threatening and cajoling he managed to regroup the pack and push them into a half-hearted attempt to catch up with the elk, but Swift would not leave Root. He could not believe the young wolf was dead. He reached out and stroked Root's muzzle with his paw, anger raging inside him. How would he tell Fallow? Only that morning she had spoken of her fears for her cub. Since his initiation into the wolfrahm he had changed, she'd said. Swift had witnessed the changes but without surprise. Young wolves had been systematically introduced into the alpha wolf's body-guard and indoctrinated with Talon's radical philosophies over a period of several years. He'd seen similar results before. Previously well-balanced cubs had become arrogant and brutal.

Leaf returned from the chase and sat down next to him. "He gave us the slip," he said.

"Good, he didn't deserve to die any more than Root did. The elk fought well for his life, Root didn't stand a chance."

"It's a tragedy, should never have happened," said Leaf.

"He was no more than a cub. Thorn should have known better."

"He'll say he was only following orders to provide

venison for the wolfrahm."

"That doesn't give him the right to do this." Swift stroked Root again. "You'd better go before Thorn comes back," he said.

"What about you?"

"I'm staying with Root. They can do what they like."

"That's what I'm afraid of. You put the wind up Thorn today, he won't thank you for that. Anyway someone's got to tell Fallow."

"I will tell her, but I can't just leave him."

Swift sat beside Root's body in bewilderment. Yesterday's sunshine had promised so much; all around new leaves were unfolding from bulging buds and the first spring flowers graced the forest floor in pools of colour. From where he sat beneath the oaks he could see the vivid gold of celandine growing on the margins of the elk trail and above them the snowflake blossom of the blackthorn and the yellow stripes of hazel catkins. He looked down at Root's body in disbelief. His young life had been snatched away in one moment of folly.

The warmth and the light faded and a cool breeze ruffled the silver-grey fur of his mane, chilling him despite his dense winter coat. He licked Root's muzzle tenderly then reluctantly left him to the carrion eaters. He knew it had to be, it was nature's law that nothing be wasted. Root's soul had gone to the heavens but his body was of the earth and must be consumed to live again.

He made the journey back to Tannon Valley

dreading his meeting with Fallow. Someone may have already told her, he thought, and deep down that is what he hoped for. He hurried on, oblivious to the forest around him. He searched for the right words to say but there were none.

When he reached her den it was getting late but the moon had not yet risen and he could barely see the track in front of him. The oaks and the ash that dominated the forest were now but dark, lifeless shapes offering him no solace, and the shrubs along the path seemed to close in on him menacingly. The den was dug in a sandy bank. Its entrance, a round hole two feet across, lay beneath the jutting, moss-covered roots of an oak tree. He hesitated for a moment then called her name. She emerged immediately, the light grey fur of her head and ears speckled with earth where she had hurried through the den's entrance tunnel. Her eyes, wide with expectancy, appeared large in the fine features of her face.

"Swift, what are you doing here? Where's Root?" Swift had rehearsed some words but none came. "Something has happened to Root," Fallow said, the pitch of her voice rising.

"Fallow I'm sorry, there's been an accident. It was on the hunt. Root..."

"No, don't say it."

"He was very brave. He..."

Swift broke off. Fallow had turned away, muttering to herself. She disappeared into the den. Her reaction told him she had already sensed what had happened. He didn't want to say any more, afraid he'd make things worse. He lay down at the entrance to the den, aware of his ineptitude but wanting to be there if she needed him. The moon rose, casting a silver light across the forest, and Swift was glad of its company. The wolf is not by nature a solitary creature and the darkness left him no distractions. He saw Root's body lying cold and stiff on the frozen ground attended by the wolverine and the buzzard.

He mourned the loss of a young wolf who had been denied the chance to enjoy a second summer and felt guilty because he had not taken the opportunity to get to know him better. Above all he felt helpless. It was too late for Root, whatever was said or done. But this did nothing to diffuse his anger. Thorn must be held responsible for Root's death and exiled from the pack. He would appeal to Talon for what it was worth. During the past four seasons the alpha wolf had tightened his control in the valley as game dwindled, increasing the pressure on the pack to make every hunt successful.

He heard sobs of anguish that seemed to emanate from the earth itself, Fallow had given in to the truth. This time he didn't hesitate. He squeezed through the entrance tunnel into the main chamber of the den. At first he did not speak but pressed his body against hers where she lay on the earth. She was cold like stone in the shade and her sobbing pierced his heart but it had to be, to help shed the burden of grief.

He put his mouth to her ear. "It's alright, it's alright," he whispered. It never would be, he knew, but he had to say something. Eventually her crying subsided until the den was silent. They lay together for what seemed an eternity, Swift feeling awkward, impotent.

Then she spoke. "Tell me he didn't suffer."

"He didn't suffer, it happened..."

"No, that's enough for now. Please stay with me, I couldn't bear to be alone tonight."

"I'll stay for as long as you need me," he said.

He could feel the rise and fall of her chest against his body as she took in deep breaths to calm herself and suddenly he was exhausted. When sleep eventually came it didn't bring the release he'd hoped for, instead he became ensnared in hideous nightmares replaying Root's death. In the morning he woke with a jolt and the recollection of Root's death came back to him like a cloud passing across the sun.

He reached out for Fallow but she was not there. Alarmed, he hurried out of the den. In the half-light he searched the shadows, calling her name, but she was nowhere to be seen. He guessed she had gone to Mistle for comfort. Mistle, his mother, had listened to Fallow's fears for Root many times. He set out at a run for home. The night-time shadows dissolved with the sun's rays which lit the forest as the sun rose. Songbirds sang their medley of songs but this morning Swift wished they were silent.

He recalled the previous morning. He'd been enthralled with the forest's revival after a bitter winter, listening with joy to the blackbird that had sung in the honeysuckle bush close to his den. He'd looked ahead to the warmth of the summer months but today his thoughts were with Root and Fallow. He went south towards the river on one of the wolf trails that criss-crossed the wooded valley. Here the valley was a mixture of broad-leafed trees, mainly ash, birch, hazel, and oak. Everywhere showed signs of the forest's degeneration. Beneath the trees, the forest floor, once grazed by the elk, the red deer, the roe, and the bison was being eaten up by the creeping invasion of bramble and ivy. The open spaces were shrinking, as saplings, a delicacy of the once plentiful herbivores thrived in the gathering undergrowth. He was surprised to see Leaf. The small, tan wolf was not usually up this early.

"Swift I've been looking for you. Fallow came to see me first thing this morning to find out where Root is."

"Did you tell her?"

"Yes, she has a right to know."

"I thought it better she didn't see him like that."

"I'm told it can help."

"I'm going to find her. Would you let Mistle know what's happened? She'll be worried."

He found Fallow lying close to Root. She heard him coming and looked up. He'd never before thought of grief as physical pain but he could see pain clearly now in Fallow's eyes.

He put his paw on her shoulder. "I wish you hadn't seen him like this."

"I had to see him," she said.

"Come back with me to Mistle, stay with us for a while."

She nodded and got up wearily. She looked at her cub for the last time, her voice was a whisper. "He died for nothing and he won't be the last."

They walked in silence, tails down. Swift wanted to talk, to unravel his emotions. He decided to visit Hawthorn the wisewolf. Hawthorn was a pack elder learned in the ancient wolflore that was passed down by word of mouth from generation to generation. As a cub Swift had spent many happy hours with him listening to stories of the old days, and a bond of friendship had formed between them.

Swift left Fallow in Mistle's care and started out for Hawthorn's den. He trotted south to where the River Tannon intersected the trail that led to the Beech Wood. Here where the Tannon was shallow the wolfrahm crossed to the alpha wolf's lair in the Beech Wood. Although the water was never low enough to cross by wading, this spot was known as the ford. He did not cross but took the path eastward along the riverbank.

It was warm and he was thirsty. He stopped for a drink, taking only a cursory glance at a pair of mallards nest-building on the opposite bank. Another day he would have watched their comings and goings with interest, today he went on his way. The river path meandered between the alders that dominated the river margins. Occasionally it passed under the drooping branches of a willow overhanging the riverbank. He followed the path for a quarter of a mile or so, passing several other wolves out enjoying a morning forage, then turned off towards the badger setts where Hawthorn lived in an abandoned sett dug out to suit a wolf's proportions. The setts had been excavated beneath the protective cover of holly bushes, situated at the top of a sandy rise beneath a stand of beech trees.

Swift glanced up the slope. About two thirds of the way up he saw a movement. Instinctively he crouched down behind a clump of holly saplings. A wolf was sitting beneath a holly bush close to Hawthorn's den. At first he couldn't distinguish who it was. He crept closer and at the very moment he recognised the pale features of Thorn a twig snapped under his paw. Thorn swung round and peered down the slope, his amber eyes flitting back and forth searching for the source of the sound. Swift held his breath for what seemed an age and could not believe his good fortune when Thorn eventually turned away to resume his watch on the badger setts. Swift backtracked to the river and took a path that brought him undetected to an entrance to the rear of Hawthorn's den. Keeping his voice low, he called Hawthorn. The old wolf emerged from the entrance tunnel looking agitated. He had aged since Swift's last visit; the natural grey fur of his face was heavily flecked with white and the fur of his back and haunches had become patchier.

"Come in quickly," he said.

Swift squeezed along the narrow tunnel leading to the main chamber of the den.

Hawthorn smiled. "It's good to see you my friend."

"It's good to see you Hawthorn. I see you've got another friend keeping an eye on you."

"He's there again, is he? He didn't see you?"

"I saw him first and skirted round the back way."

Hawthorn sat down. "That's a relief."

"What's been happening?"

"It's a long story. I have something they want."

"What do you mean?"

"All in good time, cub," he said. "You haven't told me what brings you here." Swift explained what had happened to Root but Hawthorn's reaction was not what he'd expected. "Hunting accidents do happen. Root was unlucky not to be able to learn from his mistake."

Swift let his anger spill out. "It was no accident. Thorn goaded Root into an attack. He should never have been chasing elk, let alone taking first blood. Thorn was desperate to catch an elk to satisfy Talon and didn't care who he sacrificed to do it."

"I'm sorry Swift, but I had to find out how strongly you felt. I agree with everything you have said and admit I'm afraid for the future of the valley. The way we are living at the moment is not the true way of the wolf. Now this dreadful thing has happened to Root."

"Why is it all going wrong?"

"Simple! We are living contrary to our nature and there are too many of us packed into this valley. A wolf needs space to move around in. In the old days packs were small, wolves roamed big territories covering many miles and they were free to hunt as they pleased."

"That would suit me. Sometimes I feel the urge to up and go, especially in the springtime. It seems natural."

"You can change things you know, if you want to, but you will have to be strong and clever enough to outwit the negative forces rife in the valley at the moment." For a while he was silent, choosing his words with care. "The old days won't return but the future can be better for your cubs. A lot has to be done and I must warn you, it will be dangerous." The hackles rose on Swift's back. Hawthorn touched his paw reassuringly. "Earthstar has spoken to me in my dreams and I believe with his guidance we can change things. I've said enough for the moment. It's a bad time with Root's death so recent. We'll talk again later."

"Yes, I should get back to Fallow."

"Come again soon but be careful. Tell no one."

Swift left via the rear tunnel, cautiously taking his earlier route back to the river through woods dominated by oak, ash, and elm. The River Tannon flowed from east to west through the centre of the valley. Swift followed it westwards along the river path. The sun was higher now and cleared the treetops to shine downriver from the east, warming him and making him wish his winter coat had been shed. He wasted no time on the return journey and was almost home when Leaf and Moss – a close friend – intercepted him. He could tell something was wrong.

"Leaf, what's happened?"

"Talon is organising a raiding party."

"What for?"

"You've heard the rumours about strangers crossing the northern border? Talon wants to sort 'em out. It's just an excuse for a fight if you ask me, but the worst of it is you've been chosen to go."

"Me! Why me? That's what the wolfrahm is for isn't it?"

"I know. It stinks. I'm worried Swift, this might call for a moonlight flit."

"How much time have I got?"

"Till tomorrow morning, the pack's meeting on Beech Hill at daybreak. I've got to go there now to let Thorn know you've been told. I would have told him to do his own dirty work, but thought it best to keep you two apart."

CHAPTER 2

Leaf departed for the Beech Wood and Swift and Moss set out for Swift's den. Moss, a dark grey wolf with a black face lightly flecked with grey, was born on the same spring evening as Swift in the month of March, five years earlier. Swift, the more outgoing and dominant of the two, had many times guided the smaller, introverted Moss through the pitfalls of cubhood, but tonight he looked to Moss for answers.

"Surely there are enough wolfrahm to deal with the problem? What difference do they expect me to make?"

"Apparently Talon won't allow too many wolfrahm to go, rumour has it he's worried about security in the valley."

"I can't think why! He's got the strongest and fittest wolves working for him, who's left to challenge them? Anyway why choose me? I've never had any time for the wolfrahm."

"That's just it Swift, you've made it much too obvious. Everyone is talking about the way you spoke to Thorn yesterday. I know he had it coming but the wolfrahm are tightening up and I don't think they'll let this drop."

"Root was all but murdered. If I could get to Talon I'd tell him the same."

"Where will it get you? There is no point in stirring the bees' nest if there's no honey to be had. Why don't you go to Thorn and tell him you let your feelings get the better of you?"

"I wouldn't give that weasel the satisfaction."

"Look Swift, everyone who was there with the exception of the wolfrahm agreed with what you said, but why make trouble for yourself?"

"It's no use Moss, I meant what I said. Nothing will change that. I'll have to take my chances on this raiding party. There's no point in thinking about not going, you know what Talon thinks of cowards."

Moss sighed. "If you're going I'm going with you," he said.

"There's no need for that, friend. Nothing will happen to me, I'm a fast runner."

Moss didn't appreciate Swift's humour. "You are too much of an optimist for your own good," he said, "half the pack will be wolfrahm."

"You haven't been invited, you can't just turn up."

"I'll volunteer. Talon won't be able to resist anyone keen enough to go looking for a fight."

"You'd better be careful, he might offer you a place in the wolfrahm."

"No chance, I'm not big enough or daft enough. Mind you I'm not sure about the latter. I wouldn't normally go near Talon even for a leg of venison."

"Talking of venison, whatever happens we've still

got to eat, let's see if Mistle can find us something."

"I can't eat at a time like this."

"Alright, I'll meet you tomorrow at sunrise by the ford, if you insist on coming with me."

He trotted homeward, oblivious to anything but his own thoughts. At worst they might rough him up a bit. He'd just have to protect himself as best he could. Moss was a born worrier but it would be good to have him along anyway. As he neared the den his thoughts returned to Root and the heavy weight of grief bore down on him.

He turned off the trail and ducked under the hanging branches of the honeysuckle bush that grew between a crab apple tree on the left and a holly on the right, screening the den site from the trail. Mistle and Swift's father Raven had dug the den beneath the shelter of an old oak. Its huge branches, green with lichen, spread above the den site sheltering it from sun and rain.

Mistle and Fallow sat together at the den's entrance. Mistle was a bigger, more robust female than the delicate Fallow. Mistle was light grey with a white chest and muzzle; although several years older she looked the younger of the two. She sat with a slight stoop now which showed the weight of the years but she still had a zest for life and a will to succeed which Fallow had never seemed to possess. Her belly had thickened over the years, a consequence of carrying several litters of cubs, but she was still strong and agile enough to hunt. Her cubs had all left home and found mates except Swift.

Fallow's eyes were red with crying and Mistle

looked upset. "Moss and Leaf were here," she said.

"I know, they met me on the trail. It's alright, Leaf told me."

Mistle made no attempt to hide her anxiety. "What are you going to do?"

"I know you're worried but there's no need to be. What can happen? Thorn won't try anything with all the others around."

Mistle pawed at the ground as she did when she was upset. "I want you to go away until this blows over," she said.

Swift was startled. "Go where?"

"Anywhere away from here where you'll be safe. Look at Fallow, do you want me to go through what she's going through?"

He licked her face. "Calm down and we'll talk about it," he said.

Mistle's voice faltered. "Swift, there is something I must tell you. Something perhaps I should have told you a long time ago," she said.

"What is it?"

"This will come as a shock but I've no choice. It's about your father. His death, it wasn't an accident."

Swift stared at her in stunned silence and Mistle pawed at the ground. "He was murdered to silence him. He was like you Swift, spoke his mind. There was a time when a wolf could, but not these days, not since he came. He's mad, won't stop until we're all dead."

"Tell me what happened?"

"I remember it so clearly. Although it was autumn the sun was shining. Raven and I were strolling along the path near the three-trunked oak nibbling blackberries and enjoying the sunshine when Thorn came along. The evil weasel had just been initiated into the wolfrahm and thought he was something special. He ordered Raven to join a hunting party about to leave for the northern territories. He said something about needing the antlers of some rare species of deer for one of Talon's ceremonies. I argued with him but it was no use. Raven followed Thorn along the track towards the river and..." Mistle shuddered. Swift put his paw on hers and she managed to control herself. "That was the last time I saw him. The pack was away for the rest of the autumn. Apparently they covered hundreds of miles until they reached the mountains on the other side of the northern forests. They were on a high pass hunting when Raven supposedly fell."

"And you think he was pushed?"

"Yes. He spoke out against the way Talon was organising the valley and telling wolves how they should live their lives. He said it wasn't natural and he was right. Poor Root's proof of that."

Swift sat silently, trying to absorb what he'd heard. Memories of his early cubhood with Raven stirred poignantly in the depths of his mind. They had always been very close and Raven had taught him so much about the ways of the forest. He'd always thought his father's death had been an accident.

The light faded and the shadows of dusk crept through the trees and the night came without a moon. When night comes without a moon, the wolf sleeps.

A breeze bringing an evening chill ruffled his silver mane. He pressed himself close to Mistle to comfort her. Sleep did not come easily to Swift. He repeatedly went over the events of the previous two days trying to make sense of them. He could not believe his father had been murdered but understood how Mistle had come to believe it. He needed more time to think things through, to make sure of the right decisions, but time was running out, other wolves were already taking control of his life.

Without waking Fallow or Mistle, he rose at daybreak and left the den to make his way in the greyness of dawn, along the trail towards the ford. He had decided, like his father, not to run away. Mistle's conviction that Raven had been murdered disturbed him greatly but he still refused to believe it and was sure that he would come to no great harm.

In the grey half-light he took the trail to the ford. He called for Moss whose den lay close to the trail in a small stand of silver birches. He found him stretched out behind a clump of bracken.

Startled by Swift's approach, he jumped to his feet. "You made me jump, I didn't see you coming."

"Sorry friend, I didn't mean to wake you like that, I thought we'd walk to the ford together."

"You didn't wake me, I haven't slept a wink all night."

"It's not too late to change your mind you know."

"I must be mad but I'm still coming with you. I only ask one thing. Please don't say anything to Talon about Root until we are safely back in the valley, otherwise you'll just make things worse for the both of us."

He was touched by Moss' show of friendship and agreed to his request. The two wolves took the path to the ford. At the ford the River Tannon was some thirty yards wide and fairly slow moving. Although it formed a barrier to the wolfrahm's lair in the Beech Wood, it was not, in normal conditions, difficult to cross, as wolves are naturally good swimmers.

Swift shivered as the icy water touched his belly and bit into his paws but he made no comment, both wolves were silent as they swam, contemplating what lay ahead of them. Across the river they climbed Beech Hill slowly as if delaying their arrival would bring about a change of events. In the half-light, the grey, columned beeches held no cheer. Still bare of the foliage that would soften them, they stood like forbidding sentinels warning against entry into a perilous place. Halfway up the slope several wolves waited at the foot of an old beech with branches spread wider than most, giving it a stockiness and solidity which many of its companions lacked.

Swift recognised the sandy-coloured coat of Leaf. The sight of the small, lithe tracker lifted his spirits. Leaf was always a good wolf to have around and like Swift he despised the wolfrahm. Within an hour the pack had assembled, generating an air of nervous excitement as they awaited the arrival of Thorn and Talon.

"I wish they would hurry up, this waiting is driving me mad," complained Moss, pacing to and fro, tail between his legs.

"So do I, you're making me giddy," replied Swift.

Continual chatter and attempts at humour helped

relieve the tension of waiting. Half an hour after everyone else had arrived Talon and Thorn emerged from the holly bushes that encircled the higher slopes of Beech Hill, forming a natural barrier around the wolfrahm's lair. The chatter ceased as they made their entrance. Talon stood a head taller than Thorn as he did most wolves, his unnaturally short fur accentuating his muscular, athletic body. Although predominantly grey he had patches of tan fur around his eyes, ringed with darker fur which gave him great power of facial expression, a useful asset in an alpha wolf.

There were no apologies for lateness, only a warning that every wolf would be expected to stay with the pace, which would according to Talon, be brisk. Swift and Moss fell in at the back when the pack set off. They didn't anticipate trouble within the boundaries of the valley but didn't want the wolfrahm running behind them. The pack, twenty strong, trotted for several miles in a column of twos before breaking into a canter. At this pace they could cover thirty miles in a day.

Once they had warmed up, Talon pushed on, testing strength and stamina to the limits. Swift could hear Moss' laboured breathing close behind him and slowed down to shout words of encouragement to keep his friend going.

They travelled on like this to the slopes which marked the northern outskirts of the flat-bottomed wooded valley of Tannon, which spread four miles wide and six miles long. The Tannon wolves' territory extended well beyond the natural borders of the valley but wolves had settled in the valley's once opulent woodlands in a way that wolves who were naturally nomadic within their territories had never done before. They had built permanent dens, raised cubs and lived off the wealth of game and fruits, once in seemingly endless supply. For this was their promised land to which the great alpha wolf Tannon had led them.

After leaving the valley the trails became less familiar to the pack. They travelled through a mixture of forest dominated by the oak but now and then giving way to stands of silver birch and ash. Occasionally they took broad trails forged by elk and deer which allowed them to run three or four abreast, but it was hard on the legs where the ground had been churned up by countless hooves and frozen hard by the frost.

They stopped to drink whenever they came upon a stream, giving Moss a much needed opportunity to recover. As the day wore on Moss found it increasingly difficult to stay with the pace. Swift hung back in an effort to keep his friend's spirits up and eventually Talon gave the order to make camp. The pack had covered thirty miles by late afternoon but could not rest until supper had been caught. Talon divided them into two hunting packs, each to feed itself. Fortunately for Moss and Swift they were selected to hunt with Leaf, which considerably increased their chances of an early meal.

Game was plentiful and before long Leaf led the pack to a small herd of roe deer grazing on new, spring grass in a glade cleared of trees by beavers building their dams and lodges. The beaver meadow was close to the River Heron, a tributary of the Tannon. It was a place prized by deer in the springtime for its abundance of succulent grasses and saplings. The wolf prized it for its abundance of deer and the profusion of wild flowers which scented it with a feast of fragrance to tantalise the wolf's keenest sense. The meadow blazed yellow with dandelions and coltsfoot, white with stitchwort and daisies, and was studded blue with the first sweet violets. Today the scent of the roe deer dominated as the pack stalked the herd from downwind, scrutinising each animal for signs of weaknesses to be exploited. Leaf spotted a thin buck that appeared to have difficulty in chewing.

The wind dropped and a doe closest to the edge of the clearing sensed the wolves' presence. For a second she raised her head and sniffed at the air. Leaf reacted instantly, sprinting into the clearing just as the doe took flight, spooking the rest of the herd which fled with her. He was not interested in the doe but homed in on the thin buck followed closely by the pack that backed his judgement fully. The thin buck was slow off the mark, lacking the agility of the other deer, and before it could reach the safety of the trees bordering the meadow Leaf had overtaken it and leapt at its snout, gripping it firmly in his jaws and hanging on. Three faltering steps later his weight pulled it to the ground.

The pack gorged itself on the luckless animal that proved to be riddled with arthritis in its hind legs and jaw. Ironically the wolves had saved it from the slow death of starvation. Each wolf devoured at least twenty pounds of venison to replenish the energy expended on their marathon journey from the valley. Full but exhausted, they returned to a rendezvous area to await Talon's arrival and finally to get some desperately needed sleep.

The next morning they rose early to an overcast sky and began a second day of exhausting travel that brought them by late afternoon, to the northern border of Tannon territory. They made camp and waited for contact with the border patrol. About an hour had passed when Leaf called for quiet and drew Talon's attention to a wolf howl drifting faintly in from the east. Leaf listened intently until convinced it was the call of Tannon wolves. Talon ordered a response and Leaf let out a long resounding howl, signalling the location of the pack to the patrol. Soon every wolf sat on his haunches, muzzle to the sky. The crescendo reached a climax that continued for at least ten minutes. When the howling abated there was silence. The patrol was on its way.

Now and then the pack resumed howling to guide the patrol to the campsite. Their eventual arrival was greeted with much tail wagging, licking, and chasing. When the excitement died down Talon questioned them about the interlopers but they had nothing new to report. This heartened Swift and Moss who had visions of a quick return home, but Talon soon crushed their hopes with a decision to cross the border, to 'track the enemy down'. The wolfrahm greeted this with enthusiasm but the others were silent. Moss looked dejected.

"Cheer up Moss, the mood of the pack is against a fight. If we stick together we'll be alright."

"I wish I could be so sure."

"You'll feel differently after a good night's sleep,

things will look better then."

The following morning was again overcast and dull. After devouring the remains of a wild boar left over from the night before, the pack set out to search for the intruders. The patrol wolves led, along with Leaf, followed by Talon and Thorn. Dry conditions enabled them to pick up a wolf scent about a mile outside Tannon territory. Leaf judged from the signs that they were tracking six wolves and on the strength of this Talon sent a smaller war party to hunt them down, choosing ten wolves, all wolfrahm except for Swift and Leaf. Moss volunteered but Thorn refused him on the grounds that he was too small if it came to a fight.

The war party commanded by Thorn took the north-eastern trail. In an hour, much to Thorn's delight, they were within striking distance of the intruders. The pleasure on his face was unmistakable as Leaf pointed out a fresh wolf dropping on the trail. He briefed the pack. "Right, I want no talking from now on, we don't want to scare them off. We'll move at a brisk trot and we'll keep going until we see something."

The high humidity of that morning provided the perfect medium for tension to grow in. Swift sensed it in the pack, his own anxiety increased with the realisation that there was to be a confrontation that could turn into a bloody battle. The pack trotted in single file along a narrow trail winding through a small stand of Scots pines. Swift felt vulnerable without Moss behind him so he remained at the back, hoping to keep out of trouble.

Thorn spotted a broken fern at the trail's edge

where the intruders had left the path. He ordered complete silence whilst he and Leaf searched the bracken. Two minutes later they were back, the enemy were close by. Six males and four females were sleeping off a meal of red deer. Swift felt no animosity towards wolves who had done him no harm. He considered making a run for it but knew he would never be able to return to Tannon Valley again. The prospect of not going home, of not seeing Mistle again, was enough to keep him from deserting, but he didn't expect what happened next.

Thorn looked him directly in the eye and gave his instructions. "There is no time to lose, we have to take them whilst they're dozing. We can't get behind them, it would be too noisy. We go straight in and take them by surprise. Leaf and I have trodden a path through the ferns, I want you to follow me quickly in single file. I'll grab the nearest, Swift you'll come in behind me and take the next. The rest of you take them as they come and remember Talon wants no prisoners. This is our territory and we've got to make an example of trespassers. Let's move."

CHAPTER 3

A feeling of unreality enveloped Swift. He couldn't think clearly. Automatically he followed Thorn, shocked by the realisation that he would soon be fighting for his life. Suddenly he was at the clearing where the intruders were still sleeping. Thorn leapt forward, taking the first wolf by the throat before he'd a chance to open his eyes. Swift felt a shove in his hind-quarters as someone helped him into the clearing. He moved as if in a dream, a loss of power in his limbs. His victim was halfway to his feet when Swift reached him. The wolf reacted quickly, ducking under Swift's muzzle and at the same time lunging to grip Swift's throat in his jaws. Caught off balance Swift lost his foothold and rolled onto his back. He felt the weight of the wolf pinning him to the ground. He struggled frantically to free himself but the wolf's grip tightened, choking the breath from him. Swift feigned unconsciousness, afraid that he would rip out his own throat by resisting, and hoped desperately that his opponent would release him. But there was no relaxation of the crushing pressure on his windpipe. He tried again to wriggle free but any movement intensified the pain and the wolf's grip tightened. Deprived of oxygen, his consciousness began to ebb away. He couldn't summon the strength to fight back.

The intruders had reacted quickly and fought back, biting savagely to defend themselves. A stocky tan and grey male fought furiously against Husk, a young wolf who like Swift, had failed to take advantage of his initial attack. He was pulled to the ground by the scruff of his neck as though he were a hare. Yelps of pain split the air as carnassial fangs drew blood and bruised bone in a flurry of wanton savagery.

Darkness fell across Swift's consciousness as the life drained from his body. Then as if by a miracle, life-giving air rushed through his swollen throat and a black veil was lifted from him. He rolled onto his side, retching and coughing. Fearing another attack, he staggered to his feet in time to glimpse his opponent disappearing into the pines with Leaf in close pursuit. Yelps of pain and moans of despair filled the air as wolves lay bleeding on a rough bed of fallen pinecones, others fled, pursued by those lusting for more blood. Several Tannon wolves licked bleeding wounds and Husk lay on his side whining, a foreleg broken and bent at right angles and blood pumping from a jagged tear in his throat. Swift gasped for breath, his tongue lolling, blue and swollen but his swollen flesh still intact.

He thanked Earthstar the spirit of the oak for his life. Leaf emerged from the bracken, a smudge of blood on his muzzle. He looked at Swift anxiously.

"Are you alright?" Swift opened his mouth to speak but could not utter a word. He nodded in answer to Leaf's question.

"Don't try to talk, I'll find some water." He looked

over at Husk. "Poor sod's had it, nothing we can do," he said.

The sounds of battle diminished and Swift saw the carnage around him. Some wolves licked their wounds others stood bemused, staring from glazed eyes. Wolves seldom fight for real among themselves and this was a new experience for most of them.

Thorn and Nightshade, second in command, returned from the chase in a state of euphoria, congratulating themselves over the ease of the victory.

"That taught them a lesson they won't forget in a hurry," Thorn gloated.

Swift glared at them, eyes alight with anger. Thorn felt their intensity but looked away to where Husk lay. "How bad is Husk?" he asked. Nobody answered and he understood the mood of the pack. "There are bound to be casualties when you defend your territory, it's the price you pay for holding on to what's rightfully yours." Swift couldn't reply, he merely shook his head.

Leaf had found a stream nearby. "Come on, let's drink and clean ourselves up, it's not far."

Thorn growled, exposing fangs stained crimson with blood. "Hold it, tracker," he said. "I give the orders."

Leaf didn't hide his contempt. "Worried about a counter attack? Anyone who survived that won't be within ten miles of here now."

"Keep your mouth shut, tracker. Tannon's security has to be maintained. And we'll drink when I say so." Inspired by Leaf's composure Swift stood next to

Leaf as a gesture of defiance. Thorn glared icily at him but did not hold Swift's gaze. Instead he gave the order to head for the stream. In those few moments, Husk had died.

Swift lapped up a mouthful of water and tipped his head back to allow the cool liquid to run down his bruised throat. The cold, sparkling water revived them and several of the wolfrahm talked about 'the victory'. Thorn talked of Tannon's heroes returning in triumph to the valley. Swift had hoped they'd be cured of any further desire to fight but he could see the glint of greed in the eyes of some when Thorn mentioned the fruits of victory. He thought of Husk, whose body had not yet gone cold, and Fallow's words came back to him. 'Root would not be the last,' she'd said. How soon her prophecy had come to pass.

When they'd finished drinking they made their way back to camp where Talon greeted them as conquering heroes, immediately sending out a hunting party in their honour. Within an hour a roe buck lay at the feet of the victors. They feasted on venison, some talking about their success and anticipating their triumphant homecoming, others subdued, the horrors of the conflict fresh in their minds. Swift wanted to be back in Tannon Valley with Mistle; Moss sat beside him, keeping him company in his silence.

The following morning Swift woke with aching limbs and a searing pain in his throat. He wanted to lie still until he was ready to get up but Thorn roused the pack on Talon's orders. The alpha wolf wanted to address them. Fur ruffled and heavy-eyed, they assembled reluctantly, forming the traditional semicircle. Talon returned from his morning stroll, strutting into camp head held high, tail erect, displaying the kind of self-assurance borne only by the alpha wolf.

He took up his position in the centre, facing the semicircle, and sat down on his haunches. For a moment he surveyed them, blinking occasionally almost lazily. Swift was, as always on the few occasions when he'd seen him, struck by his sheer size. There wasn't another wolf in Tannon Valley who could match his physical power and he'd remained unchallenged since the day he had taken the alpha position. But Swift knew that Talon's size was not the only reason for his survival as alpha. He appeared to be constantly thinking and planning. Planning in isolation the fate of the valley.

Talon cleared his throat. "Wolves of Tannon, yesterday was a great day in the history of Tannon Valley. You showed courage and determination in dealing with what was a very real threat to the valley's security. The wolf population on our island is growing rapidly but territorial boundaries must be maintained. There is only a certain amount of game available to us and most of this, as you know, now grazes on our territory surrounding the outskirts of the valley. This game must be protected at all costs from intruders who trespass on our land. I said at all costs. And yes, the price we had to pay yesterday for that protection was high. Although I regret the loss of Husk I believe it is inevitable that there will be casualties in this kind of situation. You can be proud of what you did and return home with heads held high. Thank you."

The remains of the roe buck were devoured, leaving only a few chewed bones for the ravens who squawked their displeasure as the pack left the campsite. Thorn led the wolves who had seen combat back to Tannon Valley. Talon, who had other plans, remained in the northern territory. The journey back to Tannon was made at a leisurely pace with frequent stops to hunt and rest. By the time the pack trod the familiar trails of home, bellies were full and spirits raised and the horror of the conflict pushed to the backs of their minds. The news travelled fast and since entering the Bluebell Wood wolves had been turning out to greet them. Thorn revelled in the attention and made as much capital from the victory as possible.

Swift decided not to mention his part in the battle to Mistle. Thorn's attempt to get rid of him had failed and he wanted to forget it. At the first opportunity he left the pack to head for home. He found Mistle at the mouth of the den, waiting where she always waited for him; she looked thinner and her eyes seemed to have sunk in her face. When she saw him she bounded towards him like an exited cub. He realised then that she hadn't expected him to come home. They nuzzled each other, licking and nipping playfully, chasing in circles, back and forth, tails wagging. Soon they lay close together, panting, neither one speaking.

Eventually Mistle got up and went into the den to fetch a hare which she laid at Swift's feet. Swift licked her face. "It's good to be home," he said.

"I've been so worried."

"I'm sorry you had to go through that again, I shouldn't have gone but I didn't know what else to do."

"You're like your father, he spoke his mind, couldn't bear to see another wolf harmed. I'm proud of you cub, but the wolfrahm is evil, please don't take any more chances."

"In future I'll try to keep my opinions to myself. Your happiness is what counts now. You look tired, why don't you sleep while I do some hunting around here for a change?"

"I want to know what happened, Swift."

"Can we talk in the morning?"

She smiled and licked him. "Alright, but why don't we hunt together tomorrow? You look as though you could do with a good night's sleep as well."

The night was warm so they slept under the stars. He watched Mistle curl up, nose under tail, then lay down hoping he could shut his mind to the events of the past few days. The whole episode repulsed him. Wolves had been murdered for no more than straying into Tannon territory. He needed to talk, to unburden himself of his guilt, but decided not to tell Mistle everything for her own good. Sometime he would go to Hawthorn.

Finally he fell into a restless, dream-filled sleep, waking up several times during the night, throat throbbing, then drifting back to nightmare images of savage, biting jaws and the grinning face of Thorn.

In the morning he awoke to the sound of birdsong, the music of dawn which had roused the forest each morning since the beginnings of time. He recognised the voices of a robin, a blackbird, and a song thrush that seemed to answer each other's songs as if in melodic conversation.

He rose slowly to his feet, yawned and stretched. First his hind legs then his forelegs, then shook himself vigorously to free his fur of soil and leaves. This woke Mistle who followed the same routine. Above the forest canopy the sky was already a dazzling blue and both wolves were lifted by the morning's freshness.

"Let's go and find some breakfast," suggested Swift.

"It's about time you did some hunting around here," Mistle replied playfully.

"What can I get you, madam?"

Mistle laughed. "A nice juicy bison would suit me fine, thank you."

"I'll see what I can do for you, madam," he said, trotting off down the track.

Mistle cantered after him. "You don't think I'm letting you out of my sight again, do you?"

Swift sprinted away, tail outstretched, inviting Mistle to chase him. The two wolves loped along the densely bordered trail where tangled brambles sent forth tendrils of new growth to usurp yet more of the woodland floor. The wood opened up among the silver birches at the north-west end of the valley. He had led her to Silver Birch Wood because he knew how much she loved the magical, silver-white hue of the trees' bark that seemed almost to glow. He knew how she enjoyed the open spaces between the trees where she could leave the path and wander on spring grasses unhindered by brambles and ivy. She'd often brought him here as a cub before Raven had died, but now its memories were no longer painful, they helped make sense of her life.

Several times they glimpsed red deer and gave chase but couldn't match their speed or agility. After an hour they strolled to Silver Brook for a drink. Close to the stream they came across an abandoned lynx kill. The venison was fresh and Swift suspected their approach had disturbed the lynx as it fed.

"Looks like our lucky day," he said. "Let's fill ourselves before we drink."

They settled down to feed in the warmth of the spring morning. There was a refreshing breeze in the woods, just enough to occasionally stir the leaf buds newly formed on the birches. Swift glanced at Mistle and thanked Earthstar again for his life. Gorged with venison they quenched their thirsts in Silver Brook, lapping up the stream's cool water before searching for a comfortable spot to lie and doze. Mistle found a honeysuckle bush to lie under.

"Swift this will do fine, I only wish it was in flower." She inhaled deeply and sat down.

"This is marvellous, why can't it always be like this?"

"It was in the old days when your father was alive. We roamed here and there, hunting and digging dens wherever we wanted. It was always in or around the valley but it was far less crowded then, you can't move for wolves these days. Just lately I've felt hemmed in. I want to go somewhere else for a while. I feel so lucky to have you back safely and I don't want to give them another chance to harm you."

"I know how you feel, but moving away won't improve things, they will just get worse. Talon is changing everything without consulting anyone and the ordinary wolf has got to do something about it."

"What can anyone do now? It's too late to stop him."

"We can't just give up."

"It's best to accept things as they are or leave the valley."

"What I saw sickened me, innocent wolves were murdered and I was part of it."

"It wasn't you, cub. You could never do anything like that."

"But I was there and I never want to be in that situation again."

Mistle sighed. "Go to Hawthorn, he will know if anything can be done but I think you'll be wasting your time."

Swift heard the weariness in her voice and knew her advice was against her better judgement.

CHAPTER 4

In the northern territory Talon sought the services of a wisewolf whom he could manipulate so he had been tracking the wolves that had escaped Thorn. A week had passed since the battle when the pack finally caught up with its prey – three females and four males – resting under a cluster of Scots pines just off the main trail. On sensing the Tannon wolves' presence they scrambled to their feet, teeth bared, ready to defend themselves. Talon and the Tannon wolves lowered their ears and tails in a display of subservience as a ploy to avoid an attack but Talon knew it would not work for long. He would have to speak.

"Before you do anything hasty, please hear me out," he said. There was no reply, only a guttural growl. "We wandered into your territory by accident to escape an attack by wolves from the territory to the south, show us the way and we will leave."

The largest of the males, a dark grey wolf, stepped closer, exposing the full length of his fangs. "Where are you from?"

Talon crouched lower, almost touching the ground with his belly to show his servility.

"From the south west, a territory which borders

the Tannon Valley," he lied.

"Why were you attacked by the Tannon wolves?"

"For no reason at all. We were hunting deer well inside our own borders when we were ambushed."

"Where are your females?" demanded the dark grey wolf.

"Several of them are with cub. We were hunting game to take back to the den." On hearing this, the grey alpha wolf seemed to relax slightly and Talon took full advantage.

"Is there a stream close by?" he asked. "We need to drink."

"How do we know you will leave, when you've drunk your fill?"

"Come with us to the stream, alpha wolf, and then escort us from your territory." The alpha wolf nodded and ordered the female wolf to lead the way. She was followed by the Tannon wolves except for Talon, who walked at the back with the alpha wolf who proved to be very talkative.

"Like you, we were attacked by a pack from the south. We think the rabies was in them, we lost four good wolves."

"We were more fortunate," replied Talon, "they were upwind of us and we were able to make a run for it, but they didn't give up the chase easily. It was a close call, a very close call. It would seem living in small packs is not safe these days. Perhaps we should hunt together. There would be safety in numbers."

"I think we should get to know each other a little better before we make any hasty decisions."

They came to a shallow, fast-flowing stream and lapped up its cool water to quench their thirsts. After they had drunk, the grey alpha wolf turned to Talon with a suggestion.

"It's getting dark, perhaps you would like to camp with us tonight, we could talk some more in the morning."

"It would be an honour to accept the invitation of such a generous alpha wolf."

"First you must eat with us."

"We wouldn't dream of imposing ourselves," replied Talon.

The alpha wolf was warming to his role of benefactor. "Game is not scarce here, although we are careful not to waste anything. We have a kill near the pines where you came across us. A red deer stag, enough for everyone."

"Again you honour us, alpha wolf. I think this could be the beginning of a long and fruitful friendship between our two packs. It's time we introduced ourselves, I'm Talon."

"Sallow."

Talon found it difficult to suppress a smile. "Good, we'll get to know each other sooner if we begin on a friendly basis."

Sallow's wolves were not so easily convinced of Talon's good intentions and were reluctant to chat to the Tannon wolves who had warmed to Talon's performance and were making their own efforts to force friendly conversation. Sallow led the way back to a small clearing in the pines where a half-eaten stag lay on a bed of fallen pine needles. The Tannon wolves feasted hungrily, consuming more venison than the others to make up for the spartan meals they'd made do with on the journey north. Talon noted that this was making them even less popular with their hosts.

He turned to Sallow. "Do excuse our manners, alpha wolf, we were about to make a kill when we were attacked and haven't eaten for days."

Sallow tore a chunk of flesh from the stag's haunch and continued eating, nodding his head in reply to Talon's comment. Talon resumed eating and nothing else was said until every wolf had finished. By this time the sun had given way to a full moon which sent down silver rays to penetrate the pine wood and light the night enough for the wolves to see each other in the darkness.

The wolves made themselves comfortable amongst the fallen pinecones. They sat in the customary semicircle, Tannon wolves next to Sallow's wolves. The night was quiet and the air scented with the smell of pine sap.

Sallow addressed the assembly. "The moon god smiles on our meeting. We must entertain him with stories from the wolflore." Next to Sallow sat a wolf of an unusual grubby cream colour. "Loach is our wisewolf, he has many stories of our history which go back to the beginnings of time before the days of the ice when the wolf did not need to roam the land in search of his food."

Loach raised his muzzle to the moon and let out a long high-pitched howl. One by one each wolf joined in until an eerie chorus warned every creature for miles around to steer clear of the gathering. The howl lasted for several minutes, then Loach stopped as abruptly as he'd begun, signalling an end to the crescendo. He waited until no sound could be heard in the night-time stillness except for the distant hoot of a tawny owl.

"Once, many moons ago, there lived far to the south in the land where the sun never ceases to shine, a wolf pack who had suffered badly from a drought. The sun had blazed down, baking the earth for season after season, withering the trees and the grass and drying the streams and the rivers until there was nothing left for the animals to eat and barely enough water to drink. For a while the wolf pack revelled in the amount of game that fell at its feet. But eventually there came a time when the abundance of dying animals became too much even for the wolf packs to consume and many a carcass was left to the buzzards, the ravens, and other eaters of carrion. But then the abundance was no more and even the ravens could not find food.

Wolves grew thin and ragged, falling prey to sickness and disease, and they turned to Tannon their alpha wolf for salvation, and the alpha wolf prayed to Earthstar for deliverance from the famine. Earthstar replied to him in a dream, telling him to lead the pack northward to a land where the game teemed, where the rivers flowed and the trees went on forever.

The alpha wolf gathered his pack around him to tell them of his dream and the very next day, after as good a night as their empty bellies would allow them, they set off for the promised land. It was a journey beset with difficulties, traversing the territory of hostile packs, snatching game here and there, not knowing where the next water was coming from. The further north they travelled the denser the forest became and the more plentiful was the game. But the alpha wolf would not let them rest until instinct told him they had reached the heart of the land of plenty.

Never had the wolves seen such a multitude of game, red deer, roe deer, wild boar, bison and beaver and many more and not another wolf to be found. They rejoiced and thanked Earthstar for bringing them to a paradise rich beyond their dreams. A river valley of immense proportions spread around them, clothed with all manner of trees, oaks, beech, silver birch, alder, and ash to name but a few. The wolf pack named the valley Tannon in honour of their alpha wolf."

At this point Loach stopped his monologue to study the faces of his audience, looking in turn at each Tannon wolf, until his eyes came to rest on Talon. It was then Talon realised the wisewolf had guessed their identity. He prepared himself for trouble but to his surprise Loach continued with his story. Talon glanced at his wolves, it was obvious they were uncomfortable at the mention of Tannon Valley but it was quite likely they'd never heard the story before. After all, he'd outlawed the wolflore many years ago. He studied Loach through narrowed eyes and wondered how much he knew.

The wisewolf concluded his story and Talon was the first to compliment him. "Ah yes, marvellous story, one that improves with time. I daresay some of my younger wolves haven't heard it before. If I may say so it was very well told."

Loach nodded theatrically. "Thank you, alpha wolf, it was a pleasure to speak to such an attentive audience."

Sallow stood up and spoke. "The night is young and the moon still rises. Let's make the most of it."

Loach continued with legends and stories of the ancient wolflore until he and the others could no longer keep their eyes open. Talon was the last to fall asleep, his mind intent on a plan for the next day. He stared across the camp at Loach. "Sleep well, wise wolf," he murmured, "there is much to do in the morning."

The following day Talon woke first; the sun was already warming the air beneath the pines and the morning chorus was past its best. He didn't raise his head from his paws but lay still, checking each wolf to be certain they were all asleep. When he was satisfied he rose silently and trod carefully across to where Loach lay. He touched the wisewolf gently on his shoulder with his paw. Loach woke with a start, staring up fearfully into Talon's smiling eyes.

Talon kept his voice to a whisper. "I would like to speak with you, wisewolf. I found your stories last night very interesting. Perhaps you would walk to the stream with me."

It was clear to Loach that he had no choice in the matter. He rose stiffly and began to stretch but Talon cut him short, indicating the need for silence with a narrowing of his eyes. Talon led the way with Loach following closely. Talon stood at least four inches taller at the shoulder than Loach, which increased his sense of power over the cream wolf. He sensed that Loach was intimidated by his size as most wolves were. Taking advantage of this, he looked down aloofly at him.

"That was an interesting choice of story last night Loach, the one you began with."

Loach swallowed. "Yes, from the moment you arrived it has been in my head. I felt compelled to tell it."

"Have you any idea where Tannon Valley is?"

"I believe it's somewhere in the southern territories."

"The southern territories, isn't that where the wolves who attacked you came from?"

Loach's nose began to twitch nervously. "Yes, it had occurred to me."

"Then aren't you worried that it might happen again?" Talon watched Loach from the corner of his eye. He saw the cream wolf's nose twitch again.

"It had occurred to me but I thought if it were you and you'd wanted to attack us you wouldn't have wasted time getting to know us."

"Very clever Loach, you are a wisewolf indeed. You've told no one else of your thoughts I trust."

"No, I thought I'd better let things develop."

"I suppose it's entirely up to me whether I believe you or not. If you've told no one then all I need do is, shall we say, get rid of you, and no one will be any the wiser."

"But I can be of use to you, alpha wolf. I can help

you get whatever it is you came for."

They reached the stream. Talon lapped at the water, quenching his thirst whilst Loach stood by nervously pawing the ground.

Talon stopped drinking and smiled sardonically. "You can stop squirming and drink your fill, I might find a use for you yet," he said. Loach drank warily, keeping one eye on Talon. When he'd finished Talon began questioning him.

"Would your pack join me if I offered them freedom of movement here and over the border in Tannon territory, in exchange for their allegiance?"

"Some of them might be persuaded but Sallow and Broom, they wouldn't know what was good for them."

"Is there another wolf capable of taking the alpha position?"

"No, the others are too young."

Talon pondered for a moment. "That's of no consequence, it will suit me to bring in someone from the wolfrahm."

Loach was still nervous. "The wolfrahm?" he said.

"You'll find out soon enough about the wolfrahm. This is what I want you to do for now."

Talon issued his instructions as they strolled back to camp. He anticipated another meal on the bones of the stag with the pack remaining close to camp. This would suit his purpose perfectly. Sallow was waiting for them but Talon had anticipated his question. "We woke early and took a stroll to the river, it's a beautiful morning."

Satisfied with this, Sallow stood up, stretched and yawned. "Your wolves are welcome to feed on what's left of the kill."

"That is most kind of you, alpha wolf. I think perhaps after we've eaten we should have a talk about our position here."

"What have you in mind?"

Talon smiled ingratiatingly. "May I suggest we find somewhere more private? What I have to say is of considerable importance and at the moment for your ears only."

Sallow's ego fed on Talon's implied flattery. "I know a nice clearing ideal for soaking up the spring sunshine."

"This is fine," said Talon. "I'll come straight to the point. I think our packs need each other for mutual security. It would seem we have a common enemy in the Tannon wolves. As separate units we can never feel safe but together we can defend ourselves against attack." Talon watched Sallow closely and glimpsed a spark of interest that merely needed to be fanned. He went on. "If we did decide to join forces there would only be room for one alpha wolf which would of course be your good self. I would take the unusual step of fully supporting your claim to the alpha position." Talon fought to stifle a smile. Sallow was almost drooling. "There is no reason why the pack shouldn't prosper, making you a very powerful wolf," he added. He waited expectantly for Sallow's reply, detecting a glint of excitement in the alpha wolf's eye.

"It would certainly put us in a position of strength," Sallow replied. "And times are changing.

We've both suffered unprovoked attacks. What's to stop it happening again?"

"I must agree, together we could organise a defence against these barbarians. May I make a suggestion, alpha wolf? Why not find out what the others think? If there is one wolf in particular whom you trust, ask his opinion and perhaps he could help you persuade the others if necessary."

Sallow smiled. "That sounds reasonable. I'll talk to Broom, he's an old friend with plenty of common sense."

Talon pushed his luck whilst it held good. "Why not fetch him now? No sense in wasting time."

Sallow strode off towards the camp and Talon smiled, it was up to Loach to do his bit now. Talon was certain Loach would be afraid to cross him but was unsure of whether he would be capable of carrying out his part of the plan. Shortly he heard Sallow and Broom approaching through the ferns. Talon assessed Broom as he approached, he was older than Sallow and much smaller; his forehead and back were grey, his flanks and muzzle tan. He had an aura of self-confidence that unsettled Talon. Sallow introduced him and invited Talon to explain their plan. Talon could not easily judge Broom's reaction to what he said which somewhat marred his performance. The older wolf merely listened inscrutably until Talon had finished.

Sallow prompted his friend. "Well what do you think?"

"I think we should take time to talk this over. It's a big step to take."

"That's alright with me," replied Sallow. "Talon, allow us some time to discuss this alone."

Not used to being told Talon winced but managed to hold his act together. "Yes alpha wolf, I'll join the others and wait for your decision." He disappeared into the ferns, cringing, but stopped within earshot. It had not taken him long to realise that Broom was cleverer than Sallow. He decided to move quickly, hurrying through the ferns to the pines where he lay under cover on his belly out of sight whilst Loach spoke to the rest of Sallow's wolves.

As he waited he watched a pair of red wood ants carrying a dead caterpillar. One at the head, one at the tail, their yellow and black carrion gripped firmly in powerful mandibles. They lugged it towards a nest of pine needles that bustled with action as their comrades toiled in unison to build and maintain it. Talon admired their sense of purpose and interdependence and thought of his vision for the future of the wolf. One day they would work for each other instinctively in the same way. Their future depended on it. He gave Loach time to say his piece then emerged from the ferns to sit down under the nearest pine.

Loach broke off and trotted over to him. "Good news, alpha wolf. They agree it would be in their best interests to join you but they are worried in case Sallow rejects the idea."

Talon frowned. "Sallow is persuaded, he thinks it is a marvellous idea. Of course I had to say he would be alpha wolf."

"But surely you will be alpha wolf?"

"Of course I will be, fool. There's no room for Sallow in my plans. Anyway Broom is already talking him out of the idea. We will have to move quickly, lead the others to the river and wait for me there." He watched Loach and Sallow's pack depart then called Thorn.

"Yes master."

"I want the following done quickly, quietly, and with no fuss." He explained his plan to Thorn and sent him with his orders to the wolfrahm. Shortly after this Sallow and Broom arrived and Talon hurried towards them.

"What is your decision alpha wolf?"

Sallow had lost some of his self-assurance. "We can't decide, we need more time to think things over."

"Take as much time as you need," replied Talon, "we are in no hurry."

"It's not something we wish to rush into," said Sallow.

Whilst Talon kept them talking three wolfrahm had moved unobtrusively around to the rear of them. At a pre-arranged signal from Talon they closed in. Sallow heard them and swung round. "What's going on?"

"I'm afraid you've taken too long to make your decision and the offer is no longer open to you after all."

"What do you mean?"

"It's obvious you're not happy with my proposal, Loach has spoken to the others and they have already agreed to join us."

"It's not up to Loach or the others. As alpha wolf it's my decision."

"I am afraid you are no longer alpha wolf, unless you wish to challenge me for the position?"

"But you said..."

"I don't care what I said. Unless you are prepared to fight for the alpha position I advise you to leave now. I want you out of my territory."

"This is outrageous. It's treachery!"

"You heard what I said, if you are not prepared to fight, leave now."

Sallow heard the note of finality in Talon's voice. He exchanged glances with Broom, scowled at Talon and resignedly trotted away with Broom close behind him. Talon watched them until they were clear of the Scots pines then led his wolves to the stream where Loach and the others waited for them.

Talon spoke to them. "Sallow and Broom wanted no part of our plan, so I had no choice but to ask them to leave. I could not allow them to put our survival in jeopardy." He turned to Thorn. "You are to take charge as temporary alpha wolf in the northern territory until other arrangements can be made. I want to leave immediately for Tannon."

CHAPTER 5

The sky was a deep cloudless blue and the sun's rays rested on the glade where Swift dozed. A bumblebee brushed the tip of his nose and he woke up and watched it land on a nearby pussy willow catkin. The catkin, laden with pollen, swayed under its weight as it hung on to feed. A brimstone butterfly of almost translucent yellow rose from a catkin close by and crossed the glade in fits and starts, skimming low across a patch of celandines, its pale yellow momentarily accentuating the rich gold of the celandines' petals. Swift stood up slowly and stretched his body then shook himself. He wandered lazily, stopping now and then to sniff the ground or to investigate a paw print. He stepped over a fallen silver birch half submerged in the ivy that blanketed the surrounding woodland floor. He flopped down onto the ivy's coolness.

He lay dozing until the sound of an animal crashing through the undergrowth tore him rudely back from the brink of sleep. He leapt up, ready to defend himself. A she-wolf, face contorted with fear, raced through the undergrowth towards him. When she saw him she changed direction and disappeared through a cluster of hazel saplings. Swift stared after her, bemused at first and wondering what to do, but the smell of her fear stirred him into action. He sprinted after her. She left the undergrowth and took to the main trail. In the open Swift soon gained on her, his powerful legs driving hard against the firmness of the track. He called out to her as he ran.

"Don't be afraid. I won't hurt you, I want to help."

He drew alongside her. She was small and lithe. He urged her to stop. She snapped at his ear and spurted forward. Swift accelerated, catching her with ease. Almost effortlessly he pulled ahead of her and crossed her path. She attempted to change direction but stumbled. He was on her quickly, pinning her to the ground. Her terrified expression made him feel clumsy and brutal and he wanted to reassure her.

"Don't be afraid, I want to help you," he said again. "Tell me what you are frightened of." He felt some of the tension leave her.

"That's better," he said. "Promise me you won't run away?"

Her voice trembled. "But I must get away."

"Who from?" he asked.

"The wolfrahm."

"What do they want with you?"

"They're trying to kill me."

Swift saw terror in her eyes as she uttered those words and the hackles rose on his back.

"Why should they want to kill you?" he asked, trying to sound calm. Tears wetted her eyes and she looked around fearfully. He stepped aside and let her stand up. "Come on, I know somewhere safe where we can talk," he said.

Swift led her to a hollow in the ground beneath a cluster of silver birches. She glanced around her nervously as she followed him in. "We are safe here. I come here when I want to be alone." She watched him, her eyes wide and staring. "You have nothing to fear from me, he said.

"Thank you," she said. "I'm sorry."

Swift smiled. "Do you want to talk?"

He could see her anguish as she spoke. "The wolfrahm murdered my brother. I pleaded with him to leave Tannon but he wouldn't listen. Two days later he was..."

"Why did they do it?"

"He refused to join them."

Swift's expression hardened. "The wolfrahm is no place for a decent wolf."

"He told Stone, Talon's second in command, what he thought about his thugs. He must have been out of his mind."

A tear rolled down her face. He thought of Mistle telling him about his father's disappearance and he regretted bitterly doubting her words. The anguish in the she-wolf's eyes brought him back to the present.

Swift touched her paw. "I'm very sorry about your brother," he said, "but what do they want with you?"

"I told everyone what had happened. Stone denied it and accused me of subversive activity. They said my brother had been killed by a bear. Then they started watching me. I was so frightened, I couldn't stand it anymore, so I ran."

"You are safe here."

"Thank you."

"You must be hungry?"

"I'm so tired."

"Sleep here, no one will find you. I'll hunt before dark."

She stood up. "Please don't leave me alone," she said.

"Alright, I'll keep watch whilst you rest. What is your name?"

"Moon," she said.

"I'm Swift. Rest for as long as you like. I'll be just over there if you need me."

Swift sat on the edge of the hollow, straining to detect the slightest sound. He thought over what Moon had told him, every so often glancing down to where she had curled up tightly with her nose tucked under her tail. The time passed by and he realised how exhausted she was. He heard the shuffle of a small creature in the undergrowth about ten metres from where he sat. He thought Moon would need something to eat when she woke up. Crouching, he crept towards the sound to find a red squirrel scratching in the leaf mould at the foot of an oak tree.

Swift was three yards away when the squirrel sensed his presence. For a split second the startled animal stared at him in surprise, then scurried up the trunk of the oak. Swift leapt too late and landed in an ungainly heap where the squirrel had been standing. Embarrassed by his own clumsiness he scrambled to his feet, self-consciously looking about him. He stopped still at the sound of voices. Before he had time to react two wolves appeared through the ferns. His heart began to thump and he cursed himself bitterly for his negligence. Both wolves were heavy, one tall at the shoulder and the other stocky. The tall wolf had a dark, almost black face and spoke bluntly.

"We're looking for a she-wolf who came this way earlier today. Have you seen her?"

Swift hesitated before replying. "I've seen no one today."

The stocky wolf sensed Swift's nervousness and sniffed at the air. "You're lying. There's been a female round here sometime recently," he said.

Swift's mind raced. "Yes, my mother was here at midday."

The dark-faced wolf bared his teeth and growled threateningly. "You'd better be telling the truth. We'll take a look round."

Swift was determined to protect Moon, he had promised her she would be safe. He leapt forward and bit deeply into the stocky wolf's shoulder. The stunned animal recoiled, yelping with pain. Swift let go and ran for the main trail in an attempt to lure them away. He dashed through the brambles, ignoring the thorns that tore at his legs. At the main trail he headed north but soon realised his plan had failed, only the stocky wolf had given chase.

He stopped suddenly and turned to face his pursuer. Taken by surprise the stocky wolf stumbled and Swift was on him, sinking his teeth firmly into his left hind leg, catching him below the fleshy part of the thigh. The bone cracked audibly and the stocky wolf fell to the ground yelping. Swift knew instinctively that the leg was broken and the wolf finished. Not wasting a moment, he raced back to the hollow, his heart beating wildly, but there was no sign of the dark-faced wolf and the hollow was empty.

Frantically he looked about him but there was no sign of Moon or the dark-faced wolf. He took several deep breaths and fought to contain his panic, telling himself that they couldn't have gone far. He examined the hollow and thanked Earthstar there were no signs of blood. He noticed a clump of flattened ferns and a broken maple sapling where they had left the hollow. He felt his strength returning and wanted to run after her, to free her, but checked himself. A broken cobweb led him further and the screeching of an outraged magpie disturbed by someone or something confirmed that he had taken the right direction. He increased his speed, guided by the bird's cacophony. He glimpsed a movement ahead and the adrenaline pumped through his body. He had a peculiar dual feeling of wanting to attack and run away at the same time, but there was never any doubt in his mind that he intended to rescue Moon.

He closed the gap between them and it became a matter of choosing the right moment to strike. Moon and the dark-faced wolf emerged into a glade where a fallen tree barred their path. Swift wasted no time in launching his attack, hitting the dark-faced wolf at speed and throwing him back against the fallen tree. He shouted to Moon to run but she stood her ground. He bit into the dark-faced wolf's shoulder but he recovered quickly and forced Swift off balance. Swift lost his grip and his advantage. The dark-faced wolf was up, facing him, teeth bared. He lunged for Swift's throat. Swift drew back, the wolf's jaws clamped shut on the skin and thick fur of his throat, narrowly missing his jugular. The dark-faced wolf fought to improve his grip. Swift resisted but felt himself being forced back under his opponent's weight. Moon leapt to his rescue, sinking her teeth into the dark-faced wolf's neck. He loosened his grip on Swift who took his chance, pulling himself free of his opponent's jaws. He made a swift counter attack, this time making no mistake. He gripped the dark-faced wolf by the throat, cutting the air off from his lungs until his body went limp and his legs buckled under his own weight. Swift released his hold and stared in horror at the body lying at his feet. Moon came to him and gently licked his wounds, murmuring words of reassurance.

She led him silently away from the corpse to a stream near the hollow where they drank and bathed to cleanse themselves. The stream intersected the path not far from where Swift had fought the stocky wolf and he was afraid that he may still be a danger. As they bathed in the stream's coolness he kept his eyes and ears open and he heard a moaning sound coming from around the bend in the stream. He warned Moon to keep quiet and edged his way along the bank, slowly making his way round the bend. Beyond the bend the stocky tan wolf lay at the edge of the stream trying to manoeuvre himself into a position where he could drink. His injured leg hung limply at his side.

Swift ducked back out of view, he tried to shut thoughts of the injured wolf's pain out but without success, and remorse swept over him. He sensed Moon beside him.

"It was them or us," she said.

"It's not easy to do that to another wolf."

"Swift, you saved my life, if it weren't for you I..."

"I know I had no choice."

The injured wolf's moaning intensified. Moon looked anxiously at Swift. "Come on," she said, approaching the stocky tan wolf.

She stopped a few feet from him. Sensing their presence, he ceased moaning and turned to face them. For an instant his eyes were wide with fear then he growled and instinctively tried to stand. Moon spoke quietly but firmly to him.

"It's alright, we won't harm you." The wolf eyed them suspiciously. "We want to help you," continued Moon.

The stocky wolf stopped growling but watched them through narrowed eyes. "Why would you want to help me?"

"Not all of us have the stomach for killing," said Swift.

The wolf averted his eyes. "They told me she had committed crimes against the spirit Havnar and it is our duty to defend Havnar's honour."

Swift shook his head slowly, in dismay. "It's the wolf's honour that needs defending."

"Talon says Havnar is the wolf's saviour and

should be treated with respect at all times."

"That kind of indoctrination is causing havoc with normal life in the valley," said Swift.

"You must rest quietly," said Moon.

The stocky wolf winced. "I'm desperate for a drink," he said and dragged himself towards the water's edge. He stretched down to lap the water, choking in his haste to quench his burning throat.

"Take it slowly," cautioned Swift, "there's no hurry."

When he'd finished he lay on his side. Swift allowed him to recover before pointing out a hazel thicket, some fifteen yards away. "Can you make it over there? In the open you'll be easy prey for a bear." The wolf nodded.

"What's your name?" asked Moon

"Stag," he said.

"Swift and I will find you something to eat."

They followed the stream to where it intersected the path. After taking a drink they headed north. Moon broke the silence. "Swift, do you think we are doing the right thing?"

"I don't know, but I can't stand by and let him die."

"I'm afraid they will kill you too."

Swift smiled reassuringly. "Don't worry about me, let's find some food, we'll talk later."

Swift knew of a small herd of roe deer that had been feeding on the spring grass in a nearby glade.

Several deer were grazing on the far side of the clearing. The wind changed direction, putting the wolves upwind of the deer. They appraised the herd quickly, assessing the physical condition of each animal. They spotted a yearling with an open wound in his shoulder and looked no more. They moved up confidently to the clearing's edge and the nearest roe buck raised his head to test the air and unwittingly signalled the attack.

The speed of it caught the herd by surprise but reflex action and agility took them into the cover of the trees. Oblivious to the movement of the others, Swift and Moon homed in on their victim, their minds focused for the kill. An hour later they arrived back at the hazel thicket, exhausted but carrying dismembered limbs of the roe buck in their jaws. They tore prime pieces of meat from the carcass and fed them to Stag who had made himself as comfortable as possible underneath the hazels.

Swift and Moon ate voraciously, replenishing energy they had used on the hunt. Satisfied, they laid down and wolf napped. A squirrel chattering and swearing in a nearby oak woke Swift, who rose stiffly and stretched. Moon, who'd endured several nightmares, jumped into wakefulness, eyes wide with fear. Swift spoke soothingly to her.

"Don't be afraid, it's only a squirrel squawking." She stared about her, uncertain of where she was until she saw Stag. Swift saw the fear in her face as it all came back to her. He moved closer to her and put his paw on hers. "It's alright, you are safe here. He won't harm you."

"Thank you, thank you for helping me."

Swift licked her muzzle and smelled the fragrance of her deliciously soft fur. "Thank Earthstar I happened to be there at the right time," he said. She was about to reply when Stag groaned in his sleep. Moon looked at him anxiously.

"What are we going to do when he recovers? He'll betray us to the wolfrahm."

Stag opened his eyes. "You've nothing to fear from me," he said. "I'm lucky you saved my life. I didn't deserve it but Stone ordered us to hunt you down as an enemy of the pack. He said you and your brother had defiled the name of Havnar. My only consolation is that I had nothing to do with your brother's death."

Moon's eyes filled with tears. "Why did they do it? What possible danger could we have been to the mighty Talon?"

"In the Beech Wood there are always training sessions and ceremonies taking place, a wolf doesn't get time to think but now that I'm away from it I can see things more clearly. I'm still new to it all but I've seen enough to know that nobody thinks for themselves. Talon, Stone, and Loach do their thinking for them. Everything revolves around worshipping Havnar."

"Why Havnar? The yew has never been our friend. Its berries have always been poison to the wolf. The oak gives most to the creatures of the forest."

"Earthstar of the oak has never been mentioned at any of the ceremonies I've been to. Havnar is the saviour of the wolf."

"What happens at these ceremonies?"

"The wolfrahm form a semicircle around Loach, who offers a prayer up to Havnar which everyone must repeat, thanking him for the special regard he has for the wolf nation."

Swift frowned. "But what about the other creatures of the forest? We can't exist without them. Surely they should be treated equally."

"No other animals are mentioned. Loach says they're all here to serve the wolf."

"The wolflore says all creatures depend on each other."

"The wolflore is taboo. The wolfrahm only know what Loach tells them, they are cubs when Talon gets hold of them and contact with the wisewolf Hawthorn is forbidden."

"Hawthorn is a recluse thanks to Talon, it's not surprising the old customs are being forgotten. Talon pleases himself."

*

The days passed slowly but peacefully and Stag's leg grew stronger by the day. Swift and Moon hunted together, leaving Stag under cover of the hazel thicket. They were constantly on the lookout for strangers, expecting the wolfrahm to come looking for their missing comrades. Moon did not stray from Swift's side.

Moon told Swift how she had come to the valley. Her father was an old wolf who had become ill and unable to hunt with the pack. She and her brother refused to leave him and they set out to find shelter until he recovered. Inadvertently they had wandered into Tannon Valley where they had met some friendly wolves who invited them to stay, saying that game was still plentiful on the outskirts. Her brother was young and Stone wanted him for the wolfrahm but he refused.

Swift hoped that in time Moon would be forgotten and left in peace.

Another March day dawned to the sound of songbirds. Tired of living on hares and rodents, Swift and Moon cantered to Sliver Birch Wood in search of bigger game. Stag had convinced them that the wolfrahm were only interested in her brother and would not be coming after Moon. It was Musk, the dark-faced wolf, who wanted her dead because she had recognised him as one of the wolves who had taken her brother away.

Swift breathed deeply, enjoying the freshness in the air. He glanced at Moon, sensing her appreciation of the change in the atmosphere. His body and mind were gradually recovering from his recent experiences and he felt a new vitality. When he reached the trail he didn't wait for Moon but ran off at a canter.

"Hey wait for me," she called indignantly and gave chase. Swift allowed her to catch up, feeling her nose touch his tail, then spurted ahead.

"Slow down," she called.

Swift laughed. "Try and catch me, slow paws."

Spurred on by his jibe, Moon caught him up again. Swift stopped suddenly. Moon more by luck than judgement managed to avoid piling into the back of him. She sat back heavily on her hindquarters and Swift ran on then stopped to laugh at her dismay. She stood up with a determined expression on her face. He splayed his front legs and ducked his head down in a playful challenge. She leapt at him and he dodged to one side. Then she challenged him. They ducked, bobbed and chased like a pair of overgrown cubs absorbed in play.

Moon leapt into the bracken; brown and tinder-dry, it crackled under her paws. Swift crashed after her. She wove skilfully through the oaks, parting the shoulder-high ferns with ease. Swift marvelled at her nimbleness, delighting in her lithe body as she changed direction with subtle ease. The birches around them showing the tips of new green shoots seemed to Swift, willing participants in the game being played out at their feet. Here where the ground cover was light and free from hidden dangers the two young wolves leapt and ran, tails held high in sheer exuberance. Butterflies took to the wing, mice scurried for cover, a jay screeched its annoyance somewhere in the branches above. Swift revelled in all these things but his amber eyes never left Moon. Suddenly he had a desperate urge to be near her, to smell the sweet fragrance of her fur. He called to her.

"Moon, stop, I'm puffed out."

It was Moon's turn to laugh. "Come on old slow paws, you'll have to catch me."

He ran on, she looked back to tease him and didn't see how the ground sloped away in front of her. Without warning she tumbled head over heels into a hollow in the ground, landing on a cushion of ferns. Swift leapt in after her. On seeing that she was unhurt he could not contain his amusement and Moon, infected by his high spirits, smiled with him.

He sat down next to her, panting. For a moment they were both too breathless to speak. Moon stretched out, resting her head on her paws. Swift lay next to her, exited by her presence.

"I owe you my life. Thank you," she said.

Swift placed his paw on hers. "Moon I should be thanking you, you've brought meaning to my life that wasn't there before. Life in the valley has been deteriorating over many seasons, everyone is despondent. You have freed me from this."

"Swift, if only it could go on like this forever. Sometimes I think it will but at other times I am so afraid."

"Don't be afraid, Stag is sure the wolfrahm won't be looking for you. You'll be just another wolf who wandered into the valley and I've taken you for a mate."

"Does that mean I can stay with you?"

"If you want to," he replied.

"Of course I want to."

"I hoped you'd say that. I've enjoyed these last few weeks more than anything I've ever done before."

"I'll stay for as long as you want me to."

They licked each other's faces. "Let's forget the future for today and just enjoy being together," said Swift.

On this day they hunted and played as one.

CHAPTER 6

Hawthorn emerged cautiously from the rear entrance to his den and sniffed the air for signs of the wolfrahm's presence. A breeze blew up the slope from the direction of the river bringing with it the odour of damp leaf mould and the scent of an unknown wolf. It had rained an hour earlier but now rays of sunlight turned wet leaves into glistening, green jewels that stirred lightly in the breeze. When he was certain he couldn't be seen he left the den, taking care not to slip on the mossy bank. He turned westward at the river following its course through the valley until he reached the ford where he began the gentle climb north to the Bluebell Wood.

The brown and grey shades of winter that dominated the flora of the valley were being transcended by the lush, green tufts of the emergent bluebells that garnished the woodland floor for as far as the wolf could see. Sunlight caught long slender leaves, casting shadows, showing many shades of green. The gusting breeze rippled them, continuously changing the emphasis of the shades. Green buds tinted with blue were poised on burgeoning stalks, preparing to transform the wood into colourful splendour and proclaim the pinnacle of spring.

At the centre of the wood grew the Ancient Oak, said to be the home of the spirit Earthstar, harbinger of light and growth. Dominated by the oaks, the Bluebell Wood abounded with life, its soil being the most fertile in the forest. Its rich humus perpetually replenished by fallen oak leaves breaking down, returning to the soil to restore vitality to the earth itself.

Finding reassurance in the presence of the ancient oak, Hawthorn sat beneath it and licked its bark reverently, enjoying its roughness on his tongue. The oak's closeness calmed him and he began to relax for the first time that morning. The sun's rays filtered through to warm his back, easing its stiffness. He took this as a sign of Earthstar's approval and it gave him the confidence to pray with anticipation. He looked up into the tree's branches and took several deep breaths before beginning.

"Earthstar, force of life that is within me and all creatures. I open my heart and mind to you in the belief that you will fill me with the power and energy I will need for the task ahead. Give me the strength of body and mind to resist the negative forces that will threaten me in the weeks and months to come. I pledge myself to your service mighty Earthstar, and pray that you will give the wolves of Tannon Valley the courage to do your bidding."

Hawthorn closed his eyes and pressed himself closer to the oak, feeling its solidness against his body. He breathed deeply, filling his lungs and distending his belly, forcing oxygen into every cell in his being. Calmness came over him and he opened his eyes. His mind and body were filled with the certainty of what had to be done, but he knew he could not do it alone. He was an old wolf, too old for the long struggle that lay ahead. His duty was to ensure the survival of the ancient wolflore. For months he had waited for the right time to arrive. He could wait no longer. He must pass on his knowledge before it was too late. It was time to visit Swift.

Now the decision had been made, he was happier, yet he regretted having to put Swift in danger. He had grown very fond of his protégé when Swift had visited him at the badger's setts and there were no foregone conclusions to the conflicts to come; much would depend on the outcome of extra-terrestrial battles. Swift would have to be lucky as well as clever to survive.

He took the path leading back to the river knowing what had to be done. At the river he turned west on the trail to the three-trunked oak which grew in the centre of the valley. Once wolves used to gather there of a summer's evening to gossip and listen to the wolflore. The three-trunked oak was the best known landmark in the valley. From an enormous bole grew three trunks of huge proportions, giving the tree a curious and awesome presence.

Once all trails led to the three-trunked oak but now many of them were overgrown with brambles. Now the Beech Wood had become the focal point of the valley's activities. Swift's den lay just off the trail about a quarter of a mile from the oak. It was still early and Hawthorn made the journey without encountering another wolf.

He found Mistle outside pulling moult hairs from her paws with her teeth. She looked up, pleased to see him.

"Hawthorn! It's been a long time."

"Things have been a bit difficult lately but I'm here now and you look marvellous," he replied.

"Thank you. Come and sit down." He smiled and sat down next to her.

"What brings you to see us?"

"I want to talk to Swift about something important."

Mistle's eyes narrowed. "I think I can guess what it's about but I hope I'm wrong."

"I know it won't be easy, Mistle, but Earthstar has made his choice."

"But why Swift?"

"He is the only wolf capable of doing what needs to be done."

"Isn't it enough that I've lost Raven?"

"I think he would be proud of Swift."

"I don't want to lose Swift as well."

"Swift will have the power of Earthstar with him."

"Will it be enough?"

"It will if we have faith."

Swift returned carrying a hare in his jaws which he put it down at Mistle's paws.

He greeted Hawthorn. "This is an honour, wisewolf."

"I hope you'll feel the same after you've heard what I've got to say."

"What is it Hawthorn?"

Mistle interrupted them. "I don't want to hear it, I'm going to call in on Fallow."

Hawthorn watched her depart. "I'll come straight to the point. Earthstar has chosen you to succeed me."

Swift sat down. "Why me?"

"You have shown courage and have always been willing to learn about the old traditions."

"Hawthorn, as much as I love the old stories, I've been wondering what relevance they have to what's happening in the valley. The wolflore has been outlawed and already there are cubs who know nothing about it."

"Swift, the wolflore is a way of life, lived by wolves since the beginning of time. Unless we return to it I don't think we will survive."

"But how can we undo the damage that's been done?"

"We must have faith in Earthstar and he will guide us. He has spoken to me in my dreams. Havnar is close to gaining a foothold in the valley. This would mean disaster for everyone. I think Earthstar will intervene but he can't stop Havnar without our help, so he has entrusted me with a secret that promises the gift of immortality. This gift is not meant for me but for a wolf worthy of its potency."

"If it came to you in dream how do you know it's real?"

"I didn't, until Talon came along."

"What do you mean?"

"Let me explain. It happened several years ago

when you were still a cub. One day Talon stopped me on the riverbank, I was on my way to see Mistle. Talon was about two years old then, just fully grown. He said that Havnar had come to him in a dream telling him about a gift from the spirits and that he was to come to me and demand it in the name of Havnar. Of course I had no intention of telling the first wolf who came along about a gift as precious as this. Besides it had been Earthstar who had spoken to me not Havnar. Earthstar said I would know who the recipient is to be when the time comes."

"Do you believe Havnar wanted Talon to have the secret?"

"Yes I do, otherwise Talon wouldn't know of its existence. Only the spirits know of it."

"But why Talon?"

"I believe Havnar brought him here for a purpose. It all began the day Tannon died. I remember it as though it were yesterday. It was one of those rare occasions when I joined the hunt. I'd had a premonition that something was about to happen. We travelled west through Silver Birch Wood, it was a damp overcast day in October. I remember my joints were playing me up terribly. We were approaching the far side of the wood led by Tannon when his hind legs buckled and he fell. His heart had finally given out. He was far too old to be out leading the pack on a hunt but he wouldn't listen to reason. We were all very distraught. There had never been an alpha wolf to match him. His wisdom and judgement were respected by every wolf. Even the toughest among us stood and wept. Then we howled a lament that we were told later could be heard everywhere across the valley. Everyone knew long before we returned that Tannon was dead. When the howl ceased there was total silence. It was unnatural. No birdsong, no voles scurrying in the undergrowth, nothing. Until I heard a pathetic whimpering sound coming from somewhere close by in the ferns. It spooked me, yet I felt drawn towards it. I found him under a clump of ferns by the path where Tannon had fallen. He was still blind, maybe deaf as well, but he had forced himself up onto his forelegs, his head bobbing unsteadily on a thin outstretched neck. There was something loathsome about this cub that made me growl and my only thought was to kill it. But before I could Thorn was beside me. 'It's an abandoned cub,' he said. 'Let's take it back to the valley with us otherwise it will die.' I said, 'We should kill it.' He accused me of being rabid but I insisted. Most of the others agreed with me. In those days I commanded some respect. But Thorn wouldn't allow it. He stood between me and the cub, teeth bared and a strange look in his eye. He was making his stand for the alpha position. It was generally thought that he would take over after Tannon. No one would take him on so I tried to talk him out of letting the cub live.

"I reminded him of the ancient wolflore that prophesied that a cub would come among us as if by magic. A cub, whom we should take in at our peril. He accused me of being an old she-wolf who hid from reality behind the mumbo jumbo of the wolflore. Without any warning the others turned against me to a wolf. I was deeply shocked and to this day I think they would have torn me to raven scraps if I'd protested anymore. The body of Tannon wasn't yet cold and already Talon's power could be felt."

"Do you think he was born with this power?"

"No, I believe Havnar is using him."

"What Talon wants from you can't he get from Havnar?"

"It would seem not."

"Talon has brought in a wisewolf from the northern territories called Loach. Maybe he will have the answers Talon wants."

"I suspect this Loach has knowledge of the spirits which Talon could use for his own good."

"Just what is Talon up to?"

"I don't know but we need to find out."

"Stag says Talon prays to Havnar at the giant yew every night," said Swift.

"Then we'll go to the Beech Wood."

"There is a small matter of the wolfrahm."

"We'll cross the Tannon at Badger's Bend and come into the Beech Wood from the other side. They won't expect us to come that way."

"Let me take Leaf with me, it's a long swim at Badger's Bend."

"You think I'm too old then?"

"We may have to make a run for it."

"Aright I see your point, but don't take any unnecessary chances."

*

Swift and Leaf took a concealed path which ran parallel with the river, meandering between the trunks of towering oaks, tall grey-barked hornbeams, wide spreading ash, and the occasional billowing lime. Apart from the ash which is one of the last trees to come into leaf, new growth was well advanced, providing the two wolves with some cover. The ground was soft beneath their paws where it had rained earlier and occasionally they had to wade through puddles.

The river was high and they heard the rush of its movement as they broke from the trees. The water level had risen, half submerging bulrushes growing along the river's edge. Here the ground was marshy where yellow kingcups decorated the bank. Swift and Leaf stopped at the water's edge and looked across to the Beech Wood which came down to meet a belt of willows lining the far bank.

The Tannon was at its widest here where it turned through almost ninety degrees to follow the course of Tannon Valley. They scanned the beeches for signs of movement until convinced they were unobserved. The water was cold and Swift shivered when it touched his belly. Two yards out they began paddling away from the bank, eyes fixed on the Beech Wood. Occasionally they were distracted by a trout that broke the surface to take a fly or by the flash of iridescent colour as a kingfisher darted downstream.

About midstream Swift busied himself by looking out for a suitable place to go ashore. An otter left the water through the reeds a little way upstream and Swift decided it would be as good a place as any. He paddled towards the bank and pushed his way through the reeds with Leaf close behind him. A narrow track ran under hanging willow branches parting the reeds, profuse on the bank. They stopped to vigorously shake the water from their coats before taking the path.

The ground below the willows was soft but became drier where it rose steeply at the beginnings of the Beech Wood. The height of the beeches even eclipsed that of the oaks dominant on the other side of the water. The beeches had no competition from other trees, forming the forest canopy in its entirety. The emergence of pale green oval leaves softened some of the harshness of the wood. Despite his allegiance to the oak he found himself admiring the pristine green of the beech leaves. At the beech hanger's margin, wood anemones blossomed taking advantage of the light before new leaves on the beeches would cast growth-stifling shadows.

The leaf litter was soft beneath their paws as they went inland. The wood was largely silent except for the occasional screech of a jay or chatter of a squirrel. Whenever they disturbed a jay or a pigeon they stopped instantly, afraid they had alerted someone. They travelled in silence, aware of how their voices would travel in the quiet of the beech hanger. Swift was glad of a head wind that made enough noise to cover any sounds they made and at the same time carried their scent away from Beech Hill. They took a narrow trail in single file. Here they made less noise where the beech mast and leaf litter had been scuffed away by the tread of many wolves using the path. Visibility was good, most of the branches grew high on the trunks and there were few under storey trees or shrubs apart from some holly and yew but not much else.

When they reached the west side of Beech Hill they left the path and climbed up to the plateaux away from the trail. From there they could see the dark bulk of the giant yew at the centre of the hilltop. In the distance to the north coming from the brow of Beech Hill the sound of voices carried on the wind. Leaf took the opposite direction, leading Swift tree by tree in a wide arc away from the wolfrahm's lair. At each tree Leaf paused to test the air for signs of danger. Swift followed him one tree behind, confident Leaf would find the safest route.

When they were within five or six trees of the yew Leaf motioned for him to stay put. There was nothing to do now but wait. They lay down silently in the leaf litter, aware that the slightest movement would give them away. Time dragged and Swift became tense as his body stiffened from lying in one position. He was considering stretching his limbs when he glimpsed activity on the brow of Beech Hill. The powerful figure of Talon strode into view, making towards the giant yew.

The alpha wolf stepped under the branches of the yew and onto the darker soil that was devoid of fallen beech leaves, beneath the thick cover of the enormous tree. He looked searchingly into its branches. Its dark green fronds hung down like the mantle of a huge eagle taking him under its wings. Suddenly Talon came to life, placing his forepaws on the gnarled trunk, stretching his long body out as though he would climb the tree. Instead he let out a long, low howl that raised the hackles on Swift's back. Swift shuddered involuntarily, unable to take his eyes from the outstretched form of Talon that in the failing light blended perfectly with the yew's darkness to become an extension of the tree itself. Talon's howl cut through his head, reverberating in his consciousness until his head felt that it would burst. It seemed to go on forever but then ceased abruptly, filling the forest with silence.

Then Talon spoke. "Omnipotent power of darkness, I stand before you as your servant to do your bidding and to bring your presence to Tannon Valley. Omnipotent power come among us to strengthen the might of the wolf nation. Make us invincible when the invader comes and we will serve you eternally. Mighty Havnar I beseech you to guide me, your servant on earth that I may prepare the way for you. I await a sign of your presence and make ready to do battle with your enemies."

For what seemed an age to Swift, Talon remained silently gazing up into the branches of the yew. Finally he howled a low eerie howl that chilled Swift's blood. Swift glanced at Leaf whose grim expression brought the full import of Talon's words home to him.

At last Talon took his paws from the trunk of the giant yew. He stood rigidly, staring into the darkness to where Swift and Leaf hid. His nose twitched as he scented the air. His ears pitched forward to detect the slightest sound. An eternity passed before Talon turned away to disappear like an apparition into the dusk.

Swift and Leaf waited until darkness in the Beech Wood was complete. They made their way back to the river in silence. To Swift every shadow seemed to conceal a demon sent by Havnar to torment them and frighten them from opposing Talon. It was a great relief when they entered the river at Badger's Bend and left the beech wood behind, but Swift still felt unnerved. They would need to find somewhere safe away from prying eyes and ears to formulate a plan. Leaf suggested the swamp and Swift agreed. They met Moss and headed west along the Tannon. A mile down from the ford the Tannon ran across a clay bed that held surface water on either side of the river, turning a large area of the valley into swamp land. This was a place shunned by wolves, who dig their dens where it is dry.

Leaf had hunted beaver and otter there many times and knew it well. He led Swift and Moss along a trail that disappeared into the muddy waters of the swamp. They reached the edge of a reed bed and entered the water. Leaf saw the grimace on Moss' face and smiled. "Watch out for the swamp monster, Moss," he said.

"How deep does it get?" asked Moss.

"It's not the water you've got to worry about, it's the mud. Don't stand around for too long."

Moss moved along more gingerly, detesting every footfall in the sucking mire. "I hope you know where we're going. I can't see a thing through these reeds. What if we get stuck?"

"Don't keep worrying, just follow me."

Leaf led them through a tangle of alders that grew across most of the swamp thriving in the wet conditions. He took them out of the reeds and through some brackish water towards a small island of raised ground covered in bulrushes. Moss was relieved to get his feet on firmer ground.

"I'm not going any further," he said.

"Alright, stop moaning, this is it."

"Couldn't be better," said Swift, "nobody will find us here."

"At least we should be uninterrupted here, can't imagine any other wolf wanting to join us," said Moss. "But I'm still not sure why we are here."

"We are here because things are hotting up. Talon is out to get Havnar's enemies and he has called on Havnar to help him do it," said Swift.

"I don't like the sound of it," said Moss.

"I believe Hawthorn is in great danger, the wolfrahm are watching every move he makes. We've got to do something before it is too late."

"What can we do?" asked Moss. "The wolfrahm are too well organised."

"We need to be one step ahead of them."

"We're nowhere near them at the moment, let alone one step ahead," said Leaf.

"We can be if we get some inside help," said Swift.

"Who are you going to ask, Thorn?"

"Stag."

"Stag, how do you know you can trust him?"

"Instinct."

"But he went back to the wolfrahm after you saved his life."

"He didn't want to leave the valley, he had no choice. He was a different wolf when he went back to the Beech Wood. I'm sure of it."

"Alright, it's up to you but I've got my doubts," replied Leaf.

CHAPTER 7

The first rays of dawn lit the Beech Wood as Talon stood at the brow of Beech Hill looking out at the dark mass of trees that populated Tannon Valley. Unable to sleep, he paced under the beeches, his brow furrowed. He couldn't rest whilst Hawthorn was missing.

"Curse that old flea bag," he muttered and resumed his pacing. He couldn't accept that only one old wolf stood between him and the realisation of his dream, especially as there was nothing he could do about it. Not for the time being anyway. He tried to cheer himself up by concentrating on his successes. He had formed the wolfrahm without too much opposition, enlisting all potential alpha wolves, buying their allegiance with favours to keep them satisfied. Not that he was afraid of them. He wanted them to be content, living a lifestyle they wouldn't want to give up too easily. Plans had gone well on the whole even though he had been forced on occasions to take drastic measures, but these were a small price to pay to secure the future of Tannon Valley. Determined to maintain the impetus he decided to address a full assembly of the wolfrahm to unfold more of his plans for the future.

Everything he had envisaged had materialised with

consummate ease but lately there was something in the back of his mind bothering him, like a flea incessantly biting behind his ear. It wasn't just Hawthorn. It was something else, something threatening. He searched his consciousness for an answer but couldn't pinpoint anything. Suddenly he felt compelled to go down into the valley as though if he were closer he might understand what caused his uneasiness.

He made his way down the slope, through the beeches, and emerged through the holly bushes into the mixed woodland at the foot of the hill. He stopped and stared in the direction of the ford as if he was trying to pick up a signal. Whatever was happening out there it bode ill for him, he was certain of that. He stood for some time under the hanging branches of a silver birch, watching and waiting, but nothing came to him to enlighten him or to relieve his anxiety. He decided not to delay and trudged back up the hill to Loach's den. As he went he cursed a blackbird singing cheerfully, high in the branches of a beech close by.

There was no sign of Loach. He peered into the darkness of his den. "Loach you lazy good for nothing it's time you were up."

Loach stumbled out, squinting in the daylight, fur ruffled, trying to stifle a yawn. "Er, sorry alpha wolf, I seem to have overslept."

"Well you had better wake yourself up pretty damn quick," Talon growled, "there is something in the air and I want to know what it is."

"What sort of thing, alpha wolf?" asked Loach, puzzled.

"I don't know, fool, which is precisely why I've come to you."

Loach cowered submissively, tail between legs. "Yes alpha wolf, we should pray to Havnar for guidance. I suggest a full assembly of the wolfrahm."

"How can I have a full assembly when half of the wolfrahm is out chasing one cursed wolf?" Talon stared maliciously at the grovelling wisewolf, acutely aware of the feeling of annoyance which usually accompanied their meetings.

"May I make a suggestion, alpha? Why don't we make our way to the sacred yew and pray to Havnar for guidance?"

"Alright, let's get on with it."

The sacred yew grew in the centre of the Beech Wood plateau and was the main reason for Talon's choice of headquarters. The yew was said to be the home of the spirit Havnar who like Earthstar went back to the beginning of time making them the most powerful spirits in the wolf world. Few trees can survive in the shade of the towering beeches but the sacred yew was believed to be the oldest tree in the Tannon territory, its huge fluted bole testimony to its long life. Thick dark branches twisted and stretched in every direction, their bark lined by the deep fissures of age. Squat, wide, solid, and permanent it stood in stark contrast to the vulnerable, smooth-skinned, straight-backed beeches which surrounded it like sentinels watching over it.

Even Talon was in awe of its magnitude and felt uncomfortable in its presence. Deep down he did not like visiting it. It made him feel insignificant and dispensable when standing in the shadow of its wide spreading fronds. He looked at Loach and felt better, unlike him he wasn't afraid of the yew, he merely resented cowering reverently in its presence as wolves were expected to do. For Loach it was easy to hang his tail between his legs but for the alpha wolf it was repugnant, besides he always felt that Loach was secretly laughing at his reluctant submission to the tree.

Head bowed, Loach spoke reverently to the yew. "Mighty Havnar, lord of the forest, spirit of the trees, master of time, it is to you that we have come to seek wisdom. In return we offer ourselves to you as humble servants that we may do your bidding. Give us a sign, Lord, that you hear our prayer." Nothing stirred in the Beech Wood. The breeze ceased to ruffle the leaves and the birds were silent. Talon desperately sought approval from the spirit of the yew and sensing contact with him, intensified the appeal.

"Eternal master, timeless one, I Talon, alpha wolf, your devoted servant, come to you with your interests in my heart. I implore you to empower me to remove all obstacles which impede your path to power in the valley and in the forests beyond."

The sound of howling came from the direction of the Beech Wood slopes and interrupted Talon's monologue. He looked at Loach quizzically.

"We'd better find out what's going on."

Talon raced back towards the slopes leaving Loach in his wake. He smiled in triumph at the sight of Stone leading Hawthorn into the Beech Wood. Restraining himself, he waited for Stone to bring the prisoner to him.

"Ah Hawthorn at last, my wolves have been looking for you everywhere. Where have you been hiding?"

"It's none of your business where I've been."

"We shall see about that, you have your breaking point like every other wolf."

"It's no use trying to frighten me Talon, you've tried that before."

"I might just try again, this time a little harder."

Hawthorn looked away dismissively. "Do what you will," he said.

Talon growled, no wolf annoyed him like Hawthorn; his impulse was to get rid of him for good there and then, but instead he dismissed Stone, much to the black wolf's annoyance, and spoke to Hawthorn alone.

"The wolflore says it is your duty to pass on its teachings to a worthy successor. If you fail to do this it is also said that you will not ascend to the forests of the spirits but instead will exist forevermore in the wastes of Falhallen, damned for all eternity." He looked searchingly at Hawthorn and smiled. "Even you, Hawthorn, would not relish that. You are an old wolf, I would judge that you haven't much time left to pass on your secrets but pass them on you must. If you don't tell me what I want to know I will find out from your successor, if he refuses to tell me, the secrets of the spirits will die with him."

"Your threats don't bother me, Talon. You wouldn't have the nerve to destroy the holder of the secret because you want it so badly. You would rather die yourself, than have no hope of finding it."

"We shall see about that, from now on every move you make will be watched and reported to me, your only chance to avoid eternal damnation is to tell me what I want to know."

Talon called Stone. "Stone, let the old fleabag go but watch him constantly, day and night, and report to me every move he makes."

"Let him go? The entire wolfrahm has just spent the last three days looking for him, and you want to let him go after a five minute conversation?"

"Stone, you forget yourself. I don't expect you to question my decisions. Now do as I say, I'll speak to you later."

Within two days of Hawthorn's arrest and release all wolfrahm patrols had been called in to comply with Talon's order that the entire wolfrahm should attend a ceremony in honour of the spirit Havnar. The last wolves had returned from the more distant outposts earlier that day, many on the verge of exhaustion, after travelling non-stop to avoid Talon's wrath.

Talon surveyed the wolfrahm from across the Beech Wood plateaux, the elite of the pack, chosen for their size, strength, and speed. They were the pick of the Tannon Valley litters, selected at an early age by Talon and Stone who lost no time in their indoctrination. Talon congratulated himself on how well it had paid off. Of course he had to keep them happy with the pick of the spoils from the hunt and so on, but he was satisfied with the allegiance they had shown him.

Tonight however, they would be entering new territory so to speak. This would be a real test of their commitment. He watched them form columns of two under Stone's instructions. He considered the black wolf a useful ally but felt it necessary to keep an eye on him, sometimes his attitude was questionable.

The April sun had sunk close to the treetops, it was time to make haste. He signalled to Stone who took up his position at the front of the pack. The black wolf led them down from the Beech Wood and across the ford where they turned east along the river path moving at a steady trot. Talon and Loach followed some twenty paces behind discussing the arrangements for the ceremony. By the time they reached their destination the light was fading fast.

The site Loach had chosen for the ceremony was a beaver meadow close to the river near a deserted beaver dam. In building the dam the beavers had cleared a large patch of woodland that was now a grassy glade rich in plant life. It was a favourite feeding ground for deer and as such had great potency in the eyes of the wolf. On the far side of the clearing amongst the ash and the alder that predominated were three ancient yews, their dark fronds shadowy in the half-light. Stone led the wolfrahm into the centre of the meadow. Talon and Loach did not follow, instead they sat in silence at the edge of the clearing watching as each animal took his place in the semicircle.

The moon was full and poised above the darkness of the treetops, flooding the woodland arena with an eerie silver light. Talon detected anxious glances in his direction as wolves fidgeted nervously, waiting for his entrance. He would keep them waiting awhile yet, building the atmosphere. With their senses heightened they would be more receptive. The sky abounded with stars, glittering jewels studding a black, velvet sky. Talon could smell the tension building in the meadow and sensed Loach fidgeting nervously beside him. Loach's cream fur gave him an unnatural spectre-like appearance in the moonlight. Talon smiled, the scene was set. "Do your stuff Loach, tonight we must have a sign."

Talon strode into the clearing followed closely by Loach. They faced the semicircle of wolves who waited expectantly against the moonlit backdrop of ancient, wizened yews. Talon saw the fear in their eyes; they were unaccustomed to being away from their dens after dark. Each wolf watched him intently and he felt a surge of power run through his veins.

"Brother wolves, you have been selected to serve in the wolfrahm. This is an honour to which not all can aspire. Only the best amongst the pack are so honoured. It is your duty to uphold the position of the wolf as master of the forest. I believe the wolf has been chosen to be its custodian. Your task as wolfrahm is to secure the future not only of Tannon Valley but of the wolf nation. It will not be easy or something we can do alone for I believe there is a threat of such magnitude that only by invoking the help of the spirits can we survive. I have prayed for this help and my prayers have been answered." Pausing for effect, he stopped speaking and surveyed his audience. "Brother wolves, my prayers have been answered by the might spirit of the yew, Lord Havnar." The murmur of whispered conversation rippled through the meadow at the mention of Havnar's name. Talon continued, "Do not be afraid brothers, Havnar will not harm those who are his servants, on the contrary they will be rewarded. Only those who do not serve him need be afraid..." He paused again. "There are those among us in Tannon Valley who are his enemies, they must be sought out and dealt with. He saw furtive glances between wolves who understood the implications for them and their families. "We must be strong, brothers, and do what we have to do."

He stopped speaking and silence fell like a heavy weight on the clearing. No breeze stirred and they stood as if in a vacuum. The wolfrahm were transfixed, united in fearful anticipation of what was to come. Eventually Talon spoke to Loach. "Servant of Havnar, I command you to invoke the presence of our master."

Loach raised his muzzle to the sky. "Lord of the night, stir from your slumber and awaken your wrath. Spirit of the night, rouse your power to smite your enemies. I beseech you to wake the dormant seeds of aggression so that your work shall be done. Your servants seek a sign from their master."

An all-pervading silence filled the beaver meadow. Talon walked reverently towards the stand of yew trees, head bowed; wolves in his path shifted nervously aside at his approach. He stopped beneath the middle yew and sat on his haunches staring into its dark, twisted branches. "Hear my plea Havnar, the wolf nation is ready to receive you," he prayed. "The heart and soul of every wolf gathered here is open to you and awaits your bidding. Give us a sign, Lord."

Talon felt a chill penetrate his fur. The temperature had begun to drop in the meadow and it was getting rapidly colder. A wispy mist was forming at the edge of the clearing. Gradually it began to creep across the glade from all sides, surrounding the semicircle of wolves. It began to move almost imperceptibly towards them, blanketing the surface of the meadow in its path. He turned towards the pack, many wolves were shivering. He began to shiver. Some wolves collapsed, a layer of frost whitening their fur. Talon tried to stop his teeth from chattering and to resist the effects of the frost but his legs were so cold he could hardly stand up. Despite his efforts his hind legs buckled beneath him but he tried desperately not to fall. His eyes widened in disbelief as he watched the mist swallow up fallen wolves. Some moaned in agony as the frost froze their bones. The advancing mist had destroyed his wolfrahm in a matter of minutes. The wolfrahm lay scattered across the beaver meadow like victims of a massacre. That night the meadow became an icy tomb that no other creature dared enter.

The thaw began the next day with the sunlight that came with the dawn. It was some time before the life-giving rays spread far enough across the clearing to warm Talon's frozen blood, but when they reached him he was the first wolf to recover. He yawned as though coming out of a long and deep sleep. Eventually he struggled to his feet, his consciousness a whirlpool of confusion. He tottered dizzily for a moment then promptly sat down on his haunches to give his head time to clear. Slowly the horror of the previous night came back to him. He looked around to see the clearing littered with frozen bodies. For a second he thought they were all dead. He glimpsed a movement and then heard a cry of agony as frozen limbs came painfully back to life. He had not expected this. He knew it would be a dangerous game playing with Havnar, but he had not expected this. This was a raw demonstration of his supernatural power. At the moment its effect on the wolfrahm was difficult to calculate, but he would tread more carefully in future.

CHAPTER 8

A week had elapsed since the first meeting on the island. Swift, Leaf, and Moss had met since and decided to try and enlist help from inside the wolfrahm. They had agreed to contact Stag who Swift had assured them could be trusted. Most of the wolfrahm were stationed in the Beech Wood engaged in the various duties which Talon had assigned for them, but Tannon Valley was constantly being policed by wolfrahm patrols. The size of patrols varied but there were never less than three. Stag believed that if ever a wolf tried to desert there were always two other wolves to deal with him. To contact Stag, Swift decided to keep the main exits to the Beech Wood under surveillance. If Stag left with a patrol Swift and Leaf would follow, looking for an opportunity to speak to him alone. After four days Stag left the Beech Wood with three other wolves, crossing the river to head north.

Swift and Leaf followed them at a discreet distance to Silver Birch Wood where the patrol stopped to drink from a stream. Swift and Leaf lay in the undergrowth, flat on their bellies, watching Stag and the others drink their fill before crossing the stream. The patrol looked around for a campsite, settling for a spot beneath a magnificent ash tree. Swift expected them to hunt but they settled down to nap without posting a sentry.

"It'll be dark soon Swift, we must try to wake Stag without waking the others," said Leaf.

Within half an hour it was dusk and the two wolves crept through the ferns with just enough light to see their way. Swift crawled to within a few inches of Stag. The three wolfrahm were asleep. Swift blew into Stag's ear, it twitched but he didn't wake up. Swift pulled himself closer and nudged Stag's shoulder with his nose. Stag stirred, changed position and continued sleeping. Swift nudged him harder, he woke with a start. Swift raised a paw to silence him. Stag stared wide-eyed in disbelief. Swift beckoned to him to follow.

Stag shook his head. "In the morning," he mouthed.

Neither Swift nor Leaf could relax sufficiently to be able to sleep well. The night seemed interminable and both wolves were glad when the first rays of daylight penetrated the woodland canopy. During the night they had moved a safer distance from the wolfrahm camp but could still see Stag. They watched for signs of movement. Eventually Stag stood up and held a brief conversation with his companions before leaving the campsite.

He trotted off in the opposite direction away from where Swift and Leaf waited but eventually turned up behind them. He gestured to Swift and Leaf to follow him and led them to a spot out of earshot of his comrades.

"What in Earthstar's name are you two doing here spying on a wolfrahm patrol?"

"We're not spying, we've come to talk to you," said Swift.

"Well it's a dangerous thing to do. Stone's been paranoid lately about rebels in the valley."

"We couldn't think of another way to contact you," interjected Leaf.

"Alright, but you'd better make it quick."

"We need your help," said Swift.

"Say what it is you want Swift, you know I am indebted to you."

"We want you to help us get rid of Talon."

"What! I'm willing to help, but I can't do the impossible."

Swift frowned and considered his reply. "I believe, that with the right planning and organisation, along with Earthstar's help, we could do it."

Stag turned to Leaf. "Do you believe this, Leaf?"

"All I know mate, is either 'e goes or I do. And I've got no plans to leave."

"Talon has an army of wolves at his disposal, and he knows everything that goes on in the valley."

"That's where you're wrong Stag, he doesn't know about us," replied Swift.

"Well it's only a matter of time, he finds out everything eventually." Stag glanced nervously over his shoulder. "They say he conspires with Havnar."

"All the more reason to stop him," said Swift.

"Do you really believe we can stop Havnar?"

"Yes, with the help of Earthstar."

"Earthstar. What's he ever done for us?"

"You forget the wolflore, Stag, remember Earthstar led us to Tannon Valley."

"What do I know about the wolflore? I've been with Talon since I was a cub."

"Stag where are you?" A shout came from one of the patrol wolves.

Stag jumped to his feet. "They're getting hungry, I'm supposed to be hunting."

"You had better get back, but will you help us?"

Stag looked bemused. "Alright, I'll be in touch," he said, and slipped off through the ferns.

A week later Stag arrived at Swift's den. It was in the early hours of the evening and Swift asked Moss to contact Leaf and join them on the island in the swamp. An hour later the four wolves met on the island. A heavy mist hung over the marshes.

Stag shivered. "Who chose this as a meeting place? It's the last place I'd have chosen."

"Exactly," said Leaf, "nobody in their right mind comes here unless they have to."

"I don't know what's worse, the stench or the cold," said Stag.

"If you smelt it in the summer you'd have something to complain about. Trouble with you wolfrahm is you get it too easy."

"Alright Leaf, let's not start any arguments between

ourselves," interjected Swift. "Stag has risked his life by coming here. Let's hear what he's got to say."

"Yes, tell us what has happened. I hope it's nothing serious," said Moss.

"It's Talon, he's been acting very strange lately; he knows something is going on, I'm sure of it. Sometimes I feel he is watching me. Stone has been ordered to tighten security in the valley. Gatherings of more than three wolves at any one time are forbidden."

"Whoops we're in trouble then," joked Leaf.

"This is serious, Leaf," said Moss, whilst glancing over his shoulder.

"That's not all," continued Stag, "there was a ceremonial meeting of all senior wolfrahm last night."

"What happened?" asked Swift.

"I don't know exactly, but apparently some very strange things took place which convinced Talon that Havnar is very much on his side."

Moss swallowed nervously. "Havnar and Talon, I don't like the sound of that."

"An evil combination," said Swift.

"Yes, but what does it all mean?" said Leaf.

"It looks as though Talon is about to unleash the forces of Havnar on us."

"And what are we going to do about that?" asked Leaf.

Swift didn't show the fear he felt inside, and looked his friend in the eye. "We get rid of Talon."

*

During the succeeding weeks it became increasingly difficult for Swift and the others to meet. Talon had imposed a curfew during the grey hours before dawn and after dusk. The daylight hours were too busy with wolves going about their daily business under the scrutiny of wolfrahm patrols, for the conspirators to meet without fear of somebody seeing them. They lived in fear of being stopped and questioned. They agreed not to flout the curfew because Talon had ordered the immediate arrest of any wolf doing so. Swift had hoped to come up with a plan before things tightened up as he guessed they would but Talon had moved quickly. He felt uneasy. It was as though Talon knew of his intentions.

Swift grew frustrated with waiting and decided to risk a visit to Hawthorn. It was noon and exceptionally hot even for August. The heat was oppressive and most wolves were resting in the shade. Even those that Swift met on the trail were sullen and none stopped to pass the time of day. The heat was getting to everyone. He became more and more depressed as he travelled through the tinder-dry valley. He reached the river and hurried along the path, squinting at the sun's reflection from the surface of the water. The closer he got to the badgers' setts the more nervous he became. He took to the undergrowth to avoid running into wolfrahm spies sent to watch Hawthorn.

He sensed danger and felt tempted to turn back but forced himself on. He worked his way cautiously to the mouth of Hawthorn's den, treading carefully to avoid the thorns of fallen holly leaves. As he got closer he picked up the scent of several wolves that he did not recognise. There was no one in sight but the den's sandy entrance was a mass of paw prints. He listened intently and sniffed at the air before entering. The smell of blood mingled with the smell of strangers rose from the den. He hurried along the entrance tunnel on the verge of panic and stared into the gloom. When his eyes adjusted to the light he saw that the den was empty. He sniffed at the blood soaked into the sandy floor. It was wolf, and fresh.

He hurried out into the sunlight and took several deep breaths to calm himself before searching around the entrance for more clues to what had happened. He followed the tracks through the holly bushes to the trail which traversed the northern edge of the valley. The scent of wolves grew stronger but something was wrong, it was too quiet. He sniffed the breeze and peered upwind along a straight stretch of track. Several wolves came into view, moving swiftly towards him. He felt panic pulse through his body and a single thought ran through his mind. *How did they know?*

A voice from behind sent a shiver down his spine. "Ah Swift, what a pleasure." Swift turned to find Stone grinning with cold pleasure. He experienced a sinking feeling in his stomach and felt as though he was shrinking away under the black wolf's penetrating gaze. "I rather hoped I'd bump into you. You see I have some questions to ask you. Now will you come quietly or will we have to persuade you? We had to persuade your friend, poor thing is not feeling too well now."

"What have you done to him? You evil weasel."

"Come and see." Stone led him round a bend in the path. A wolf lay on his side, the fur on his face and neck matted with blood. It wasn't Hawthorn as Swift had expected. It was Moss. Swift ran to him and nudged him with his muzzle.

"Moss, it's Swift," he said.

"A friend of yours?" said Stone, still smiling. "It's alright, he's not dead, plenty of time for that. First he has to answer a few questions."

"What have you done to him?"

"You'll find out if you don't co-operate. He'll have to stay here until he's well enough to travel. You will come with me now."

"Where to?"

"Why, to the Beech Wood of course."

Swift's mouth was dry but he tried to sound calm. "I've done nothing wrong."

"Did I say you'd done something wrong? Guilty conscience is it?" Stone smiled at Swift's discomfort. "We just want to talk to you."

"What about?"

"Don't fret wolf, all in good time." Stone continued to grin but his eyes remained icy. "You will come with us."

Stone set a fast pace with Swift following behind him flanked by four hefty wolves. Swift agonised over his predicament. He knew how dangerous it would be if he let them take him to the Beech Wood but if he escaped, Moss would be alone in their clutches and left to Stone's whims. He could not desert him, not after what they had done to him, yet the prospect of being held in the Beech Wood frightened him more than most things.

Stone led them along little-used paths where there were no witnesses to his capture. He increased the pace and Swift drew in gasps of air through his gaping mouth and his heart began to pound as they neared the ford. Heavy rain had swollen the river to overflowing which meant it would have to be swum. Swift, being a strong swimmer knew it was a last opportunity for escape but his conscience would not allow him to leave Moss at Stone's mercy.

They wasted no time in crossing the river, stopping briefly on the Beech Wood bank to shake the water from their fur. Swift felt sick, it was too late now, he was in wolfrahm territory. As they ascended the forbidding slopes of the Beech Wood he prayed to Earthstar for courage and deliverance. In the half-light of the evening the fringe of holly bushes at the base of Beech Hill became a dark, sinister wall beyond which hidden dangers lurked. Inevitably they entered its darkness, following a path between dense holly leaves. He winced as sharp thorns pricked his nose and pierced the pads of his paws.

They emerged into the openness of the Beech Wood and Swift's paws sank into the thick litter of beech leaves. Nothing grew beneath the towering beeches except a few holly bushes and to Swift it was barren and alien in the gloom of dusk. He found it difficult to grip on leaves soaked by several days of heavy rain but Stone would not slow down until they reached the ancient yew, where Talon waited as though he was expecting their arrival. Swift was struck by the alpha wolf's physical stature, as he was every time he saw him. His muscular frame, accentuated by unusually short fur, was twice the size of the average wolf. Stone opened his mouth to speak but Talon cut him short.

"Where's the other one?" he said.

"He met with an accident. He'll be with us a bit later."

"We have them all then?" It was more a statement than a question. Talon turned his attention to Swift. "I had a feeling I would be seeing you again."

"Why have you brought me here?"

"Come, come, I think you know the answer to that one."

For a moment Swift expected Talon to smile but he didn't.

"I've no idea what you're talking about," he replied.

Any hint of humour left Talon's face. "Rest assured you will soon find out. Stone, see that he is watched at all times."

Stone led Swift to a small holly bush with drooping branches that spread out touching the ground to form a dome. He ordered Swift inside. The hours dragged as he pondered over his fate and watched for Moss' arrival. He kept going over the events of the past week, wondering where it had all gone wrong. Just before nightfall a wolfrahm patrol returned, bringing with them a badly limping Moss who looked barely able to stand. Swift regretted involving him and felt responsible for the danger he'd placed all his friends in. Perhaps he had been too hasty and had underestimated

Talon's power. And what about Leaf? Talon had said he'd got them all. He watched Moss being led through the beeches towards the yew. His attention fixed completely on the outcome of Moss' meeting with Talon, he did not notice a group of wolfrahm approaching the domed holly.

A big grey wolf with an unusually deep voice startled him. "Come on, this way, the alpha wolf wants you."

Swift stood up his legs stiff from inactivity. He walked the same path to the yew as Moss had done a few moments earlier. His heart sank, the small figure of Leaf stood next to Moss. Swift stood next to them and they waited in silence, exchanging nervous glances, but Leaf managed to wink at Swift. This encouraged Swift for a moment but Talon soon put an end to that.

"Good, now that you are all together I can tell you why you are here. It is quite simple. I am in need of certain information which only Hawthorn has. In order to get that information I am going to offer Hawthorn the opportunity to save your lives. All he has to do is tell me what I want to know and you will go free. If he chooses not to then he will have your deaths on his conscience for the rest of his life. For the good of the wolf nation I have tried to persuade him to tell me what I want to know but he refuses, so I am forced to take drastic measures. Hawthorn is being held elsewhere where you will not be able to influence his decision. He will be told that you have been arrested and be given the opportunity to save your lives. If he gives me the information I want you go free. If not, you will be executed as rebels." Swift glanced at the others. Moss had a glazed look in his eyes but Leaf managed another wink.

Talon continued with his monologue. "I will be with Hawthorn asking the questions, Stone, my second in command will remain with you. Hawthorn will be given three opportunities to tell me what I want to know, each time he refuses one of you will be executed for plotting the overthrow of the alpha wolf. The wolfrahm are striving to bring law and order to the valley to secure the future of the wolf nation and you, it would seem, are determined to disrupt our efforts."

Swift could listen in silence no longer. "The only law we want to disrupt is your law, not the ancient wolflore, the true law of the wolf. The wolflore has grown from the law of nature. Your law has been manufactured to suit yourself."

"Pah, the ancient wolflore is nothing but the gibberings of so-called wisewolves who live in the past and can see about far as the ends of their snouts. What of tomorrow when the wolf will face the greatest crisis in his history? Only Havnar will save us then."

Swift was silenced by the look in Talon's eye, realising that nothing he could say would have the slightest effect on the alpha wolf's opinion, so he decided to save his breath. Talon turned to Stone. "Take them to the domed holly. I will send messages by runner." Without another glance at his prisoners he trotted off towards the slopes with an escort of four wolves.

"Right, you heard, come with me." Stone led them

back to the domed holly.

Leaf spoke first. "Don't look so glum, old Talon might get eaten by a bear before he reaches Hawthorn." Swift and Moss just stared at him. "Well it's no good giving up hope, is it?" he went on.

Moss looked as if he was about to vomit. Swift touched his friend's paw. "Leaf is right Moss, we shouldn't give up hope."

"All Hawthorn has to do is tell him what he wants to know and we're high and dry," said Leaf. Swift didn't know what the repercussions of that would be but guessed they wouldn't be good. To take the pressure off Hawthorn they would have to make a run for it. Even as he reached that decision Stone doubled the wolfrahm guard.

The wind had picked up and dark clouds blew in swiftly from the south west. It would be dark soon, maybe they would have a chance of escape after nightfall. Talon's first runner had not arrived yet and it was unlikely that he would travel at night. This would give them time to come up with a plan.

Leaf spoke, interrupting Swift's thoughts. "It was that weasel Stag, we should never have trusted him, he was probably working for Talon all along."

"You don't know that, Leaf," replied Swift.

"Well where in Earthstar's name is he? Why isn't he here with the rest of us?"

Swift had been asking himself the same question. Whoever had discovered them must have seen Stag at the same time. "He's probably out on patrol somewhere, he'll be for it when he gets back. At the moment there is no point in speculating about Stag, we've got to find a way out of here. I think our only chance is to make a dash for it after dark."

"I agree," said Leaf, "the darkness will be a great leveller, none of us or them will be able to see what we're doing. With those rain clouds coming over it'll be darker than Stone's backside."

Swift managed a laugh. "We might have a chance yet," he said.

The south-westerly was now rattling the holly leaves fiercely and getting noisier as it whistled through the branches above their heads. It had become chilly and some of the guards lay down to shelter from the wind. The darkness intensified simultaneously with the velocity of the wind which swept under the drooping branches of the domed holly, lifting them into the air. The prisoners cowered to protect themselves from prickly whips that lashed back at them when the wind temporarily abated.

The noise in the Beech Wood grew with the wind's fury, intensifying with each gust. Swift looked up warily, trying to pinpoint the sound of two branches rubbing together, grinding out an ominous tune. Even the mighty beeches were dancing silhouettes in the darkness straining against the onslaught. Swift felt the movement of their roots straining to retain their grip in the earth but still the wind had not reached its climax. It moved through the trees with the sound of thunder, its roar frightening the inhabitants of Tannon Valley who cowered in their dens. Close to the holly a yew sapling bent double then whipped back in a moment of brief respite before being doubled over again. Swift had never known a wind like it; he, Moss, and Leaf huddled together, seeking refuge from its assault. From further down the slope they heard the terrifying sound of roots being torn from the earth followed by a thunderous crash as an old beech lost the struggle to remain upright. Then another crashed, this time closer.

The darkness intensified their fear but Swift took heart from the storm. "This is a gift from Earthstar, let's take advantage of it, the wolfrahm are cowering in their dens. If we make our way down the slope we are bound to reach the river. When we do, we follow it to the ford where it will be less swollen. We'll cross there, and tomorrow, all being well, we'll meet on the island. He sensed Moss' fear. "Come on Moss, take heart, Earthstar is with us."

"How can we possibly make it to the river in the dark? We'll all be killed."

"Moss, it's our only chance, if we stay here it's certain death. Hawthorn can't save us and we can't afford to waste time or we'll be numb with cold. I'm frozen already."

"Come on you two, cut the cackle and let's get going," growled Leaf.

Leaf in front and Swift at the rear, they crawled on their bellies in single file under the hanging branches of the holly and down the slope unchallenged. Once clear of the holly they stood up and continued down the slope, each losing sight of the others in the pitch black of the night. Swift called to them but his voice was lost in the roar of the hurricane. Continually he had to check his footing on the sodden beech leaves as the wind tried to force him headlong down the slope. Holly leaves tore at his face, scratching his nose as he stumbled through the holly bushes forming the periphery of Talon's stronghold. The rain stung his eyes and the wind took his breath away. From every direction came the crash of falling trees and he prayed to Earthstar for Moss and Leaf's safety and his own deliverance from the hurricane.

An enormous gust slammed him against a beech tree, knocking the breath out of him. He lay on the saturated ground panting, incredulous at the storm's ferocity. He staggered to his feet and felt his way around the tree, edging down the slope to the valley floor where brambles sunk their thorns into his snout, tearing his skin. Numbed, he stumbled on, determined to leave the Beech Wood as far behind him as possible.

The ground levelled out beneath his feet and he hoped to make better progress in his bid to reach the river. He tried to orientate himself in an attempt to find his way to the path which led to the ford. He made his way westwards around the base of Beech Hill, his paws submerged in rainwater flowing in rivulets down the hillside. Visibility in the rain was non-existent and he continually collided with branches and stumbled into potholes. His progress was brought to a sudden halt by a huge beech which had been torn up as though it were a sapling. It took what seemed a lifetime for him to circumnavigate its bulk and pick up the trail to the river again. The hurricane tore through the forest, keeping Swift in a constant state of fear that he would be crushed by a falling branch or tree. Progress was tortuously slow.

He wanted to find a bolthole and lie low until the storm had blown itself out but was driven by the greater fear of his fate if Talon caught up with him.

The roar of the wind was petrifying and when it gusted through the branches above his head he cowered with fear, barely able to contain an urge to run somewhere, anywhere to escape the wind and the fear of being crushed to death, but there was nowhere to run. He told himself to keep calm and head for the river. He concentrated as best he could but the crack of a branch above his head stopped him. Within a split second a branch hit the ground only feet away. He whimpered like a lost cub searching for its mother, ears flattened against his head in a posture of total submission, unable to take another step to secure his freedom. Then he thought of Moon and the cubs she was carrying.

An overpowering fear that he would not live to see his cubs gripped him and dragged him to his feet, driving him on toward the river until at last he glimpsed a break in the canopy where the river cut a swathe through the forest. When he reached the riverbank he hardly recognised the sleepy, slow-moving Tannon which had transformed into a tidal wave sweeping through the heart of the valley. His only hope of crossing safely was at the ford where the water would be shallower but time was running out, another downpour would swamp the river path and cut him off. The light near the river was a fraction better and he moved more quickly along the river path, but his progress was continually hampered by fallen debris. Eventually he turned the bend to the ford but found a dark swirling mass of rushing water.

He hesitated, his fur parted and flattened against his body by a wind of such power it threatened to blow him into the river. For the first time in his life he was afraid to enter the water. He considered lying low until the storm blew itself out but he knew his only real chance of escape was to cross the raging torrent that once was the Tannon. He tried to force himself forward but his legs remained rigid. He turned away from the river and stared into the darkness which shrouded Beech Hill, and the fear he'd felt in the domed holly came back to him. An image of Moon suckling her cubs flashed into his mind and he knew he would have to cross if he were ever to see them.

The roar of the hurricane thundered through the treetops and another branch crashed to the ground nearby. Suddenly the river seemed like a safer place to be. Without another thought he turned quickly and plunged into the water. Its coldness took his breath away and he gasped for air as the current immediately swept him away from the bank and downstream. At the river's whim he was spun this way and that and dragged down by the swirling undercurrents which tugged at his legs.

He couldn't believe the water's power, like the wind it had gained strength beyond anything he'd ever experienced before. At first he kicked and struggled frantically only to be dragged down again and again, his lungs bursting. Against his natural instinct he forced himself to relax. With a few well-timed kicks he pushed his way up through the swirling blackness to resurface in mid-stream, gasping for air. He opened his jaws and sucked in deep breaths, fighting to stay on the surface long enough to get his bearings and to begin his push for the far bank. Gasping, he struck out using all his strength, his gaze fixed on the distant bank. He made some progress on a diagonal course and took heart from this concentrating his mind on his objective and off the terrors of the river.

The closer he got to the far bank the greater the impression of the river's speed. He wondered how he would ever pull himself out if ever the opportunity arose. He caught sight of a fallen willow downstream where the current was sweeping him. He careered into it, grabbing at its branches with his teeth. His legs hit a branch below the surface of the water, blocking his progress. He gripped a branch in his jaws and hung on, his heart pumping furiously, adrenaline flowing. He knew this would give him strength but he had to calm down enough to clear his head to think. It wasn't natural for a wolf to climb in trees.

The bank was now only feet away and the sight of land encouraged him enormously. Using his strong jaws and powerful neck muscles he pulled himself up and got a foothold on a branch. He steadied himself, drawing in deep breaths of air. The wind rocked the branches of the tree and he was afraid a gust would blow him back into the water. He manoeuvred his forepaws up onto a branch, gaining a precarious purchase on the willow and with a massive effort of will pulled his hindquarters out of the water and onto the branch. The tree swayed but he held on.

He decided to jump for it but waited for the wind to drop a fraction. He leapt for the bank, landing in an undignified heap half submerged in freezing muddy water. His hind legs slid back into the river but he scrambled up the bank, dragging them free, driven by fear of the river's awesome power. He lay shivering, panting for breath, too exhausted to worry about the danger of falling branches. It was the fear of being discovered that finally forced him up onto shaking legs. Instinctively he shook the weight of the water from his sodden fur and staggered into the undergrowth to lay hidden beneath a clump of bracken, curling his body and covering his face with his tail.

He fell into a fitful sleep and the night passed in a series of fragmented nightmares in which he struggled desperately beneath the surface of the water, watching helplessly as Moss and Leaf were swallowed up by the maelstrom. He woke up trembling with a mixture of fear and cold. The storm had blown itself out and dawn began, gradually, to illuminate the devastation it had left behind. Swift stared in disbelief at what he saw; fallen branches littered the forest floor and fallen trees lay in every direction. The river remained swollen but had lost some of its power. It seemed now to be the only thing which was moving. The forest was motionless as if in a state of shock at the ferocity of the hurricane's assault. Not a bird sang or animal stirred.

Swift stood up slowly, his joints stiff, and shook the moisture from his fur. He stretched aching limbs. His right forepaw throbbed with pain where a claw had been partially torn out during his leap to safety from the willow the previous night. Wincing, he licked dried blood from it. The horror of the storm dominated his thoughts he was the strongest swimmer of the three and had struggled to cross the

Tannon safely. Surely it would be a miracle if Leaf and Moss had survived, he thought.

He stared across the river to Beech Hill. On the hill the shallow-rooted, lofty beeches were particularly vulnerable to the hurricane's power and the Beech Wood had suffered severely in the storm. Everywhere trees lay, uprooted. There were no signs of wolves.

He remembered their plan to meet on the island but wondered whether it would be safe. Talon seemed to know their every move. Despite the dangers he decided he had no choice but to go. It was a tortuous journey, every path was blocked by fallen trees. Time and again he skirted round trees which were once familiar landmarks, old friends which now lay impotent and dying. He met and talked with many wolves, all of whom had a tale of horror to tell about friends or relations who had been crushed by a fallen tree or had been trapped under ground. Nobody had seen Leaf or Moss.

Swift was ravenous after his energy-sapping ordeal but would not stop to hunt. Getting to the island obsessed him. He felt responsible for Leaf and Moss' safety, blaming himself for the perilous situation they had found themselves in. The torrential rain had caused flooding on the periphery of the marshes, making the path to the island almost impossible to follow, much of it being underwater and the rest a quagmire. The closer he got to the island, the deeper the water, until it eventually touched his underbelly. It became increasingly difficult for him to withdraw his paws from the clinging, sucking mud. He'd just made his mind up to turn back when he heard a familiar voice from behind.

"You'll catch cold if you stand around in there for too long."

He turned to find Leaf and Moss behind him.

"Leaf! Moss! Thank Earthstar you are safe."

He pulled free of the mud and waded back to firmer ground where he licked his two friends profusely.

CHAPTER 9

Hawthorn could not believe his good fortune. The fallen oak which had crushed his two guards to death had left him unscathed apart from shock which had caused him to tremble violently for some time afterwards. The tree had crashed to the ground only minutes after Talon had left him to return to Beech Hill. Despite his shock he was quick to depart to a safer spot. He had suffered extreme torment, knowing that his friends' lives depended on a decision of his, and never wanted to find himself in that position again.

He headed for the swamp, hoping the others would find their way there. Surely if Earthstar had sent the hurricane to free them he would guide them to a place of safety. He picked his way through the debris left by the storm, his arthritic hips aching in the dampness, but he would not allow himself to complain.

The storm had come to save them. Swift had shown strength of character and leadership qualities which Earthstar had recognised. It was up to Hawthorn to harness those qualities and to impart the knowledge which Swift would need to fulfil his responsibilities to the wolves of Tannon Valley. It was time to entrust him with Earthstar's secret. As a cub

Hawthorn had heard the stories of the two-legged creatures known as man: how they sent sticks and stones through the air to murder the wolf and steal his food; how they were the agents of Havnar and how they were poised across the big water waiting their opportunity to pillage the island of the wolves.

Tannon had brought the pack north many years ago to escape their advance before the waters had risen as the great icecaps had melted. This was the land that Earthstar had promised them, but Havnar had entered it and the minds of its wolves through his agent, Talon, upsetting the delicate balance of the habitat, and now there was no longer enough prey in the valley to feed the ever-growing wolf pack. The bounty of the valley was close to being exhausted and Havnar's grip was crushing the spirit out of the Tannon wolves. Talon had to be stopped before it was too late.

He crossed the valley to a point beyond the bend in the river from where he could hear the floodwaters roaring like an enraged monster rampaging through the forest. The wind had dropped considerably, enough for him not to worry about falling trees as he picked his way through the debris strewn across the valley. He remembered the route Swift had shown him and stuck with it as best he could. Eventually he came across paw prints left by Swift and the others on the edge of the swamp. Excitement released a surge of adrenaline, putting new life into him. Then something stopped him. A sound, or was it? He stood stock still, listening and staring into the tangle of alders which grew in the swamp. He saw a movement, something grey. He dropped to the ground, the earth was damp on his belly and the rank smell of the swamp filled his nostrils. He wanted to find cover before it was too late. He began to edge his way backwards, scarcely daring to breathe, when he felt the sudden pressure of a paw on his back and his heart sank.

Slowly, he looked back over his shoulder to find Swift, paw raised, to silence him. Swift led him to drier ground, where he spoke to him in a whisper. "Sorry to frighten you but I had to make sure you weren't being followed."

"Swift, thank Earthstar you are safe. Where are the others?"

"Moss and Leaf are over there, come on, let's go and join them."

"Swift, before we join the others there is something I have to say to you."

"What is it, wisewolf?"

"Swift, you've been chosen by Earthstar to uncover the secret of the spirits which could save us wolves from self-destruction."

"I'm not sure I'm capable of that, wisewolf!"

"I think you are our only hope." Hawthorn saw the anxiety in his friend's eyes. "Swift, don't be afraid. Earthstar will guide you and you will be invincible."

"I'm lucky to be alive, let alone invincible."

"It wasn't luck that you were freed from Talon's clutches. Don't underestimate Earthstar's power."

"What will I have to do wisewolf?"

"You will have to leave the valley and travel to the

distant mountains of the north where you will seek out a wisewolf called Moondreamer."

"What then?"

"Moondreamer will have the answers you need."

"When would I go?"

"Tomorrow."

"Tomorrow! What about Moon and the cubs?"

"Don't worry, Mistle and I will provide for them with Earthstar's help." Hawthorn saw Swift's torment at the prospect of leaving Moon. "She will be safe with us," he said.

"What can you and Mistle do against the wolfrahm? As long as Moon is in Tannon Valley she'll be in danger."

"She will have to leave the valley."

"Nowhere is safe, Talon won't rest until he's had his revenge."

"Let's talk to Leaf, he will know of somewhere."

The two wolves joined Leaf and Moss in their hiding place where they spent the evening recounting their escape stories and talking about the future. They decided that Leaf and Moss would accompany Swift on his journey. Swift was subdued and Hawthorn knew he was worrying about leaving Moon and thinking about the cubs. Leaf suggested several escape routes and hiding places for Moon, and Moss seemed pleased that someone had at last made a decision for them to leave the valley. Although they had agreed that no one should leave the safety of the swamp. Hawthorn was worried about Swift's agitation over

Moon's safety. "Swift, go to Moon and bring her here after dusk. We will wait for you," he said.

In the dwindling light of dusk Swift made his way from the swamp to the den as quickly as he could. The nearer he got to home the more anxious he became. Moon needed him to help look after the cubs and he was about to leave on some fantastic mission to where no southern wolf had ever been before. The more he thought about it the more ridiculous it seemed. It crossed his mind to take Moon and run, just disappear without trace and start a new life, but what would become of the valley? He had to do something, besides he couldn't live with himself if anything happened to his friends and loved ones and he'd done nothing. What would become of Mistle if he just upped and left? She had given him so much when his father had died, there was a huge debt to repay.

He was honoured that Earthstar had chosen him but any feeling of satisfaction was overridden by fear of the enormous responsibility placed on his shoulders. He left the path and ducked under the hanging honeysuckle and down the slope to the bank. He stopped at the entrance to the den. He could hear Moon humming to herself. She sounded content, at last beginning to get over her brother's death, now he was about to destroy her happiness again.

She appeared suddenly in the den's entrance and he saw her as if for the first time, beautiful, everything he'd ever desired. He wanted to stay with her, protect her, not go gallivanting off to some distant country with a half-baked idea that he, Swift, could save the wolf nation on his own. Her look of surprise at finding him there turned to one of anxiety and he realised that he was staring at her. He licked her face and rubbed his muzzle against hers.

"What is it, my darling?" she asked.

"I have to leave the valley."

"Why?"

He hated the incredulousness in her voice. How could he tell her? "Moon I have to go on a journey."

"We can go together, just as soon as the cubs are old enough."

"I'm afraid what I have to do can't wait, my love."

"What is so important that you can't wait to see your own cubs born?"

Swift told her about his meeting with Hawthorn. For a while she was silent as the full import of his words sank in. He agonised at her silence, feeling he'd betrayed her.

"When are you leaving?" she asked, her voice flat.

"Tomorrow," was all he could say.

"Tomorrow! But you can't! What about the cubs? What about me? You just can't walk off and leave us as if we don't exist. We're your responsibility now, you know. You could at least wait until the cubs are born."

Her anger tore at his conscience and pierced his heart but he said nothing, just stood like a naughty cub, letting her unburden the terrible pain his news had caused her. Desperately, he wished he could change things, but there was nothing he could do. It was for all their sakes.

Perhaps in time she would understand.

She began to cry and he moved close to comfort her, half expecting her to pull away from him but she didn't, she buried her face in the thick fur of his chest. He whispered comforting words, trying to calm her.

When she stopped crying he explained what had to be done. "Moon, you will have to leave the valley as well. I know it's terrible that I should leave now, but Earthstar has chosen me. If I stay I can be with you whilst the cubs are born but what after that? What kind of life will there be? If I could choose, I wouldn't have it this way for anything, but I have no choice."

"Yes I know, you should go. You have no choice." She sounded deflated, resigned.

Swift licked her face, grateful for her courage. "I'll be home as soon as I can. Before we go Leaf will find you somewhere safe to have the cubs and Mistle and Hawthorn will look after you." He saw her look wistfully towards the den which she had dug lovingly for her cubs, and understood how she must feel at leaving it. "We'll dig you another one before we go," he promised.

"That's she-wolf's work," she said, with a touch of defiance.

"I know my love, but you are the wrong shape for digging holes at the moment." Despite her anguish, she smiled and he felt better. They chose a little-used track, glad of the dusk to shield them from prying eyes. For safety they walked in silence but neither felt like talking anyway. It was as if there was no more to be said. Fate had decreed they should be parted and each was left now to carry their own burden of sadness.

At the hideout they found a very nervous Moss on sentry duty. "Thank Earthstar you are here, I thought something had happened to you," he said.

"Every path has a fallen tree lying across it," explained Swift.

Moss licked Moon. "How are you?" he asked.

"I'm alright thank you, but these cubs are getting heavy."

"Come in and make yourself comfortable. If you are hungry Leaf has caught a couple of hares."

Hawthorn and Leaf greeted Moon, and Swift was heartened by her pleasure at seeing them. Between them they devoured even the bones of the hare and made plans for the following day until the conversation finally petered out and they drifted into sleep.

*

The next day they were up before the sun to begin the gradual climb up the northern slopes of the wooded valley, towards Silver Birch Wood. Swift and Moon strolled together at the back cherishing each other's company whilst they could. They entered Silver Birch Wood which appeared a ghostly grey in the half-light of dawn. Occasionally they glimpsed a red or roe deer but there was no time to give chase, their objective being to get as far away from the valley by sunset as possible. Swift constantly watched Moon for signs of fatigue or distress and for her sake they rested occasionally.

Every now and then she would wince when one of her cubs became restless and Swift would ask her if she was alright, but she would tell him light heartedly not to fuss, hiding the discomfort she was feeling. On that morning Silver Birch Wood had an eeriness about it which bordered on the sinister. It was a place which seemed to change character with the time of day or year and a wolf's mood. He remembered their pleasure when they had first come there together in the springtime, how they had watched new leaves turn gently this way and that in the breeze and sparkle in the sunshine. Today it held no comfort for Swift or the others but evoked a sense of foreboding. It was as though they were walking through it out of one life and into another, filled with uncertainty and danger.

Swift wanted to be clear of the wood but for Moon's sake suppressed an urge to hurry the others along. Frequently he glanced over his shoulder, expecting to find Talon behind them, only to see a void where nothing moved. At times he wondered if even they were really moving – the wood seemed to go on forever.

Eventually, as promised, Leaf led them to a secluded spot north of Silver Birch Wood, far away from the main trails where he found a sandy bank which was an ideal den site for Moon to safely give birth to her cubs. Swift immediately made a start with the digging whilst Moss and Leaf hunted, and Moon, Hawthorn, and Mistle rested beneath a beech tree which had taken advantage of the sandy soil of the bank and grown tall amongst the ash hazel and oak which predominated in the surrounding woodland. The den would normally be built over several weeks by the she-wolf but Swift knew there was no time to waste in case Moon had the cubs early. If he gave them a good start Hawthorn and Mistle would be able to take over and dig deep enough for Moon to have the cubs in comfort and safety. If necessary it could be extended later if Moon had a big litter. When Moss returned from hunting he worked in shifts with Swift helping to dig out the main chamber.

It was agreed that the three wolves should leave at sunrise, needing a good night's sleep after a day of hard physical labour. Leaf and Moss had caught an elderly wild boar that had been injured in a territorial clash. This provided them with a nutritious meal in preparation for their long journey northwards. Swift and Moon lay together among some bracken a short distance from the mouth of the den. Swift was enjoying the warmth of Moon's body; he pressed closer to her, acutely aware that there were many lonely nights ahead of him. He had no idea of how long he would be away or whether he would survive to come back. He could feel their cubs moving inside her and was afraid he may never see them. He put his paw on her belly and felt its firmness. His heart ached when he thought of the plans he had made for helping them discover the rich wonders of the forest.

CHAPTER 10

After Swift had left Moon in Silver Birch Wood, he, Moss, and Leaf had made good progress and were close to the outskirts of the northern territories. A week had passed without incidence and they were resting after a steep climb up an ash-covered rise when Swift spotted Stone and a dozen wolfrahm approaching the foot of the slope. He motioned to Leaf and Moss to get down.

"What is it?" asked Leaf.

"Wolfrahm, down the hill."

"If they spot us now we're done for. I'm going to draw them away, you and Moss keep heading north. I'll catch up when I can," said Leaf.

"Leaf, I can't let you do it."

"If you don't, you can say goodbye to a return journey to Tannon."

"Alright, if anyone can do it you can."

"I'm going to show myself and draw them along the slope. You stay put until we're out of earshot."

"Good luck."

They watched him trot along the top of the slope beneath the hanging fronds of the ash trees. Almost instantly they heard barking from down the slope. Leaf increased his pace and disappeared around the hillside. Swift and Moss held their breath in the leaf litter. When the barking faded they headed north at a canter.

*

Two weeks had passed since Leaf had left them in the ash wood, they had made good progress through forest that was new to them, travelling twenty to thirty miles a day from dawn to dusk, stopping only to drink. They hunted at first light, catching anything from squirrels to deer, sometimes eating as much as twenty pounds of meat each at a single meal.

Over the previous two days the forest had begun to thin out. The fugitives had left the lowlands of the south to climb the foothills of the Pennines, their daily mileage falling because of the hilly terrain. For several days the sun had blazed down, heating the humid atmosphere until it was too hot to travel after mid-day. Swift decided to rest in the afternoon and travel in the early evening when the temperature had dropped.

He lay down on the grass, enjoying its softness – it reminded him of the grassy glades of Tannon where he had lain with Moon in the sunshine, enjoying the thrill of being together. As they ascended the trees had become sparser and were giving way to grasses that thrived at the higher, more exposed altitudes. He had never seen so much of the sky and wondered how much higher they would have to climb. It was at quiet times like this that his thoughts returned to Leaf. He prayed to Earthstar for his safety.

He got to his feet to explore; they were in need of a good meal but had seen no game all day. He left Moss sleeping and wandered from the camp. He had gone about two hundred yards when he came across several large paw prints in a damp patch of earth on the banks of a stream. They looked fresh. Swift sniffed the air but detected nothing unusual. He heard a twig snap behind him. He swivelled round but too late, the bear was on him.

A sweeping blow to the temple knocked him sideways. For a moment his senses were scrambled but instinctively he leapt to his feet, at the same time crouching low to avoid another bludgeoning swipe from the bear. He barked loudly, hoping to intimidate his attacker but the bear merely rushed at him again. Swift leapt aside with only a split second between him and oblivion. He felt a rush of air as the bear's huge paw swept past his head. He darted out of the bear's range. In his haste to get away he trod awkwardly on an exposed tree root, turning his ankle. The bear was on him in a flash, grabbing a hind leg to drag him backwards. Swift tucked his head down to avoid the death blow but it never came.

A resounding roar stopped the bear in mid-swing. Another bear of even more enormous proportions had appeared from nowhere to launch a vicious attack on Swift's tormentor. Swift cowered beneath them as they tore into each other with a ferocity Swift had never encountered before. Biting, clawing, and scratching they fell to the ground only yards away from where he lay. Swift's attacker squealed with pain as the bigger bear's claws ripped into its flesh. Unable to defend itself it struggled violently to break away from the bigger bear's grip. Eventually it pulled itself free and sprinted on all fours at high speed through the trees with the larger bear in pursuit.

Swift stood up and shook himself, unable to believe his good fortune, but his sense of relief was short lived. His saviour had given up the chase and was on its way back. Swift turned to run for cover and to his astonishment the bear called his name. "Swift, wait." Swift thought he'd suffered brain damage during his encounter with the bear. It wasn't possible. Then the bear spoke again. "Do not be afraid Swift, I will not harm you." Swift nervously watched the bear approach but strangely did not feel the urge to run. The bear stopped a yard from him and he was dwarfed by its size.

"Who are you?"

"I am Crag, servant of Earthstar. I am here to warn you of great danger. The hordes of evil are gathering, intent on destroying you. The bear that attacked you was a manifestation of Havnar himself."

"I owe you my life."

"On the contrary, it is I who owe you. The path you have chosen is fraught with dangers yet still you choose to walk it."

"It is not me you should thank, it is the wisewolf Hawthorn."

"Yes, Hawthorn has also done much. He had a narrow escape helping me."

"Is he alright?"

"Yes, but I am sorry he has remained in the valley, there are many dangers lurking there."

"Why has it gone so wrong in the valley? Its beauty and abundance were unrivalled but now it is jaded, and riddled with treachery."

"The wolves of Tannon Valley have become complacent, they allowed Talon in when it had been prophesied he would bring nothing but death and destruction with him. Only Hawthorn opposed him."

"Is it too late to save the valley?"

"Only you Swift can save the valley from Havnar's evil. You have heard the words of the wisewolf. You must keep your nerve and shut out any thoughts of defeat. Above all, be on your guard against the agents of darkness."

"Crag, can you give me any news of Moon and the cubs?"

"I am sorry, I can tell you no more. Remember, believe in yourself." With those parting words the huge animal turned away, took three steps, and faded into the ether.

When he had regained his composure Swift thought over what the bear had said to him and he felt bitterly disappointed he'd had no news of Moon. He thought about what faced her in the valley and shuddered. Had he done the right thing to leave her? This was the question now uppermost in his mind. He even began to wonder if Earthstar might merely be using him to defeat Havnar.

He wandered back to camp trying to make sense out of the confusion which his life had become, his good mood of earlier gone. He wanted to turn back, go home and take Moon and his cubs to a place of safety, away from Havnar's contamination where nothing could harm them. Only Crag's words stopped him but the weight of responsibility bore down on his shoulders and threatened to crush his spirit. Back at camp Moss lay head on paws watching him return. Swift didn't speak but sat quietly down at the foot of a Scots pine.

Moss trotted over to where he sat. "Swift, what's happened?"

Swift reluctantly described his encounter with Crag, wanting really to be left alone. He glimpsed the disbelief in Moss' eyes and thought his sanity was in question. Maybe he was mad. How could he be sure of what was real anymore? He answered Moss' questions as best he could then excused himself.

Walking helped to still the maelstrom of thoughts swirling in his head and gradually his attitude became more positive. He went over again what Crag had said, looking at it from a different perspective. His faith in Earthstar returned when he thought of Tannon's beauty. If he went back with nothing, evil would destroy it and his life would be over.

The future of the Tannon Valley wolves depended on him finding the gift of the spirits before Talon. Moon's vulnerability still dominated his thoughts but he put a brave face on for Moss.

"Hello friend," he said, "I'm back and ready to eat."

Moss wagged his tail. "Good, there's plenty of venison, let's have a feast."

Swift smiled. "Good idea, a good feed followed by a long nap, then we strike out for the north."

The two wolves passed the evening talking of happy

times spent together as cubs. They had explored the valley together, eating the fruits of the forest, sloes, bilberries, blackberries, and anything else which was edible. They would follow the river for miles marvelling at the new plants and animals they discovered, chasing butterflies and sniffing out voles living beneath the undergrowth. This was the valley that Swift wanted for his cubs, a valley without danger, save for the odd bear or lynx passing through. These happy memories of past times inspired him and gave him a new determination to stick to his task and succeed.

Dusk fell and shadows filled the forest. Swift found a comfortable spot and curled up. He closed his eyes and whispered a prayer to Earthstar, affirming his newfound strength. Seconds later, he was asleep.

*

The following morning they finished what was left of the roe deer, stuffing down as much as they possibly could, not knowing what the hunting would be like in the hills and when they would eat again. They trekked all morning, climbing continuously until gradually the trees became sparser. It was a strange world but Swift was excited despite his apprehension.

When they had first climbed above the treeline they had marvelled at the extent of the forest behind them but on reaching the top of the first of the foothills Swift felt exposed and vulnerable. The mountain peaks stretched out ahead of them into the distance and the two wolves saw the earth's vastness for the first time. Swift realised how insignificant his life was against the magnitude of the planet, but he could see the earth's splendour as never before. Forests filled the valleys and his mind was awed by the abundance before him. His valley was one among thousands, yet Havnar had chosen it to evoke the earth's negative forces. It occurred to him that once Havnar had a foothold, all of these valleys would be at risk.

He pushed thoughts of Havnar from his mind before the huge responsibility could threaten his morale again. Chatting with Moss gave him a feeling of security so they discussed everything from the mountain peaks to the lushness of the grass. The lowland was the kingdom of the trees but the hills belonged to the grasses where it was too exposed for the trees to survive the onslaught of winter gales. They found the mountains deceptive. When the end of a climb was in sight they would reach a peak only to find another rising higher beyond it, revealing an ever more distant horizon. The feeling of vulnerability never left them but they developed a sense of freedom which they had not experienced before. There was an abundance of hares which were not wary enough of the wolves to make catching them difficult. They were well fed on the luxuriant grasses and consequently bigger than their woodland brothers, making them a reasonable snack for a hungry wolf.

For three days they trekked along the Pennine Mountains, hunting at dusk and dawn when the hares were more active under the cover of twilight. On the fourth day the temperature began to drop. By midday the sky was overcast with low, grey cloud and it was chilly. By mid-afternoon they were shivering and

Swift sensed something was wrong. At first he'd thought the lower than normal temperatures were characteristic of the mountains but now it had become cold, too cold for late August. It was cold enough to be December. The wind, no more than a breeze at dawn, was flattening the fur against their bodies and cutting into their faces as they crossed yet another peak. They could not have been more exposed and had no choice but to continue crossing the mountain in the hope of finding shelter in the next valley.

The first snowflakes were small and almost undetectable in the driving wind and Swift ignored the first two or three that landed on his nose, but before long they had grown bigger and fell more densely. Swift looked at Moss in disbelief; suddenly the hills had turned hostile. The snow settled immediately on tinder-dry grass and there was no shelter to be had anywhere.

"This is unbelievable, freezing cold in August. What on earth's going on?" said Moss.

"I don't know but we'd better get off this mountain and look for some shelter."

The wind's speed increased perceptively and developed an eerie howl. It whipped the snow into their faces, stinging their eyes. They strained into the gusts, eyes mere slits, unable to see far into the thickening blizzard. Swift lost his sense of direction but was aware that they were still climbing. *Surely we should be over the peak by now*, he thought. He wondered whether there was any point in carrying on, not knowing where they were going, but to stop would be to freeze to death.

Moss had taken on a ghostlike appearance, his dark face now white with freezing snow. Swift stopped to shout some words of encouragement then put his head down and pushed on. For an hour they forced their way on like this, the bitter wind sapping reserves of precious energy. Swift felt Moss nudge him. He turned to find his friend barely recognisable. His fur carried a thick blanket of snow. He spoke but Swift could not hear him above the screech of the wind. He watched him lay down in the snow. Swift shouted at him, nudging his shoulder violently, forcing him back onto his feet. They staggered on into the blizzard, their feet frozen to numbness. The next time Swift looked back Moss had gone.

He shouted into the storm but the wind tore the words from his lips and scattered them in the blizzard. He backtracked but before long there were no tracks to follow. Fighting to hold down the panic rising in his stomach, he retraced his steps.

As he searched, the snow filled his own tracks, obscuring his trail and any possibility of him re-retracing his direction. He was close to giving up hope when he stumbled across a mound in the snow. He dug frantically at the already frozen crust and uncovered Moss' body. Swift tried to rouse him but without success. Close to exhaustion, he knew that if he left Moss to find shelter he would never find him again. He also knew that if he lay down beside him they would both die. But he had to rest if only for a moment. He lay down beside his friend, curling himself round his body in an attempt to warm him. It was then he realised the only chance of survival was for the storm to blow itself out.

He tried to stay awake but his mind drifted towards unconsciousness. He would drag himself back only to slip away again. He tried to keep himself awake by licking the frozen snow from between his paws. Images of Moon and Hawthorn flitted across his mind's eye. He imagined a bear lifting him, its colossal strength crushing the life from his body. He saw a white hare bobbing before his eyes mouthing silent words. He leapt up to give chase and saw his body below him shrouded in snow. He sped across the snow, keeping the hare's bobbing tail in sight. Onwards and onwards into eternity they raced until the hare stopped and rose onto his hind legs. He pointed with a forepaw. Swift squinted, trying to focus in the blizzard. A few yards away he could just make out a small cave in the hillside sheltered by an overhanging rock. The hare spoke to him. "Take shelter, there is food and bedding inside."

Swift lurched towards the cave, barely able to summon the strength to move his frozen legs. He fell onto the lush grass bedding lining the floor. He wanted to drift off into sleep to escape the pain of frozen limbs but remembered Moss. He tried to stand but his body would not respond and the urge to sleep finally overpowered him. He fell into a sleep which could have been mistaken for death itself. Many hours later when he first woke up he did not recall where he was but then the full realisation of what he'd done hit him. He'd left Moss to die alone in the blizzard. A wave of remorse swept through him, making him feel physically sick. Although he had no hope of finding him alive he determined to find him or die in the attempt.

He peered from the cave's entrance. It had stopped snowing. A flicker of hope touched him and he hurried out into the daylight. He stared at the landscape, there was not a snowflake to be seen. Mile upon mile of lush green grass rippled in a warm summer's breeze. He turned to check the cave. It was still there. He hadn't imagined that, but how had he got there? He stared up at the mountain racking his brain for answers. He remembered the hare. Fragmented memories came back to him and he began piecing them together, but had they really happened?

There was no time to think about it, he wanted to find Moss. He tried to run but the slope was too steep and he'd exhausted his reserves of strength. He looked up to judge the distance he would have to climb. At the top of the rise he saw the silhouette of a wolf.

His heart leapt with expectation and he limped up the slope calling his friend's name.

The wolf began to move down the slope towards him.

Suddenly he realised that it was not Moss, but Leaf. "Leaf, thank Earthstar you are alright. I can't believe it's you! Something terrible has happened, I think Moss is dead."

"I don't know, I can't leave you two for five minutes without you losing each other. But don't worry I found Moss on the other side of the hill."

"Is he alright, Leaf?"

"He's a bit worse for wear but he'll survive. He thinks you're dead. I don't know, all you've got to do is stroll in the sunshine and you end up in this state."

"It's a long story, Leaf. Let's get Moss and I'll tell you all about it."

Reunited, they lay on the hillside in the sunshine, enjoying each other's company.

"What happened after you left us?" Moss asked Leaf.

"Well it was a close thing I can tell you. I had to let them get a glimpse of me so as to draw them away from you two. I'm built for stamina not speed, but I ran like a hare. Who wouldn't with Stone breathing down his neck? Eventually I pulled away from them and settled into my running. I thought if I stayed ahead for the first five miles I would be alright, but they didn't give up easily, believe me, they wanted Swift badly. They tracked me for days. I had to keep far enough ahead so they wouldn't twig they were chasing the wrong wolf.

It was near impossible getting enough food to keep me going. I lived on mice and berries. I didn't know how far they were behind me so I couldn't risk stopping for long. I guessed they would sleep at night so I kept going till after dark. If the moon was out I could see well enough and I'd be up and away first thing. Of course I was in territory I'd never seen before, travelling eastwards drawing them away from you. Eventually I came to what they call the big river where water stretches for as far as the eye can see. I'd heard of it from the wolflore but it's got to be seen to be believed. I was dying of thirst so I ran to the water and took a drink but it tasted disgusting. I couldn't believe it, all that water and nothing to drink.

The place was infested with squawking, white

birds. I ran along the water's edge following the rise and fall of the land. Soon the water was a sheer drop below me and the earth was golden dust along its edge. The water moved in slowly to cover the dust then moved out again. I kept going along the bank of the great water for several days. On the sixth day a storm blew up and the water sounded like thunder. The rain was driven by a wind so strong it stung my face. There was no shelter so I decided to move inland. And that decision saved my life. When I turned away from the great water I saw them coming, Stone and the others. When he saw that it was me and not you I saw the hatred in his beady little amber eyes. They split into two packs to cut me off. I headed back towards the big water. I was hardly moving in the headwind and they were gaining on me. I glanced back over my shoulder and could see Stone's face thirty yards behind me. I was knackered, as weak as a new-born cub. I could run no more and resigned myself to a fight to the death, probably mine.

Then I found myself plunging through the air headlong to the rocks and the great water. Next thing I know I was waking up with a thumping headache, halfway down the tall bank on the narrowest ledge of rock you've ever seen. It was a miracle, I was still alive. I ached all over but amazingly nothing was broken. I'd hit the ledge and didn't bounce off. Stone must have thought I'd ended up in the great water."

"How did you get down from the ledge?" asked Moss.

"With great difficulty. I couldn't move for two days I was so badly bruised, and it didn't stop raining for three days. Good job really or I would have died of thirst. As it was I ended up with a stinking cold.

"When I was able to look over the edge it was not a pretty sight. Below me were jagged rocks surrounded by what looked like very deep water. I hadn't been swimming since the night of the hurricane, when we crossed the Tannon, and I didn't fancy doing it again. Just my luck I thought, surrounded by all this water and I die of thirst.

Then the weirdest thing happened. This ruddy great white bird flew in and perched on the ledge. Its wingspan was about the length of a bear's back and its beak as long as a heron's. And, wait for it, it spoke to me. Said its name was Crag and it was a messenger from Earthstar. I know birds can't talk but this one did. I wondered whether the blow on the head when I hit the ledge had mashed my brains. But I didn't complain, the next day it turned up with a fish for breakfast. I didn't care what it said after that."

"But how did you get down from the ledge?" repeated Moss.

"Alright I'm coming to that. Thought you'd be impressed by a talking bird. Anyway I'm soon up and about with all the fish I'm being fed. Well as up and about as you can be on a ledge that size. I looked over the edge the day after the bird arrived and saw that the water had shrunk back, uncovering more of the golden dust. I thought if I could get down there I might find a gap in the bank where I could get away.

"The next day the bird turns up again and he's already figured out how to get me down. He was some bird, this Crag. If it wasn't for him I'd be a pile of bones suspended in the middle of nowhere. He guided me down the cliff. Cliff, that's what he called it. At first I was petrified, but the further we got the more I realised he knew what he was doing. And I believed in him. That's when we started to make real progress. I can tell you, it was good to get my feet on that golden dust. What was it he called it? Sand, I think.

We travelled a mile or so on the sand, and the water began to creep back in again. I could see me going up that ruddy cliff again but luckily we came to a gap where a river ran out into the great water."

"But how did you manage to find us?" asked Moss.

"That bit was easy, I just followed the bird. He'd lead me so far then disappear into thin air, but he always came back again, until this morning when I found Moss. One minute he was standing there, the next minute he'd gone, without a word."

Swift thanked Earthstar for their safety and told Leaf about his encounter with the bear.

CHAPTER 11

Moon winced, her contractions were becoming more frequent. "It's alright my loves, it won't be long now," she said softly.

She forced herself to her feet and eased her bulk through the entrance tunnel and into the coolness of the den. In the darkness she felt more secure, besides she had to get used to spending time below ground for the safety of the cubs. As always her thoughts reverted to Swift, she missed him every time she thought about the cubs. They would need a father's guidance to avoid the pitfalls of life in the forest. She shifted her position, lying stretched on her side to relieve the pressure on her swollen belly. She pushed her fears to the back of her mind as best she could. "Come back soon my love," she whispered. She tried to be positive. As long as the location of the den remained a secret she thought they would be safe whilst Swift was away.

A tawny owl hooted from a nearby holly tree, announcing the onset of darkness and bringing Moon back into the present. She sniffed at the air, it seemed an age since Hawthorn had departed to fetch Mistle back from a hunting trip and she desperately wanted someone to share the birth of her cubs with.

Suddenly she felt helpless, everything seemed beyond her control and she wanted to scream but she wouldn't let herself go, the cubs would need all her strength. They were her strength, giving her the courage to carry on from day to day without Swift.

Her contractions came more frequently now. "Don't come yet my darlings, soon but not yet, please wait for Hawthorn and Mistle," she whispered. It was getting darker, no daylight penetrated the den and she grew increasingly agitated. She listened for signs of their return, perhaps they had waited for nightfall before beginning their trek back. Yes, it would be safer but she wondered how they would find their way through unknown territory in the dark. What if the wolfrahm followed them? Her mind struggled with a flow of morbid possibilities which she couldn't stop. She knew how much Talon hated Swift and believed nothing would stop him taking his revenge. Visions of the wolfrahm descending to surround the den tormented her and she sat up, straining to hear what lurked outside in the darkness.

Tension spread through her, intensifying the discomfort in her belly. Her contractions were relentless now and she could no longer stop herself from pushing. The pain in her abdomen became excruciating. She took several deep breaths and pushed with all her strength, wanting to be free from the pain. She repeated this many times until at last the head of her first born emerged from her loins and she felt relief.

She took another deep breath and forced him free of her body. For a moment she panted for breath, then instinctively she bit through the umbilical cord as though she had done it a hundred times before. She gave her first cub his first wash, carefully licking away the afterbirth from his fur. She nudged her newborn towards her waiting teats, feeling a surge of love as his warmth touched her. She could feel him in the darkness, searching and probing her belly. Then she felt him suck at her swollen teats, his paws kneading her, coaxing out her sweet warm milk. She had imagined the scene many times before, hoping she would be able to cope. She wanted to relax and enjoy her success but a stab of pain reminded her of unfinished business and she focused her mind on the task ahead. She wondered how many more waited impatiently to break free of her body.

Again she felt compelled to push. Waves of pain swept through her as she forced her second cub closer to the outside world. He came more quickly than the first yet with more pain, relieved only when his head emerged from her body. She squeezed him out and severed the link to her body which had given him life and sustained him for so long. He had taken his first step towards independence already but he needed her more than ever now in the huge space, so alien from the warmth and comfort of her womb.

Moon experienced a pleasant warmth as the pain subsided and she licked her newborn clean. How wonderful they were, she thought, and wished Swift could see them; he would be so proud of her and them. She had created life and given birth for the first time, it was something she had always dreamed of. Although it was tinged with sadness she had a strong feeling of fulfilment.

Her third cub lingered for a while, as if it was not

quite ready to face the world outside, but before too long Moon felt again the overwhelming urge to push and she found herself hoping that it would be for the last time as she was feeling sore. The head of her third and last cub emerged but immediately Moon sensed something was wrong. She examined the cub's head with her tongue and realised that its umbilical cord had wrapped itself around the cub's neck.

She set to work cautiously with her teeth to unravel the cord, wishing Mistle was there and praying that she would not harm her cub. As she lifted it over her newborn's head the cub whimpered pathetically and Moon's heart filled with compassion for her. She bit the sibling's cord through with a single skilful bite. She took a breath and pushed hard and gave birth to her third cub, a she-wolf lighter than the other two. She licked her new daughter clean, greatly relieved that her work was done. She nudged her towards her teats where her two sons were already suckling hungrily. She licked them in turn, her tongue inspecting them for completeness, feeling relief and gratitude for the gift of three healthy cubs.

She was distracted by a noise from outside the den. She pricked up her ears, expecting to hear Hawthorn's voice. Instead she froze at the sound of voices she didn't recognise. Afraid even to breathe, she remained rigid for what seemed an eternity until the voices faded and silence returned. She let out her breath slowly through clenched teeth. Then she heard movement in the entrance tunnel. Frantically she gathered her cubs beneath her and prepared to defend them to the death if necessary.

A wolf called her name but although the voice

sounded familiar she could not be sure who it was. "Moon, Moon, it's Stag, the wolfrahm are close by. I have a message from Hawthorn. He and Mistle won't be back until the early hours of tomorrow morning, the wolfrahm are everywhere, watching every path. Stay in the den until Hawthorn returns and for the time being you should be safe, we shouldn't be back this way."

Moon trembled with a mixture of fear and relief; relief that her babies were safe and fear of what might have happened if Stag had not been there. Suddenly she was exhausted. She lay on her side, her cubs suckling her, and tried to sleep but sleep would not come. Constantly she listened for threatening sounds outside the den. But despite this, from time to time, her thoughts were filled with joy at her new cubs.

They fed voraciously, pumping away at her teats with their forepaws to extract the precious juice from her body. She looked forward to the morning when she would be able to see them more clearly. It would be several weeks before they would set foot in the outside world and she would be able to see them in the daylight. She dreaded that day for she knew her troubles would begin when they began to wander and explore. She would be afraid to let them out of her sight and they would resent the restrictions she would have to impose on them. If the wolfrahm discovered one of them it would be the end of them all.

Suddenly she was hungry; giving birth had consumed her reserves of energy and she had eaten very little in the last twenty-four hours. She put it from her mind as best she could.

Sure that Hawthorn and Mistle would bring food

when they returned in the morning, she yawned and then dozed until she woke at daybreak to the sound of a chaffinch singing in the oak above the den. Her cubs were all sleeping soundly, cuddled against her belly. The entrance to the den let in enough light for her to see their outline and as she admired them she remembered how she and Swift had lain in the sun choosing names for this occasion. They could only agree on two but Moon decided to let him have his way on the other. The first-born male would be Raven after Swift's father, the second male would be Finch after her brother, and the she-wolf would be called Willow, a favourite name of Swift's.

She became anxious, it was daylight and Mistle and Hawthorn still hadn't returned. She disentangled herself from the cubs without waking them and peered out of the den's entrance. She squinted in the brightness of the sunlight as she searched every direction for signs of them. She bit her lower lip anxiously and contemplated how she would manage if they didn't come back. She had to eat to provide enough milk for the cubs and be there constantly in the early days to provide them with warmth and security.

She glimpsed a movement not far off in the ferns. She stood up on full alert, ears erect, tail raised, emitting a warning growl. She cursed herself for her foolishness, whoever was coming would have seen her easily now. Two wolves broke cover and moved stealthily across a small glade about fifty yards away. With a mixture of relief and delight she recognised Hawthorn and Mistle.

She wagged her tail as they approached, both of

them looked tired and unkempt. "I'm so glad to see you both," she said.

"I'm sorry we took so long. Thank Earthstar you are safe," said Hawthorn. "There are wolfrahm patrols everywhere. How we made it back unchallenged I'll never know."

Moon glanced beyond Hawthorn into the forest. "Don't worry, I'm sure we weren't followed," he said.

Moon turned to Mistle. "I'm so glad you've come, the valley isn't a safe anymore."

Mistle frowned and nodded. "Maybe one day we'll be able to go back." Her face brightened. "What about the cubs?" she asked.

"I've got three beautiful babies."

Mistle wagged her tail and licked Moon profusely. "Can I see them?"

"Of course you can."

Hawthorn licked her face. "Well done."

Moon led Mistle into the den's darkness. The cubs were just waking and she lay down to let them feed.

"Oh Moon! They are lovely, what a clever thing you are. What wonderful cubs. Look, this one is just like my Swift. I hope you didn't have the trouble I had giving birth to him. He was hard work I can tell you. What about you? You must be worn out. You should get as much rest as you can. When the cubs sleep you must sleep. When was the last time you had something to eat? Don't worry, Hawthorn and I will bring you something, you just lie still and rest."

Moon laughed. "It's wonderful to have you here

but don't worry, I'm alright. You and Hawthorn must be tired, why don't you have a rest then go hunting a bit later?" Mistle agreed and left the den, promising to hunt later on.

Hawthorn called from the entrance tunnel. "Can I come in, Moon?"

"Yes, come in and meet the cubs." She shifted her position to make room for him. "Sit down."

"Thank you. How wonderful, you'll be kept busy now. They're a healthy-looking bunch. Swift will be so proud of you all."

Moon looked at him intensely. "Do you really think he will come back?"

Hawthorn put his paw on hers. "Swift is a very determined young wolf, you know. If anyone can succeed, it's Swift. I have every confidence in him."

"Hawthorn I need to know the truth. What are the chances of him returning safely?"

Hawthorn spoke gently to her. "There will be many dangers. All we can do is pray that Earthstar will protect him. He has everything to live for and I believe nothing will keep him away from you and the cubs."

*

A week passed by during which Moon rarely left the den and then only for a moment at a time. Mistle and Hawthorn hunted successfully, keeping her well fed. The cubs gained weight, eating and sleeping as they pleased. The adults were vigilant at all times with Hawthorn and Mistle sharing sentry duty. Whenever they left the den area to hunt they took a different route to avoid tramping down a trail which would betray the den's location.

Moon worried about Hawthorn who looked tired, but he insisted on sharing the duties equally with Mistle. Moon was amazed at Mistle's energy. She was as able as any wolf half her age. The cubs had given her a new lease of life and appeared to have taken her mind off Swift.

Many sun rises had passed since the wolfrahm patrol had come so close to discovering the den and at last Moon was beginning to relax, she didn't miss the valley and was glad to have left its torments behind. She had everything she needed to keep her cubs healthy and for the moment that was enough. Swift was never out of her thoughts but she tried to be positive to ward off the panic which lurked persistently in the back of her mind.

One morning when the cubs were sleeping, Moon, feeling the need for fresh air, left the den to stretch her legs. Mistle was hunting and Hawthorn on sentry duty. Moon could see he was finding it difficult to keep his eyes open. She was about to suggest that he took a nap when a movement in the ferns some thirty yards away caught her eye. Instantly she was alert, ears forward, tail erect. She woke Hawthorn with a muffled bark.

The old wolf struggled to his feet and stood beside her. "What is it?"

"I don't know. There is something in the ferns over there."

Seconds later, came a friendly bark, followed by the emergence of Stag. He hurried towards them.

"Moon, Hawthorn, thank Earthstar I'm in time."

"What's wrong?" asked Hawthorn.

"Talon left the Beech Wood earlier this morning and there's a strong rumour that he knows the whereabouts of Moon's den."

Moon felt sick, she couldn't believe what she was hearing they had been so careful. "How could he know?" she asked.

"It's a complete mystery to me," said Stag. "Beside me nobody knows about the den. I've told no one."

"We trust you beyond any doubt Stag," replied Hawthorn. "These are strange times, remember you found us by way of a dream. Thanks to you we are still ahead."

Moon began pacing nervously. "What about the cubs? What are we going to do?"

"If we keep calm we can get the cubs away to safety," said Hawthorn.

"Away to safety! We thought this place was safe. How could he know we are here?" she repeated. She was close to panic but forced herself to listen to Hawthorn.

"The trick is to stay one step ahead, and to do that we must keep calm, and act quickly. Moon, are the cubs fit enough to spend a night out in the open?"

Moon stopped pacing and tried to pull herself together. "Yes, for one night. It hasn't been too cold lately."

"When Mistle gets back we'll start moving them."

"We shouldn't wait, there's no time."

ROB BURNETT

"There are three cubs and we can only move one each at a time."

Stag moved closer to her. "Moon, don't worry, no one followed me. We have enough time to get you and the cubs safely away. Together we'll move them in no time."

Moon exhaled heavily as though she had been holding her breath. "Oh Stag, forgive me. Thank you for what you've done, but you must get back otherwise you'll be missed."

"You and the cubs come first. Swift is away making great sacrifices for the valley, how can I allow anything to happen to you?"

Moon put her paw on his. "Thank you," she said.

At that moment Mistle came bounding through the undergrowth, oblivious to the brambles snagging her legs. "Wolfrahm! Barely a mile away," she blurted out between gasps for breath.

Hawthorn ran for the den. "Come on we've got to move now, each of you fetch a cub. We'll go north travelling off the track, it's mainly through bracken, shouldn't be too difficult."

It was against Moon's instincts to move her cubs so soon, they were still both deaf and blind and would have no idea of what was happening to them. The last thing she wanted was to frighten them. She lifted Willow as gently as she could but still she whimpered in protest. Each of them picked up a cub in their jaws by the lose skin at the nape of the neck and followed Hawthorn.

They moved slowly and deliberately, picking their

150

way through the undergrowth, desperate not to lay an easy trail for Talon to follow. Mistle was having trouble with Finch who'd decided he didn't want to go and wriggled and kicked in protest. Moon thought it best that she took him and Mistle take Willow who was lighter. In his mother's firm grip Finch settled down to only the occasional wriggle and the group made better progress. Moon would not allow herself to look back, convinced she would find Talon right behind her. She was grateful for every step forward and dreaded the moment when the cubs would start whimpering for food.

Moon guessed nightfall was about an hour away, giving them time to put a good distance between themselves and the den. She began to feel more hopeful, when a bark in the distance froze them in their tracks. They stood transfixed, breath held. Another bark came, this time closer. Moon's expression beseeched Hawthorn to save her cubs. "We must have drifted towards the path," he said. "If we crouch out of sight they may miss us."

"Unless they are distracted they'll sniff us out easily," said Stag. "Stay here and don't make a sound, I'll draw them away."

Moon put Finch down. "Stag it's too dangerous, stay here with us."

But Stag had already made up his mind. He nodded to Hawthorn and licked Mistle's face. "Take care of the cubs," he said to Moon, and disappeared into the bracken towards the path.

They lay silently beneath the shelter of the bracken's fronds for what seemed an eternity before the storm broke. It began with isolated wuffs and grew into a cacophony of barks drawing ever closer. Moon lay in terror expecting the wolfrahm to break through the bracken at any second to slaughter her cubs. She felt the vibration of their paws in the earth beneath her body as they came closer. A silent scream drew back her lips. She smelt their stench and her heart beat so loudly she thought it would explode. But as if by a miracle they passed by. When the barking died into the distance she was unable to comprehend her good fortune and remained rigid with fear. Eventually she let go her breath and lay drained, staring in disbelief at her unharmed cubs. She looked from Hawthorn to Mistle but neither spoke. She knew their thoughts were with Stag.

Before sunset they struggled north for two miles, making camp in a thicket of ferns beneath a cluster of silver birch trees. Mistle helped Moon keep the cubs warm in the cold hours before dawn. No one slept well, protecting the cubs was paramount. At first light they continued north with Hawthorn guiding them through the undergrowth. He was worried about Moon, who jumped violently at the slightest sound. The stress she was under could impair her ability to feed the cubs, he thought. They would have to find a den site soon and start digging.

Mid-morning they stopped for Moon to suckle her cubs. Hawthorn left her with Mistle to search for a suitable den site. He found a good spot not far from a stream – an oak torn from the ground during a storm had left a gaping crater where its roots had once anchored it to the ground. Some of the roots, although bent and bowed, still held firm and it was beneath these that Hawthorn began the first excavations. Content with his choice he fetched the others and organised a rota of digging which included Moon, who insisted she do her bit. It took several days of hard labour to complete as the cubs had to be fed and the hunting done, but eventually it was finished. With great relief Moon moved her cubs in.

CHAPTER 12

Swift, Leaf, and Moss continued their journey, leaving the Peak District to travel northwards through lowland forest into what is now Scotland. They crossed the cheviot hills without incident – using knowledge they had gained from their trek along the Pennine chain. Moving on across the southern uplands of Scotland into the Caledonian pine forest which teemed with life; red deer, reindeer, bear, lynx, wild cat, ptarmigan, and capercaillie.

After the exposure of the mountains they revelled in the great expanse of the forest; following reindeer trails through the lichens and heathers of the woodland floor with the pleasant smell of pine sap in their nostrils. Guided by Earthstar they kept up a routine of hunting and trekking which took them through to the magnificent Cairngorm mountain range. Although they had become accustomed to travelling at altitude and to viewing impressive panoramas nothing had prepared them for the splendour and beauty of the highlands. Mountain peaks, the very backbone of the earth, stretched to the horizon. Swift thanked Earthstar for his guidance to what instinctively he knew to be his destination. This would be the place where the spirits first set foot on earth and this would be what would entice them grey again; fresh clean air, the purple of the heather, the dark granite rocks and endless space to wander in freedom amongst infinite beauty.

Swift saw it all in a glance. The spirits had come from the skies and alighted on these soaring peaks which stretched up to meet them from an island of wild magnificence. He wondered if Tannon the alpha wolf had realised the magnitude of the promised land when he had led the wolf pack to it from the great drought. He feasted his eyes on the panorama. Tannon Valley was a small part of an island paradise that had everything a wolf could ever dream of; a paradise where each creature and every plant had its part to play in a delicate balance of nature. It became clear to him when he thought about Tannon Valley how easy it was to upset this balance. The ever-growing population of wolves had driven the game animals away. The forest had become a tangle of bramble and ivy which had smothered the grasses which the deer and elk fed on, closing the forest down to a system of wolf trails which the bison, wild boar, and deer were afraid to tread. All this because the wolf no longer lived the nomadic life its ancestors lived, in accord with their true nature.

Swift's destiny had drawn him here but now he'd arrived he was unsure of what to do next. Whilst the others relaxed he paced restlessly, waiting for a sign, wanting to get his business done and return home. Moon was on his mind constantly and he was acutely aware of time passing. For several days they camped in the shadow of the highest mountain they had encountered and Swift believed without doubt that his destiny would be decided on its granite slopes, but the waiting played on his nerves. He became moody and withdrawn, leaving the others to hunt whilst he brooded. He would sit silently staring up at Eagle Peak watching for a sign. He felt alone, abandoned by Earthstar when he needed him most. His mood darkened and he took to spending hours away from the others.

On the tenth morning Swift left them to take up his usual position facing Eagle Peak. He was considering moving across to camp at its base when he caught sight of a movement further up the slope of Ptarmigan Crag. Some kind of creature was descending from the rocks. Swift lay flat on his belly to conceal himself as best he could in the heather.

Soon a she-wolf, the most exquisite Swift had ever seen, emerged from behind a jutting boulder. He was stunned by her beauty, her fur being luxuriant, pure white. *Like summer clouds*, he thought. She descended the mountain with the grace of an alpha female, her tail curled high in friendly confidence. He could do nothing but stare and take pleasure in his good fortune. She did not see him immediately, half submerged in the heather, but when she did.

He stood up awkwardly. "I hope I didn't frighten you," he said.

She smiled at him. "Well you did rather startle me lying there in the heather like that," she said.

Swift felt embarrassed. "Sorry, I didn't mean to I was just enjoying the heather's fragrance."

"That's alright, no harm done. You 're not from these parts, are you?"

"No."

"Where are you from?" she asked.

"Tannon Valley," he replied.

"Where's that?"

"It's in the southern forests."

"Is that far from here?"

"Far enough when you've had to walk it," he replied with a smile.

She laughed. "You must have been lonely walking on your own."

"I came with two friends."

"What brought you all this way?"

Swift smiled. "How about me asking you some questions?"

She smiled with him. "Alright," she said.

"What's your name and do you live in these beautiful mountains?" he asked.

"I'm Shade, and yes I live on the other side of this mountain."

"Are you with a pack?"

"With my family. They are the pack."

"Do you know a wolf called Moondreamer?"

A distant bark distracted her. "I'd better go, my brothers are looking for me. Meet me here at this time tomorrow." She smiled and sped off up the mountain. Swift watched until she disappeared from sight, her melodic voice still sounding in his ears. He trotted back down the mountain, tail up, looking forward to tomorrow.

Leaf and Moss were stripping chunks of flesh from a recently killed reindeer. Moss looked up when Swift returned. "Come on Swift, this is good venison," he said.

Swift smiled. "Good idea, I'm starving." The three wolves ate their fill then lay resting.

"Haven't seen you eat like that for weeks," said Moss. "In fact I haven't seen you look so well for weeks."

"I have a feeling things will be happening soon."

"It's about time something happened," chipped in Leaf, "we've been here over a week and haven't seen a soul."

"What makes you think something's about to happen?" asked Moss.

Swift scratched at his flank. "Oh just a feeling," he said.

They spent the rest of the day talking and dozing, only getting up to eat more venison. The autumn sun warmed them as they recharged themselves, building up reserves of energy ready for the next stage of their mission. Swift's thoughts continually returned to Shade; he hoped she was the link he had been waiting for and looked forward to seeing her extraordinary beauty again in the morning.

That night he slept well, rising early next morning to leave for his usual destination whilst the others slept. The sky was clear, awaiting the sun's appearance from beyond the distant mountains. As he climbed he looked out for Shade. At last she appeared on a track which wound round the mountain. She was too far away for him to see her features but he recognised her sleek frame. She had a dense ruff of fur round her neck and shoulders and her body tapered to slim flanks. She strolled confidently down the mountainside towards him, the pure whiteness of her fur accentuated against the dark granite of the mountain rocks. Her movement was rhythmic, displaying harmony with her surroundings yet setting her apart from other creatures. He guessed her to be in her third year.

She called to him. "Good morning." Her voice seemed to float on the air.

"Good morning," he replied.

She stopped close to him. "I don't know your name," she said.

"Swift."

"Swift by name, Swift by nature, is that it?"

"Only when I'm chased by a bear," he replied.

"Where you come from is very different from here?"

"Yes. We don't have mountains."

"Ugh! No mountains! I can't believe that. I bet you can't see a thing for trees. Up here you can see the whole world."

"Yes but all this climbing makes your legs ache." They both laughed and Swift felt his spirits lift. "How many wolves in your pack?" he asked.

"Seven. Come and meet them."

"Are you sure? They may not take kindly to another male wolf trespassing on their territory."

"It's alright, I'll protect you," she joked.

"I don't want to cause you any trouble."

"Don't worry, I'm sure they'll like you."

"In that case lead the way."

He followed her along the meandering track which led up and around the mountain. Now and then it disappeared and they had to climb round an outcrop of rocks or leap a chasm. Swift was astounded by Shade's agility and self-confidence. At times he had to force himself to follow her. He was not at all comfortable when faced with a sheer drop but tried to conceal his discomfort and embarrassment when Shade had to wait for him.

At last they rounded the mountain and began to descend. Swift could see several wolves in the distance. Despite what Shade had said he felt anxious, it wasn't normal for strangers to be received cordially where he came from. He dropped his tail and arched his back submissively not wishing to challenge anyone, least of all the alpha wolf.

They got within forty yards of the den before they were seen and the barking started. Four wolves raced along the track towards them, barking a warning. Swift stopped, lowering his hind quarters further to signal his submission. Shade carried on walking but her family raced past her as though she wasn't there. Swift was surrounded and under threat of attack. They closed in on him, hackles raised, tails erect. Suddenly Shade burst through them to stand by his side.

"Stop this at once, he's a friend." Swift had expected something like this to happen but had not worked out the best way to react. He looked for an escape route but quickly concluded he would probably have to fight his way out.

Shade spoke forcibly on his behalf. "This wolf is not an enemy but a stranger who has travelled miles to reach our mountains."

The alpha wolf was angry. "Everyone's an enemy, until they prove they're a friend."

"How can he prove he's friend if you tear him to pieces?"

"Shade, you know it is a bad time to bring strangers into the den."

"But Tarn, he..."

"Let him speak for himself." The alpha wolf glared at Swift. "Well, what is it you want?"

Swift felt foolish, he hadn't much idea of what he was looking for but he managed to recall the wisewolf's name, given to him by Hawthorn. "I'm looking for a wisewolf called Moondreamer." Swift thought the alpha wolf's expression softened at the mention of Moondreamer's name but his attitude was unchanged.

"Moondreamer. What do you want with him?"

"It's a long story."

"You won't see Moondreamer until I've heard it. You'd better come with us." The alpha wolf turned and trotted off down the track. Swift glanced at Shade who smiled reassuringly. He followed the alpha wolf at a respectful distance, to the entrance of a small cave. The alpha wolf gestured for Swift to sit down and then had a whispered conversation with Shade who subsequently disappeared into the cave. Swift was alone with the alpha wolf, who fixed him with a penetrating gaze. "Now tell me what you want from Moondreamer."

Swift was unsure of how much he should tell the alpha wolf but began by describing Talon's reign of terror in the valley. As he spoke he tried to gauge Tarn's reaction to what he was saying but the alpha wolf remained inscrutable. Swift wanted to avoid mentioning the secret until he knew more about Tarn and how he would react. He described the supernatural battles being waged between Earthstar and Havnar and how Hawthorn had dreamed about a wisewolf called Moondreamer. He explained how in his dream Moondreamer had told Hawthorn of a visitation from the spirit world and how he had gained knowledge of how to resist the negative powers of evil. Swift finished speaking and waited for Tarn's reaction. Tarn's reply stunned him.

"You are wasting your time. Moondreamer is dead."

It was a moment before Swift was able to reply. "Moondreamer dead! He can't be."

"I repeat, Moondreamer is dead, your journey has been wasted."

"Why didn't you say so before?"

"I am the alpha wolf. It is my duty to find out why you are here, and what your intentions are. What are your intentions?"

"I'm not sure, I'll have to think."

The white wolf stood up dismissively. "I suggest you go home. There is nothing here for you."

Swift stood up. "Can I say good bye to Shade?"

"Shade, your friend is leaving." She emerged from the cave. Her fur looked whiter than ever against the blackness of the cave's entrance. "Say your farewells, your friend is leaving for home." Swift saw disappointment and a touch of sadness in her face.

"Perhaps one day we will meet again," he said.

"Could I walk down the mountain with him Tarn?"

"There is no point. Besides I need you here." He nodded curtly to Swift and left them alone.

Shade moved closer to him and spoke in a whisper. "I'll meet you tomorrow at sunrise by the rock." Swift nodded and left the den site, his mind in turmoil. He made his way back towards camp, numbed by what he'd heard.

Moss was waiting for him at the jagged rock. "Swift, what's happened? You're walking in a daydream."

"I can't believe it. Moondreamer is dead."

"How do you know?" asked Leaf, who had appeared from behind the rock.

"I made contact with a pack living on the far side of the mountain."

"When?"

"Two days ago."

"Why didn't you tell us?"

"I don't know, I should have told you."

"You might have been killed for all we knew. That would have dropped us all in it," said Leaf angrily.

"Leaf, I'm sorry. I don't know what came over me."

"Tell us what happened."

He told them about Shade and about his encounter with Tarn.

"What I want to know is, why this Shade wants to meet you tomorrow. Did she give you any idea?" asked Leaf.

Swift shook his head. "We didn't have time to talk."

"Well anyway that's it. We may as well start back in the morning, the game's up."

"I want to hear what Shade has to say."

"I would've thought the sooner you got back to Moon, the happier you'd be."

"Of course I want to get back," snapped Swift. "But I can't just give up."

"What else can we do?" asked Leaf.

"I don't know. Wait for a sign from Earthstar."

"Earthstar! He's led us all the way up here, to find out the one wolf who can help us is dead."

"I think we should sleep on it, things may look better in the morning."

The rest of the day was spent hunting. They located a herd of reindeer on the slopes just above the treeline. Spreading out they approached cautiously from downwind. The herd spotted them but allowed them to get close, confident of their agility on the slopes. When they moved in the reindeer were ready, making a quick break down the mountain. One old stag was slower than the others and the pack sensed an opportunity. They sprinted forward, cutting him off from the rest of the herd, working effectively as a team. Leaf leapt at the animal's muzzle, gripping it firmly between his teeth, allowing his weight to hang from the reindeer's snout to pull it off balance. Swift and Moss closed in for the kill.

They feasted well in anticipation of their return home, replacing the energy expended during the hunt and stocking up for the journey ahead of them. They remained at the scene of the kill, too gorged with venison to move. Dusk became night but Swift couldn't sleep, instead he lay looking out across the valley towards the mountains and beyond, enchanted by the beauty of the stars. An unexpected optimism filled him and he felt the need to pray. This was what made the mountains special, the night sky, visible in all its glory. The universe was vast and he just a speck in its infinity, yet at that moment his life had taken on great significance. It had real substance and meaning but he was still the same wolf. He had been chosen to save others not because he was better than they but because they were worth saving. He was their servant.

The depression he'd felt during the day lifted and he relaxed, allowing the universal power to flow as he prayed to Earthstar. "Earthstar I am you, you are me, we are one. I open my heart and soul to you knowing that the positive power of life will flow through me, permeating every cell of my body with the boundless energy of the creator. Mighty Earthstar, send me your divine guidance."

He breathed in deeply, drawing the cool night air into his lungs. He did not exhale immediately but allowed the life-giving oxygen to infuse his body.

When he exhaled his body relaxed and he was ready for sleep.

*

The next day Swift was first on his feet. He stretched and yawned then watched the others slowly come to life. Leaf yawned noisily. "Trouble with these ruddy mountains, the sun comes up too early. Let's get home to the trees," he grumbled. He stood up, turned round, and lay down again.

"Come on Leaf, we've got time to eat if we hurry," said Swift.

"Does that mean you've come to your senses and we're on our way home?" asked Leaf.

"Not quite, friend, we've unfinished business here."

"Oh, you still insist on seeing this, what's her name, Shade, then?"

"Leaf, we can't just go home with nothing. I'm sure if we stay a bit longer something will come up." They finished the remains of the reindeer before departing for the jagged rock. Shade was waiting beside the rock. Swift saw her and pointed her out to the others.

"Wow! That is one attractive she-wolf," said Leaf. "I can see why you kept her quiet."

Swift felt himself flush. "I don't know what you mean," he replied.

"What beautiful fur. I don't think I've ever seen anything like it," said Moss.

"I suppose you both want to stay now," said Swift.

"Well I don't suppose it would hurt to spend a couple more days here," agreed Leaf.

Swift greeted Shade and introduced the others. "Welcome to the highlands," she said. "I'm afraid Swift didn't get a very friendly greeting from my family. I'm sorry Swift but there are reasons for Tarn's touchiness."

"I didn't expect a hearty welcome. I don't suppose you've seen wolves like us before."

"Only your colour is different?"

"Even so Tarn seemed determined to get rid of me as quickly as possible."

"Why did you come here?"

"To find a wisewolf called Moondreamer. But Tarn said that he'd died."

"That's what I wanted to see you about. Moondreamer may still be alive."

"Shade, are you sure?" asked Swift.

"I can't be certain, but there is a good chance."

"Where is he?" asked Leaf.

"I think I can find him for you."

"Can you take us to him?" asked Swift, a feeling of hope returning.

"I can't take you all. It would be too dangerous."

"Will you take me?" asked Swift.

"Yes."

"Can we leave right away?"

"If you want to."

CHAPTER 13

Moss and Leaf agreed to lie low whilst Swift and Shade took the path around the mountain to Eagle Peak to search for Moondreamer. Swift gazed up at Eagle Peak's vastness.

"What is it Swift, don't you like our mountains?" asked Shade.

"They are so big."

"Yes, but don't they give you a sense of freedom?"

"They make me feel vulnerable."

"What are you afraid of?"

"Of being so exposed, I suppose."

"In the forest you may be hidden, but you can't see who might be lying in wait for you. Besides, here you can feel the warmth of the sun on your back and the wind in your fur."

"It's a bit draughty sometimes."

"You wouldn't like to live here?"

"It would take some getting used to."

They continued their conversation until they reached the foot of Eagle Peak. Swift stared up into the mist which shrouded its apex. "How far up do we have to go?" he asked.

"About halfway," Shade replied.

Swift groaned. "It's so steep."

"It's alright, I know a good track."

They climbed for two hours on a little-used path, Swift praying he'd find Moondreamer alive.

"How much further?" he asked.

"Not far now, around this rock and we're there."

His heart began to pound. On the far side of the rock was the mouth of a cave. They stood peering into its blackness. There were no signs of life. Then a thought struck Swift.

"You never said why Moondreamer came here."

"He came here to die."

"Why didn't you tell me before?"

"I didn't want you to give up."

"It could be too late then?"

"I do hope not, Swift. I know how much this means to you."

Swift was reluctant to disturb an old wolf who had left the pack to die, but he had no choice.

Shade called out, "Moondreamer." But there was no answer. She tried again. They stood silently waiting and just as Swift was about to give up hope a voice answered, but it was too feeble to be understood.

Swift looked at Shade. "Shall we go in?" She nodded and they stepped into the cave's dimness. Light did not penetrate far beyond the entrance and they could see only dark shadows in the cave's depths.

"Moondreamer, it's me, Shade."

"Go away."

"Moondreamer, I've brought someone who needs to talk to you."

"I've done all the talking I'm going to do, now go away and leave me alone."

"Moondreamer, my name is Swift. I've come from the forests of the lowlands. I..."

"I don't care who you are, or where you come from. Go away and leave me alone."

"Moondreamer, does the name Hawthorn mean anything to you?"

"What do you know about Hawthorn?"

"He's a wisewolf in Tannon Valley where I come from."

"Did Hawthorn send you?"

"Yes."

Moondreamer sighed. "What can I do? I'm an old wolf. I've had enough."

"Moondreamer, I need your help to save my friends and family."

"It's too late for me to help anyone."

"Please, you must try. Swift has travelled hundreds of miles to find you," pleaded Shade.

"I'm not sure I can help him."

"Hawthorn said you have knowledge of the spirits which no other wolf has," said Swift.

"My memory isn't what it used to be, besides I haven't eaten for three days. I can't think."

"We can find food for you," said Shade.

"Ask me what it is you want to know then go."

Swift wondered where to begin. Not being able to see Moondreamer in the darkness was unnerving. "I want to find out what I can about where the spirits visited the earth."

"I can't entrust that information to you. I was sworn to secrecy until the chosen one comes."

"Swift is the chosen one," said Shade, "he made the journey here with Earthstar's blessing."

"How do we know he's telling the truth?"

"How can I convince you?" said Swift.

"Who was it you said sent you?"

"Hawthorn! The wisewolf from Tannon Valley," Swift replied.

"Ah yes, Hawthorn. Hawthorn has visited me in my dreams many times. He is a good wolf. Why didn't he come himself?"

Swift glanced quizzically at Shade. "He is too old to make such a long journey."

"So he sent you instead. Bit young aren't you? Well never mind that, what is it you want to know?"

"Where exactly the spirits came down to earth."

"Am I the only one burdened with this knowledge? I'd resigned myself to taking it to my grave, anyway I'm sworn to secrecy until the chosen one comes, you know."

"Swift is the chosen one," repeated Shade, "he has come with Earthstar's blessing. Hawthorn is too old."

"It's too late, I've hardly the strength to talk."

"Moondreamer, you must help me for the sake of all wolves."

"Pah! What good will it do? You've heard the stories of the two-legged creatures from across the water. They are as organised as we are and they have language like we do but worse, they have the flying sticks that kill. How can we stop them? The wolflore says they lived in our lands before the great thaw warmed the earth and the trees grew, driving the big herds of game away. One day the two-legged creatures will come back, you mark my words."

"If they come back we can be ready for them, with Earthstar's help," replied Swift.

"Look, I'm tired and hungry. If I'm going to talk to you, I need something to eat."

Swift gave a sigh of relief, at last he was getting somewhere. He turned to Shade. "Would you help me find some food for Moondreamer?"

"Yes but we'll have to keep an eye out for Tarn."

Squinting against the bright sunlight which bathed the mountainside, they left the coolness of the cave. Shade led the way to the lower slopes to track reindeer and Swift marvelled at her hunting skills. She soon located a herd grazing just above the treeline. They quickly segregated an old stag who struggled to keep up with the rest of the herd. Swift brought him down with his first charge, inflicting a fatal wound with a bite to the throat. They gorged themselves on the succulent venison then dismembered the carcass for easy transportation to the cave. Swift looked at Shade, her pure white fur now stained red with blood.

He licked her nose. "Thank you," he said.

She smiled. "Do you think Moondreamer will tell you what you want to know?"

"I'm relying on it. Without his help what can I do?"

"I want to help you all I can," she said softly.

"I don't know how to repay you already."

She licked his face. "I believe in what you are doing, that's enough."

Between them they carried as much venison as their jaws could grip, making it a long, slow climb to the cave. When they got back they were exhausted and by the time Moondreamer began to eat the light was fading; Swift could hear him gnawing on the reindeer's flesh in the dark recesses of the cave.

He lay down next to Shade and they slept the deep sleep of the exhausted. Next morning he felt Shade lying close to him and was glad of the warmth of her body on the stone floor of the cave. Some daylight penetrated the gloom and he watched his breath condensing on the cold air. He listened to Moondreamer's laboured breathing and wondered how he'd survived the night.

Shade stirred and moved closer to him. He studied her profile then gently touched the ruff of thick fur at her neck with his nose. It was exquisitely soft and sweet scented.

She opened her eyes and smiled. "Caught you

keeping your nose warm," she joked. Embarrassed, he pulled away. "Don't be shy Swift, we're friends aren't we?"

"Yes we are, and I want you to know how grateful I am to you."

"It has given me much pleasure to help you." Swift felt her press closer to him and he thought of Moon and how he had missed her warmth at nights. Shade licked his ear.

"Shade, I don't think we should," he said.

Moondreamer woke up. "Who's there? What do you want?"

Shade glanced at Swift then looked back in Moondreamer's direction. "It's Shade," she said.

"What do you want?"

"You agreed to help Swift."

"Help him with what?"

"To find out where the spirits visited earth," said Swift.

"Oh yes. Now let me see, can I tell you that? No, I was sworn to secrecy. I can only tell the chosen one."

"Earthstar came to Hawthorn in a dream and chose Swift," said Shade.

"Oh yes I remember now, but I can only tell one of you. There can only be one chosen one, obviously."

Swift put his paw on Shade's. "Would you mind waiting outside, please?" Without answering she left the cave and Swift sensed her resentment at being asked to leave.

"Are you alone?" asked Moondreamer.

"Yes," he replied, and he heard Moondreamer groan. "What is it wisewolf?"

"Old age. I'm alright until I move." As he spoke he emerged from the darkness looking as old as time itself, ribs protruding through skin which hung loosely on an emaciated body. His fur was matted and grubby and he peered at Swift from watery eyes, embedded in deep sockets. "What are you staring at? Never seen an old wolf before?"

"I'm sorry, I didn't mean to stare."

"I came up here to die in peace. You wouldn't expect me to look a picture of health, would you?"

"I'm sorry. I suppose I was curious to see what you looked like."

"Oh never mind, don't keep apologising, we've got business to attend to. Sit down, no need to stand on ceremony." Swift watched the old wolf lower his hindquarters slowly to the ground. It was obvious he was in pain and discomfort. Swift silently thanked Earthstar for helping him to reach Moondreamer in time. He listened intently to what the wisewolf had to say.

"What I know of the secret came to me in a dream. It came to me, because I am the wisewolf living closest to where the spirits descended from the heavens. It is not something I asked to be burdened with, I had no choice in the matter. I would have been happy to carry the secret to the grave. I believe immortality may benefit the individual, but not the wolf nation. It will only interfere with the natural balance of things. We live and we die. It's nature's law."

"Tannon Valley is on the verge of disaster, only a miracle can save it. Havnar is acting through the alpha wolf Talon who has already destroyed the natural way of the wolf. He is being driven by Havnar, to find the secret before I do. I was lucky to escape the wolfrahm and get away from the valley."

"The wolfrahm?"

"Talon's body-guard, he controls the valley through them."

"Did they follow you here?"

"They tried, but we lost them."

"Thank Earthstar. We don't want any of that sort in the highlands. Here we stick with the traditional ways. Now what were we talking about?"

"The secret."

"Oh yes! The secret. It won't be easy, you know. I hope you realise what you're getting yourself into."

"I didn't come here for the fun of it."

"Getting testy now are we?"

"I'm sorry, a lot's happened and my friends and family are depending on me."

"A family eh? You'd better be careful then. Shade seems to have taken quite a shine to you." Swift shifted his feet uneasily and Moondreamer carried on speaking. "If you don't fully understand the implications you could be in for a shock." Swift felt a surge of uncertainty and Moondreamer saw it in his face. "It's not too late to leave here, you know. I've told you nothing."

"How can I leave with nothing?"

Moondreamer yawned, his face etched with weariness. The energy seemed to drain from him. He closed his eyes and Swift's heart pounded in alarm; surely he was not going to die now. Swift stared in disbelief. He moved closer to Moondreamer as if it would help.

"Moondreamer, what's wrong?"

Moondreamer coughed as though he was about to choke. "I'll be alright, just give me a minute to get my breath, it's this damp cave playing hell with my chest." Swift hated prolonging the old wolf's agony, keeping him from death's peace. Moondreamer recovered his composure. "I'm sorry, now where were we? Oh yes. This is what you must do. You will visit each place where the spirits materialised on the earth, and see and understand what they saw. You will discover what they discovered, and will absorb the latent power which they bequeathed to its finder. And you will be more powerful than they are. You will have what they crave, immortality on earth. Only the spirits can choose the recipient of this power. They would take it for themselves if it were possible. Across the millennia the spirits have searched for a way to come to earth in mortal form to ensure its survival, but time is running out. That is why you have been chosen."

"If this power can only be tapped by a mortal why is Havnar so determined to know its secret?"

"Havnar would use it through another wolf who already courts the powers of darkness. This Talon fits the bill nicely. Havnar has wet his appetite with promises of everything he desires. This is how he spreads his power. Every wolf will become important only to himself, and eventually he will destroy his fellows. You are in great danger now, trust no one. Havnar will not rest until he has destroyed you."

Swift became aware of a change in Moondreamer – he seemed younger, more animated, as though new life had been breathed into him. The old wolf continued. "Don't lose heart, Havnar is only one among many. The spirits don't want the earth's beauty destroyed. They have sampled its treasures and want to protect them. They are involved in a constant struggle to maintain a balance between positive and negative forces. If these forces become unbalanced then it spells disaster for someone. Havnar is a mutant spirit who is convinced the negative forces outweigh the positive and wants to use them to gain power. For this he needs a terrestrial agent who will help him destroy nature's equilibrium. Once he has gained a foothold, it will be very difficult to stop him."

Moondreamer stood up with no trace of his former stiffness. It was as if he were a different wolf. His thinning fur had taken on a new lustre and his eyes shone with determination. He paced the floor of the cave. "Swift, only you can absorb the energy of the spirits. You must not fail. More than Tannon Valley depends on your success.

"First you must enter the Forest of the Pines at night and listen for the nightingale's song. When the song has bathed your ears you must stay in the forest and search for the honeysuckle. You must sample its scent. Then you will begin a journey to the summit of Eagle Peak. Along the way you will encounter a she-wolf who has recently given birth to a litter of cubs. You must feel the soft down of their fur, feel their warmth and care for them. When you have done this, continue your ascent. As you climb you must look out across the valleys and see the vast forests which populate them. Feast your eyes on the trees and imagine the myriad creatures which live amongst them, and know how important each species is, to the survival of the others.

"When the spirits descended to earth they saw what you will see, and, you will experience the same wonder. When you have been climbing Eagle Peak for some time you will be thirsty and your instinct will lead you to water. You will find a spring of the purest water imaginable. To drink from this spring is your final task before you ascend to the summit of Eagle Peak. By then you will have done all that the spirits did, and demonstrated your courage." Swift looked at Moondreamer in silence. Moondreamer grinned. "Any questions?"

"It seems too easy."

"I've a sneaky feeling it's going be more difficult than it sounds."

"What do you mean wisewolf?"

"You don't think Havnar is about to sit back and let you get away with this. Do you?"

"I keep hoping he's given up."

"I wouldn't bank too much on that one."

"There are times when I could give up."

"You must have faith in yourself, and in Earthstar, if you don't, what hope have you of saving yourself or your friends?"

He thought of Moon and the cubs, of Mistle, of

Hawthorn and Stag. If he didn't take a chance with his own life, they could all die. He didn't want to die, he desperately wanted to live, but what choice did he have?

"I'll ask Shade to guide me."

"You should go alone."

"How will I know where to go?"

"Alright, take Shade, but trust no one."

Swift moved closer to Moondreamer. He licked the old wolf's face. "Thank you wisewolf. I'm sorry I had to disturb you."

"Nonsense, wolves have been disturbing me all my life, for one reason or another. Why should it be any different now? After all death is just another part of life. Now I think it's time you got on your way, you've a lot to do."

Swift looked at Moondreamer for what he knew would be the last time and left the cave. He caught sight of Shade peering into the cave's gloominess, she stepped aside as he emerged, squinting into the sunlight. He looked away to hide his tears and Shade moved to his side, to touch him. "Swift, it comes to us all, Moondreamer's suffering will soon be done and he will move on to another place."

"He seemed so alone."

"It's the way of the wolf."

"Shade will you help me? I need someone who knows the mountains to guide me."

"You know I will help you."

"What about Tarn?"

"I will go home after dark and tell my sister to let him know I am alright."

"I'll tell Moss and Leaf what's going on."

By dusk they were back at the jagged rock. A full moon gave Shade enough light to return safely to her den whilst Swift spent the evening under the rock recounting his experiences to Leaf and Moss.

"Looks as though you caught Moondreamer just in time," said Leaf.

"I think Earthstar kept him hanging on," said Swift. "Without Earthstar I don't think we'd have even got here."

"Course we would. We have ourselves to thank, nobody else," said Leaf.

"Remember the great white bird, Leaf?" said Moss.

"Ah yes, well only the spirits know where he came from."

"Exactly," said Swift. They laughed and relaxed in each other's company. Swift prayed he would find Moon and the cubs safe and well when he returned home, then settled down to sleep.

The next morning as the first rays of sunlight spread across the mountain Swift woke up and saw Shade hurrying through the heather towards the jagged rock.

She called to him as she approached. "Tarn is not far behind me."

Swift woke Leaf and Moss. "See if you can hold them off," he shouted.

Leaf got up and shook himself. "You leave it to us.

Just get on your way."

They took the path down and across the mountain, Swift struggling to keep up with the she-wolf whose agility on the rocky slopes far exceeded his own. Twice he stumbled whilst looking back over his shoulder for Tarn. Finally he decided to keep his head down and concentrate on keeping pace with Shade. Soon they were down in the valley with no sign of Tarn anywhere.

"Do you want to rest?" asked Shade.

"No, we haven't time. Let's wait until we're in the forest. Tarn won't follow us there."

Swift followed Shade along the narrow track which cut through the heather on its descent towards the pine forests, a mile or so distant. In less than half an hour they entered the forest with no sighting of Tarn. Swift could sense Shade's unease at being amongst the trees but he was also conscious of Moondreamer's warning that he should act alone.

He asked Shade to wait for him at the forest's edge. "Please let me come with you, I don't feel safe here on my own," she said.

"Shade I have to do this alone. I'll come back as soon as I can, I promise."

Swift felt relieved to be back amongst the trees. The Scots pines let in plenty of light and purple heather grew in clumps amongst the soft greens of the lichens and the mosses. Here and there the yellowing leaves of a silver birch hinted at the beginning of autumn and the roar of a stag, preparing for the rut, affirmed the start of the fall.

The sound comforted him but Shade peered around anxiously. "Why do you find the forest so frightening?" he asked.

"Because bears and vipers lurk amongst the trees," she replied.

"So do deer, boar, and beaver. You learn to take the rough with the smooth."

"I feel so hemmed in."

"Why don't you wait for me on the mountain?"

"No, I'll be alright."

They made camp beneath a mountain ash laden with crimson berries. Its bark was scored by the antlers of a red deer where it had rubbed off the remains of the antlers' protective velvet, prior to the rut. The marks were made recently and for a time the two wolves sat silently, watching a pair of pied wagtails searching the lichen for bloated tics, fallen from the stag's back.

Swift left Shade to make herself comfortable whilst he hunted. He caught several wood mice which he ate himself and was lucky enough to catch a mountain hare for Shade. He wanted to venture deeper into the forest. Ever since he had set foot amongst the pines he had been aware of an invisible force trying to draw him deeper into the forest's interior. It grew stronger with the passage of time, compelling him to follow.

"Shade, promise me you'll lie low until I get back."

"Please be careful Swift."

"Please don't fret Shade. Earthstar will protect me."

Shade licked his face and rubbed her head against his. "Come back safely," she said.

For a moment he held her gaze. "I'd better go," he said.

He walked away, sorry to leave her, but drawn by a force which he found irresistible. He didn't know where he was going but knew eventually he would get there. Only the spirits could help him now but had they the power to resist the forces of Havnar?

There was enough daylight left for him to move comfortably through the trees. The smell of pine sap filled his nostrils and he acknowledged the beauty of the pine forests; the orange-tinged bark of the Scots pines and the purple heather underfoot, the delicate greens of the grasses, and the charming blue of the harebells. These were things he would never forget. But even as he absorbed the beauty around him, he thought of his wolves, and his home.

After an hour's trek the compulsion pulling him forward ceased and he stopped in a clearing. It was dusk and the forest was silent save for the sound of a small brown bird about the size of a robin, searching the undergrowth for spiders. Swift sat on the moss and watched the bird hop amongst the lichens and harebells which grew there. He closed his eyes to enjoy the silence. When he opened them he saw a bright, dazzling orb of light which hung suspended in the glade below the lowest branches of the pines. At first he blinked against its intensity, but he quickly became accustomed to it and it became soft to his eyes. Warmth emanated from it, bathing his body, and bringing with it a deep sense of wellbeing.

The image of a handsome wolf began to form in the orb, his silver-grey fur shining with the vitality of the light. His amber eyes radiated love and he looked down at Swift with compassion. "Welcome Swift, I am glad you have come. I know it has not been easy for you but through everything you have kept faith. You seek what all the spirits seek, immortality on earth. This is a gift the spirits can bestow but they cannot award to themselves. You will be more powerful than they. This is a gift we do not give lightly, but to save the earth from its own destruction it is necessary. No one deserves this more than you. You alone can bear its responsibilities. You must bring love and peace to the world through the wolf. The wolf must be the great respecter of nature and always seek to keep its fragile balance.

"You must teach selflessness and the spirit of the pack so that wolves will work for each other. You must teach the wolf how to use the positive forces and to shun the negative forces of the mutant Havnar. All wolves have to respect and cherish the power you will possess, in the knowledge that it is for all wolves. Therefore it is in their interests to preserve it. Although you will be able to resist death by all other agents you will not be able to resist it from the bite of another wolf. Before you can fully assimilate this power you must commune with the spirits where they came down to earth and absorb the latent power which they have bequeathed to the chosen one."

Swift revelled in a feeling of peace and understanding as Earthstar's words soothed his troubled mind. Everything he had been through suddenly became worthwhile but before long,

Earthstar's image faded and the orb disappeared, and Swift once again became aware of the little brown bird.

Dusk turned to night and he sat whispering a prayer to comfort him in the darkness of a night darker than he'd ever experienced before. A low-pitched melody drifted to and from his consciousness. Such was its quietness that it barely registered in his senses and he was unsure of its reality. He cocked his ears, straining to be certain of what he heard. Gradually the song became louder, permeating his mind. He became enraptured by its beauty and delicacy. As it increased in volume his whole body absorbed it like a sponge soaking up water. He wanted its effects to intoxicate him forever. Each note was the essence of clarity and purity and the forest reverberated with the nightingale's song. His pleasure was complete. Swift sat back on his haunches and let the euphoria wash over him, his consciousness lost in a beautiful melody that filled his senses.

But then something unwanted began to force its way into his consciousness. He tried to shield his mind from it, to prevent it from polluting the song's wonderful clarity. He was horrified that anything could interfere with the ecstasy he was experiencing at that moment, wanting it to continue forever, totally in accord with nature. Unaware of his own physical being his spirit had risen with the melody of the nightingale's song, but now he was aware of another sound forcing its way into his hearing to contaminate the song's purity. He felt cheated, deprived and angry as the sound increased in volume until he realised that it was a wind blowing up and gathering in strength.

The purity and resonance of the nightingale's song dwindled in its wake.

Swift's mind was filled with terrible memories of the night of the hurricane, and memories of his escape from the Beech Wood returned to him in all their horror. He cowered in fear, and the nightingale's song was forgotten in the cacophony of the wind that threatened to sweep him away. Somewhere close by a branch crashed to the ground and he felt the earth vibrate beneath him. On the brink of panic at being crushed to death he leapt up, searching for an escape route – there was none, only a wall of blackness and the deafening crash of falling trees ripped up by the ferocity of the wind.

An image of Earthstar appeared in his mind, mouthing words which Swift could not hear. Swift focused on his lips, trying to read what he was saying. With a huge effort of concentration he forced the wind's roar from his mind and read Earthstar's words.

"Cast out your fear. Be infused with courage and above all believe in yourself."

Earthstar's voice remained inaudible and the wind returned to renew its assault tenfold. Swift's fur was flattened along his back and the wind drove into his face, forcing the breath from his body. He lay clinging to the earth, his claws piercing the layer of moss and lichen, digging into the soil beneath. The wind threatened to lift him from the ground but he held firm, letting his fear go and the wind wash over him.

His fear began to lift like mist from a mountain and he stood serene in the face of the storm, his terror vanquished. The winds abated more suddenly than they had come, leaving the forest still. An inner strength he had not experienced before buoyed his spirits and his strength returned with an assurance that the power of the spirits had transfused his veins. The first rays of dawn lit his way as he calmly returned to Shade.

She waited where he had left her; she looked tired, as though she had not slept, and he knew she had waited anxiously for him. He marvelled at her beauty as he had done the first time he'd seen her. She heard him and stood up, relief showing instantly in her eyes. "Thank Earthstar, you are safe," she said. "What happened, you've been gone all night?"

"Everything's alright, I listened to the most wonderful mesmerising melody and I wanted it to go on forever, but it was destroyed by the noise of the hurricane. Shade, are you alright? The winds were so ferocious."

"Winds, what winds? The night was still and quiet."

"It was Havnar! I should have realised. But the song was real."

"What song?"

"The song of the nightingale, I had to experience its beauty, just as the spirits did when they came to earth."

"You must be exhausted, I'll hunt while you rest."

Shade caught several mice which she gave to Swift, who could not sleep. The song of the nightingale had charged him with energy and he wanted to make use of it. He ate the mice and washed them down with cool water from a nearby burn. Thirsts quenched, they lay on its bank watching a dipper perched on a rock in the middle of the shallow, tumbling water. The small, dark, white-breasted bird constantly bobbed up and down as it scanned the fast-flowing burn. To Swift's surprise it jumped into the water and disappeared. It reappeared briefly on a rock further downstream before taking off and flying upstream just above the water's surface. Although grateful to the dipper for the brief distraction, Swift wanted to get on.

"Surely you are going to rest?" asked Shade.

"There's no time and I've never felt better. Please wait for me here and I promise we'll leave the forest before nightfall."

He licked her tenderly on the nose and left her by the burn. The first path he came to led up a slope. He came to the top of the rise and stopped to listen to the sound of cascading water. He walked ahead to a chasm and looked down on a bubbling mass of white foam, tumbling and crashing down a craggy watercourse hewn out of rock. Further down, the white water was swallowed into the depths of a dark river snaking its way across a bed of granite through a deep rocky gorge.

He followed the path upstream, enjoying the coolness that emanated from the icy water. Along the rock-strewn banks of the gorge the Scots pines receded where the soil was too sparse even for them. Instead dark green bushes of broom, delicate fronds of fern, and the omnipresent heather flourished amongst the silver-white rocks that basked in the sun.

Swift began to wonder if honeysuckle grew in the pine woods. They were so different to the woods of home where he often found honeysuckle clinging to the branches of a hawthorn bush. He wasn't convinced it would still be flowering anyway. He walked on along the river, the sun at its zenith.

He came to a path branching at a right angle to the river and instinctively took it. His wolf's sense of smell caught the fragrance of the flower before he saw it. It clung possessively around the trunk and branches of an old juniper tree. The plant had climbed its host to gain height and then as if in payment, had hung its yellow, tube-like flowers to adorn it.

Swift walked reverently towards it, seeing its beauty for the first time. He lifted his head and his nose touched the lowest flower. The sweet fragrance drifted into his nostrils and he drew in a deep breath rich with the flower's perfume. His spirit soared. He closed his eyes and his mind, to everything but the scent of the honeysuckle.

He was enchanted by a plant he'd scented many times but had never experienced. The sound of the river had disappeared, only the purity of the honeysuckle touched his senses. It was all that mattered, until something touched his paw.

The spell was broken and the sound of the river rushed back into his consciousness. For a second he was disorientated. He remembered feeling a touch. He looked round, expecting to see Shade. There was no one. The hackles rose on his back. He felt a sharp sting in his foreleg. He leapt back as if a bear had swung a paw at him. At his feet, its head and a third of its length raised from the ground, a viper gyrated slowly from side to side as though it were trying to hypnotise him.

Swift glanced at his right foreleg. A trickle of blood showed where the viper had sunk its fangs in just above the paw where the fur was thinnest. He watched the viper lower itself to the ground and move sinuously towards him. For a moment he was mesmerised by its movement through the tufts of heather. His eyes were drawn to the distinct black 'V' shape on the reptile's head. He knew the viper's bite was fatal to the wolf and he was seized with an anger that dismissed his caution. With lightning speed he seized the viper in his jaws, gripping it just below the head. The startled snake thrashed its tail violently in an attempt to wriggle free. Swift closed his jaws tighter to prevent its head from moving into a position from where it could strike. He carried it in his jaws to the chasm and held it over the thundering, white water. He opened his mouth and let it go. It fell in the shape of an arc, its heavy belly pulling its head and tail after it. But it was gone before it hit the water.

Swift felt dizzy and his leg throbbed, he was hot and there was no cooling breeze in the wood. Instinctively he lay down to conserve the energy he would need to fight the effects of the snake bite. Fear rose in his stomach when he looked at the trickle of blood running from the two small puncture marks made by the viper's fangs. His chest tightened as the venom performed its evil work. His breathing rate increased as he attempted to draw more oxygen into his failing lungs. He was on the edge of unconsciousness when Earthstar's image formed in his mind's eye and he heard the words Earthstar had spoken when the nightingale had sung. 'Cast out your fear. Be infused with courage. Above all believe in yourself.'

Swift began to relax and the power of the spirits flowed through him. His strength gradually returned and with it again an inner assurance that the power of the spirits had entered his veins. He rested for a short time then walked back along the river, watching the salmon bravely leaping upstream against the white water to spawn. As he walked back down the slope he could see Shade sitting by the burn waiting for him. When she saw him she got up and cantered to meet him. Her coat was thickening in preparation for the cold northern winter and it seemed to him more luxurious than ever. As always her grace and beauty astounded him. When they met she licked his face and they chased each other like cubs in their first spring. She listened to his story and then reminded him of his promise to leave the forest before nightfall.

"We'll leave right away. Moondreamer said I would encounter a she-wolf with newborn cubs and I would be expected to care for them as if they were my own."

"My sister has a new litter but it would be dangerous, Tarn will be guarding them."

"Tarn will be out looking for us, we should do it now. We'll go via the jagged rock, Leaf and Moss will be there."

"Alright," she agreed.

They travelled cautiously, keeping watch for signs of the highland wolves. Swift desperately wanted to avoid a confrontation with Tarn now the purpose of his journey was close to being fulfilled. By the time they reached the jagged rock the weather had deteriorated to a drizzle and there was no sign of Moss or Leaf.

"Perhaps they're hiding from Tarn," said Swift.

"They will have to be at their best, nobody knows these mountains like Tarn," replied Shade.

Swift didn't want to think about that. "We'd better keep moving," he said. He was glad when he could see the entrance to the den in the distance.

"I'll go on ahead and see if it's safe," said Shade.

"Be careful."

She licked his face and trotted off towards the den. She went in and Swift waited ready to react if Tarn appeared. Shortly after, Shade called him from the den.

"It is all clear, only Beck is here. I've persuaded her to take a stroll with me, but she will not leave the cubs for long." Beck was waiting anxiously at the entrance.

Swift smiled at her. "Don't worry, I will guard them with my life. This is for all wolves." Not wanting to frighten the cubs, he entered the cave as quietly as he could. It was not deep and there was enough light to see them by. At first they looked like a bundle of cream-coloured fur but as his eyes adjusted to the light he could pick out the tips of ears and tails. They were all sleeping soundly and he crept closer, wishing they were his own. He smelt their newness as he reached out to touch them with his paw – they were soft and warm. He nuzzled his nose behind an ear and lay down beside them, feeling the warmth of their bodies close to his. Love and compassion filled him and his instinct was to protect them with his life.

They lay beside him in their purity, unsullied by the rigours of life and he wished, as if they were his own, that they could remain that way forever. He had never touched anything so soft and warm. The cub nearest him raised its head and peered at him through closed eyelids, it would be another three weeks before they were able to see and feast their eyes on the beauty of the highland world they had been born into. He wished they could remain in their innocence but losing it would be the price they had to pay for the experience of life. He understood then that they could not remain innocent and live life to the full.

Swift had never experienced such a powerful urge to protect a fellow creature. He lay enchanted by the sound of their breathing. He felt the rhythmic rise and fall of their chests and was thrilled with the nearness of newly created life. He felt more content than he could ever remember, his mind filled exclusively with the presence of the cubs. Eventually he drifted into a slumber from which he awoke now and then to further fill his senses with their closeness.

It seemed to go on forever until he was dragged back to stark reality by something which gripped his leg with such force he thought his bones would be crushed. A paw of huge proportions tore him away from the cubs and towards the cave's entrance. He spread-eagled his legs, trying to gain a foothold, but it made no difference. He spun round, contorting his body to confront his assailant. What he saw terrified him. The cave's entrance was filled with the head and shoulders of a huge bear that was determined to extract him from the cave.

Swift lunged at his attacker, biting ferociously, but only snapped thin air; he yelped as the bear increased the pressure on his leg. Digging his front paws in, he managed to slow his progress but not for long. Unable to resist the bear's strength, he sped roughly through the cave's entrance, cracking his head on rock as he went. Although painful, it didn't do any real damage, but it gave him an idea. When the bear pulled him to his chest he hung limply in the bear's paws, feigning unconsciousness. Surprised, the bear stared at Swift's lifeless body, shook it several times and then threw it to the ground in contempt.

Swift reacted immediately. He leapt up and dived away from the bear in one movement. For a second or two they stood eyeing each other, the bear temporarily startled by Swift's recovery. Swift had never seen a bear of this size before, not even Crag had towered to this height. Snarling, he turned away from Swift and in two strides was at the den, thrusting his head and shoulders through the entrance. Horrified, Swift threw himself at the bear's black hindquarters, knocking the wind out of himself but having no effect on the bear. He shook himself to clear his head and tried again, this time sinking his teeth into the bear's thigh and digging his hind legs into the ground for leverage. The bear growled, kicked out, and sent Swift crashing against a boulder. With startling speed the bear rounded on him and Swift was cornered. The bear raised itself to its full height and roared. The fear Swift had experienced when he had been attacked in the Pennines returned to paralyse him. There was no escape, this time the bear intended to kill him.

As it had done in the forest, a vision of Earthstar came to his mind's eye and he remembered what he had to do. He drew in a deep breath and cast the fear from his mind. At that moment the bear charged him, Swift leapt sideways, narrowly avoiding the bear's lunge and before it could recover Swift rounded it and scrambled into the cave. He shielded the cubs as best he could, teeth bared ready to strike back. The bear tried to squeeze his way through the narrow entrance but luckily this time, his size was to Swift's advantage, he couldn't force his bulk through. If Swift could avoid his outstretched paws then he would be safe. He growled threateningly to give himself courage more than anything and to his amazement the bear withdrew. Only the sound of the cubs whimpering broke the silence. He wanted to comfort them but could not take his eyes off the cave's entrance.

For several minutes he watched, both ears cocked, sure that the bear would return. The cubs were very distressed and he prayed the bear had gone for good. He licked each cub in turn, whispering soothing, reassuring words, acutely aware that they had come close to death before they'd had a chance to live. He felt drained and lay down limply beside them, exhausted. He thought of their mother with eternal gratitude, that he was able to face her with her cubs alive and unharmed. He owed their survival to one thing, his ability to relax in the face of danger. He pricked his ears up, someone or something was approaching the den. He sighed with relief when Beck emerged from the shadows, uttering soothing words to her babies.

Shade followed her in looking expectantly at Swift. "What happened?" she asked.

Swift glanced at Beck who was licking her cubs. "We'd better talk outside," he said.

"The cubs, are they alright?"

"Yes. Thank the spirits." He followed her outside. "I've just been attacked by the biggest bear I've ever seen. It threw me around as though I was a wood mouse. I couldn't believe its power. We had a narrow escape in there. When I think of those cubs..." He stopped speaking and shuddered.

Shade licked his ear. "Are you alright?"

"I feel terrible for taking such a risk with Beck's cubs. They could so easily have been killed."

She touched his paw. "No harm has been done. They are safe with their mother now. Forgive yourself, you are flesh and blood too, you know."

Swift looked into her eyes. "Thank you. Where would I be without you?"

Swift had taken strength from defeating the bear and the prospect of climbing Eagle Peak didn't seem so daunting, although he had the greatest respect for the mountain. He looked through the morning mist to where it towered into the clouds and wondered how they would reach its peak. Shade had admitted she'd never been beyond halfway.

They crossed the glen towards the mountain which became more imposing the closer they got to it. As they began the upward trek through the heather, Swift hoped they could get up and back before nightfall. He didn't relish the prospect of a cold night on the mountainside. Neither of them spoke, Swift being preoccupied with what might await him on the scree slopes. They had been climbing for an hour when Swift felt compelled to stop.

"What is it?" asked Shade.

"I don't know."

He was drawn towards a cluster of boulders about ten yards from the track. Using the others as stepping stones, he scrambled up onto the largest. His gaze was westward. The pine forests stretched along the great glen into the far distance. This was the world at its most magnificent: unending forests teeming with life, sheltered by vast mountain ranges bathed in fresh, clear air. He felt humbled yet ennobled by the spectacle.

As he absorbed the panorama he caught sight of a bird circling just below the cloud which obscured Eagle Peak's summit. It glided in an arc on huge wide-spread wings. Swift watched it circle for a few minutes before he realised it was moving almost imperceptibly in a descending spiral. He was captivated by the ease of the bird's movement as it cut effortlessly through the air, on its methodical downward course. From a black speck in the distant sky it was soon close enough for Swift to see the browns of its plumage and the subtle movement of its flight feathers. Its head and body appeared small in relation to its enormous wingspan.

It circled round and flew in towards him and he

saw clearly the slate grey of its huge curved beak and hooked talons. Swift followed the bird's flight path and craned his neck as it reached a point almost directly above him. He saw it draw its wings close to its sides, tuck its talons back and begin to drop.

It was then, Swift realised that he was the eagle's target. He scanned the rocks for somewhere to hide but there was nowhere. He scrambled across the boulder, keeping his head low. As he leapt for the next boulder the eagle hit him with outstretched talons, catching him off balance, and sending him sliding over the edge of the rock. The force he hit the ground with knocked the wind out of his body. He lay on his side, momentarily unable to move but watching as the eagle turned and flapped its wings to pull away from the mountainside.

It started to bank and Swift knew it wasn't going away. He hauled himself up onto shaky legs, wincing with the sting of pain in his shoulder. He looked up. The eagle was hurtling out of the sky towards him. As it closed in, it spread its tucked wings and thrust its yellow, clawed feet towards him. He threw himself to the ground, steeling himself against the impact of the eagle's talons. Instead a whoosh of air ruffled the fur of his neck and back, as the winged predator narrowly missed him.

This time he didn't watch it lift upwards, he scrambled into the gap below where the two big boulders touched, crouching back as far as he could against the rock. He peered at the sky, shaken by the eagle's attack, hoping for time to think, but it was coming again. The hatred in its eyes startled him and he remembered a time when as a cub he had been frightened by a raven. The memory of this angered him and his fear evaporated. He thought of Earthstar and relaxed, knowing he was safe under the rocks.

The eagle kept coming and the points of its talons momentarily loomed over Swift, filling the view from his refuge. The bird in its rage had misjudged its target, it banked too late and caught its wing on the boulder, spinning it sideways. Swift saw his chance. He rushed the stunned bird, barking loudly. It took two faltering steps and lurched forward, attempting to flap its wings. It recovered itself, but Swift's jaws closed like a vice on its tail feathers when it tried to take off. Swift felt the power of the bird's wings as it flapped and squawked in its attempt to escape. Finally it pulled away, but left half of its tail in Swift's mouth.

This time the eagle did not bank but disappeared abruptly, as though it had evaporated before it reached the clouds surrounding the mountain top. Swift let out a sigh of relief and remembered Shade. He wondered why she had not helped him. He looked round to see her emerge from behind a rocky outcrop.

She cantered up the mountain towards him, her face full of concern. "Thank Earthstar it has gone. Are you alright?" she asked.

"Yes. I think so."

"Please let's go before it comes back."

Swift felt pain in his injured shoulder and was forced to limp on his right foreleg. Shade licked his muzzle. "It will soon be over, there is only the spring."

He wondered how she knew about the spring. He had told her as little as possible in keeping with

Moondreamer's wishes. Perhaps he had mentioned it inadvertently, he thought. The track gradually disappeared as they ascended and the going became increasingly difficult. They picked their way round loose boulders and negotiated ledges jutting over sheer rock faces. Luckily for Swift the mist had closed in, shrouding the top of the mountain, masking the drop. Every move now had to be thought through, every foothold tested. He hoped Shade couldn't see his legs trembling when it was his turn to squeeze along a narrow ledge.

They had been climbing for three hours in the mist when visibility improved. Swift managed to stay focused on the climb, seeing just enough in front of him to break it down into small manageable chunks, but as the mist lifted his attention began to wander. He found himself looking down and then looking up at where he had to go next. Shade had to continually encourage him to move on and not look down. He wished, many times, he had his feet firmly planted on the trails of Tannon Valley.

He glanced down to find a foothold and when he looked up again, the last trace of mist had lifted. The September sun glared from a watery blue sky, lighting every nook and cranny of Eagle Peak's summit. The view across the mountains was stunning and for a moment Swift forgot his fear. "I can see why the spirits came here," he said.

"Ah! You like our mountains after all?"

He laughed. "Yes, you get a very good view of the forests from here," he joked.

Shade moved around freely, pointing out

landmarks she recognised thousands of feet below. Swift wished she would stand still. Feeling acutely insecure he sat down shakily. He could see more of the world than he'd ever seen before, and understood Shade's love of the mountains.

He heard the gurgle of running water and crossed the peak unsteadily to find its source. He peered into a cleft in the rock and saw the flow of fresh mountain water, cascading over a rock to feed a subterranean stream. The water was pure and translucent and Swift could smell its freshness and its closeness cooled him. He put his forelegs into the cleft and reached towards the water. He lapped at it delicately, respecting it for what it was, the most crucial sustainer of life. His thirst was great and it was like nectar, pure and unsullied, a gift from the spirits themselves. He felt its wonderful power to revive and refresh him.

His thirst quenched, he backed out of the cleft. Shade was no longer moving around but sitting watching him, an odd expression on her face, one he had not seen before. It was as though she had discarded a mask and he was seeing her for the first time. Somehow her beauty had suffered for it. She donned the mask and came towards him till their noses touched.

"Swift, we have become very close. I want you to stay in the highlands with me. I can't bear the thought of you leaving."

"Shade I have to go back to my family, they won't survive without me."

"I can't survive without you. I have given you everything."

"They are relying on me."

"How do you know they've survived?"

"I have to believe it."

"Swift, I didn't take you for a fool. If you go back, Havnar will find a way to destroy you."

"I'll take my chances."

"With your power and the strength of my love, we could be invincible."

"Shade, I have the greatest respect and fondness for you but I have to go back to Moon."

"Then you are a fool. You are turning down an opportunity for power beyond even the dreams of Talon."

Swift was startled. "What do you know about Talon?"

"Everything! He should be here, not you. He and Havnar have great plans for the survival of the wolf. What will you do? You will save your family, and the wolf nation will perish."

Swift stared at Shade, trying to make sense of what she was saying. "You don't really believe that do you? Havnar doesn't care about the wolf."

"Only Havnar can save us, and there will be nothing but glory for those who follow him."

"Havnar and Talon have brought nothing but misery to Tannon Valley."

"Nobody said things would be easy, Swift. You are weak and a threat to the wolf's survival, you have to be stopped now before it's too late." Swift felt the hackles rise on his back. Suddenly Shade had become unrecognisable, a hideous creature her beauty transformed. Her eyes exuded evil and her throat issued a sinister guttural growl of such menace that he stepped back from her, his heart thumping. He saw a dribble of saliva trickle from her mouth and a terrifying realisation hit him. She was rabid.

He had seen rabies once before as a cub and was horrified by his recollection of it. No wolf had ever survived its agonising death. Keeping one eye on Shade, he glanced around for an escape route. She began moving slowly, deliberately, towards him, her bloodshot eyes contrasting starkly with the pure whiteness of her coat. He looked desperately for a way off Eagle Peak's summit.

He tried to reason with her. "Shade you are sick, let me help you."

"If you want to help me, pledge your allegiance to Havnar. He is the only one who can save us now." He understood the full import of her words and was deeply saddened. She was in Havnar's power and the only way she could save herself was through his, Swift's, death.

"Shade, please let me leave the mountain and return to my friends."

"I can't do that Swift. I think you know what that would mean."

He steeled himself against an attack, desperate to avoid a bite. She leapt at him and he swiftly ducked down and gripped her throat. She squealed as he dragged her to the ground and pinned her to the rocks. She squealed again and her eyes, Shade's eyes, pleaded for mercy. Sickened by what he was doing, he let go. For a second he saw gratitude in her eyes, then, she bit his leg viciously. Instantly he recoiled. He limped across the peak, searching for the way down.

He stopped at a sheer drop which descended to a bed of rocks a hundred feet below. He swung round. Shade was closing in on him fast. She lunged at him furiously. He leapt aside without a second to spare and her momentum carried her forward. She tried to get a grip on the smooth surface of the rock. She teetered on the edge for a split second, trying to regain her balance, but slid over the edge into the precipice. Her scream cut through him like a claw through flesh, lacerating his soul, and his tears flowed in a cascade of remorse.

Her beauty was unmatched and she had been his friend. He cursed Havnar over and over again, vowing to avenge her death. The wound in his leg throbbed and reminded him of his fate. He thought of Moon and the cubs waiting for him to come home. He had failed them. Havnar had won. Moondreamer had tried to warn him but still he had taken Shade with him. He had failed everyone in Tannon Valley who had put their faith in him. He deserved to die. He staggered to the edge of the precipice that had claimed Shade's life. Her body lay dashed on the rocks, a white speck in the abyss.

CHAPTER 14

His first instinct was to get off the mountain and back to Leaf and Moss before it was too late. He started back the way they had come, his fear of falling diminishing with his haste to get down the mountain. His urge to get to Leaf and Moss drove him like a demon. He remembered that symptoms of rabies did not show for a long time after infection and this gave him hope of getting back to Tannon before he died.

It was almost dusk when he reached the jagged rock where Leaf and Moss waited for him. Subdued by the news of Shade's death they listened in silence to his story. He did not tell them about Shade being rabid. Knowing they had failed and that the journey had been wasted would destroy their morale for the journey home. Once they were home they would want to do all they could for Moon and the cubs when the end for him came. When Swift finished his story they explained how they had hidden in the pine forest to escape Tarn. After this a mist closed in around them and there was no moon to talk by so they slept as best they could in the dampness beneath the jagged rock.

*

Early the next morning they began the journey

home. Moss and Leaf were euphoric but Swift was deeply disturbed by Shade's death and the failure of their mission. She had been used by Havnar but the positive forces of Earthstar had been too powerful for her to overcome. Yet she had helped him in his quest and they had become close. Havnar had taken advantage of her desire for power and turned her into a monster. He mourned her death and prayed for her soul, asking Earthstar to forgive her weakness.

They averaged thirty miles a day and Swift began to think ahead to what they would find in the valley. This did little to improve his mood; he'd had no news of Moon since the springtime and now it was autumn. He was quiet for long periods and Leaf's jokes and Moss' concern over his health got on his nerves. He found himself snapping at them and drove them harder than he knew he should, expecting them to match his pace and travel as far as daylight and the need to hunt would allow.

For Havnar the distance from Eagle Peak to Tannon Valley was immaterial. It was this that drove Swift on until the sight of blisters on Moss' feet persuaded him to stop and rest for a day. By this time they were within a hundred miles of Tannon. Leaf and Moss talked about the valley and how good it would be to see Hawthorn and the others again.

Swift was tense and impatient. "I don't know what you think it will be like when you get back. Do you think Talon's going to give you the run of the place, and Stone invite you to supper?"

"Blimey, consorting with the spirits has done nothing to improve your temper," retorted Leaf.

It was then he decided to tell them the full story. The burden had become unbearable and he could carry it no longer. He hadn't felt well for the past two days but wouldn't admit the worst. When he'd finished, they sat and looked at him, waiting for a sign of a joke or a crumb of comfort but he said nothing more. Moss whimpered like a cub and licked Swift's nose.

Leaf stared at the grass. "It was all for nothing," he said.

They sat silently for a while, taking it in. For Swift it was as though talking about it had made it a reality. He lay down, feeling sick, head thumping. He made Leaf and Moss promise to get Fallow and Moon away from the valley. They watched over him for two days and two nights whilst he mumbled deliriously in the grip of a violent fever. When the fever subsided he lay still and his breathing was almost imperceptible. Moss prayed for his life to be spared.

Leaf began pacing. "This doesn't add up, he would be frothing at the mouth by now if he was rabid. It's nearly two moons since we left the highlands and until four days ago he was as strong as a bison. He must have been, at the rate we've been shifting. I reckon he's sleeping something off. He's over the fever. I'm going to wake him up." He nudged Swift's shoulder and gave him some time to come round before he spoke. "What was it Earthstar said about you dying only by the bite of a wolf?"

"He said, although I will be able to resist death by all other agents, I will not be able to resist it from the bite of another wolf."

"But you said Shade had bitten you in the leg.

That's not enough to kill most wolves, let alone you."

"But Shade was rabid. I'm sure of it."

"That's as may be, but rabies is not the wolf. It's a disease within the wolf."

Moss leapt up and playfully nipped Leaf's ear. He splayed his forelegs and ducked his head, challenging Leaf to chase him. Leaf couldn't resist and soon they were chasing each other's tails in excitement. Eventually they trotted back to where Swift lay. "You've beaten the mad death! How do you feel?" asked Leaf.

"Not too bad. How long have I been asleep?"

"Two days and two nights," replied Moss.

"I've had some frightening dreams. I've seen creatures you wouldn't believe could exist, all shapes and colours. Some lived in barren lands where no trees or plants grow. I saw humans! I didn't like the look of them at all, they carried the pointed sticks that the wolflore speaks of."

"Swift, can we go home now?" asked Moss.

"Moss, my dear friend. Have I not survived the mad death? We can go home now and do what needs to be done."

*

They reached the outskirts of Tannon through Silver Birch Wood. Swift stopped the others. "The wolfrahm will know we are coming, have no doubts about that. We need to make contact with Hawthorn to find out what has been going on, I don't want to go straight to Moon, in case we are followed."

"How do we find him?" asked Moss.

"I think it would be safer if I carried on alone. Earthstar will guide me," said Swift.

"But what if you bump into a wolfrahm patrol?" asked Moss.

"Alone I'll be less likely to meet anyone."

"I agree," said Leaf, "three wolves travelling together would be easy to spot."

Swift left them with orders to find a temporary den site. He decided to visit Antler, an old friend of Hawthorn's who had a den by the river, hoping he would have some information. Not sure of whom he could trust, he tried to avoid meeting anyone. Talon's policing of the valley proved to be very thorough; twice wolfrahm patrols came too close for comfort as he traversed the network of trails that criss-crossed the valley. There was an air of hopelessness about everything, no sounds of cubs playing, no wolves sitting and chatting. Every wolf looked lean and hungry, ribs protruding under lacklustre fur. Sentries had been posted at each junction where two or more of the main trails met. Swift had to backtrack several times, frequently taking to the undergrowth and cutting through shrub to avoid detection.

As he neared the river, the smell of it rekindled memories of his cubhood and a longing for those halcyon days of freedom swept over him and strengthened his resolve to get rid of Talon. Antler's den was situated in a mossy bank beneath the roots of two silver birch trees. Swift approached sniffing the air, ears erect. He was relieved to find Antler at home, gnawing on a yellowed bone.

The old wolf's eyes sparkled with pleasure when he saw Swift and he clambered to his feet. "Swift! We'd given up hope."

Swift smiled. "One thing I've learnt, is never to give up hope."

"It's good to see you."

"It's good to see you, old wolf."

"Come and chew a bone with me."

"Are you sure you can spare it?"

"Ah, you've noticed. Times are hard at the moment."

"Everyone looks so thin. And that bone you're chewing has seen better days."

"Things are pretty bad, the valley is overcrowded and there simply isn't enough food to go round. The whole place is completely out of balance. We're dependent on wolfrahm hunting parties to bring food into the valley, deer and elk won't come anywhere near us. Hunting parties are going further and further afield and to make matters worse the wolfrahm are having the pick of the food. Some wolves are living on berries and mice alone. That's no good for youngsters, they need venison."

"What are wolves doing about it?"

"What can we do? Morale is low."

"We could organise ourselves and take Talon on."

"The best young wolves are taken by Stone for the wolfrahm and they are being well fed and worse, indoctrinated with Talon's philosophies. The message is 'the wolfrahm comes before the family.' What chance does the ordinary wolf stand? There is a curfew after dark and no more than three wolves are allowed to gather in one place at a time."

"Antler, I must contact Hawthorn."

"Haven't you heard? Hawthorn is very ill. He's not expected to live much longer."

"Where is he?"

"Only Mistle can tell you that."

"Is she alright?"

"As far as I know, she's somewhere in hiding in Silver Birch Wood."

An hour later Swift, Leaf, and Moss were on the northern fringes of Silver Birch Wood combing the woods for signs of Mistle. They spread out, calling her name, and before long she emerged from the bracken to greet Swift. They licked each other profusely, tails wagging.

He nuzzled his nose into the thick fur of her neck. "You look tired," he said.

"Is that all you can say after all this time?"

He smiled. "I've missed you," he said.

"I'm so glad you are home cub."

"It's good to be here. How is Moon?"

"She is safe and well."

The relief he felt at those words drained him and he sat down. "Thank Earthstar," he said, his voice just a whisper.

"Are you alright cub?"

"Yes."

"Well there's nothing to be worried about now, you are home safe and well and Moon is fine."

"What about the cubs?"

"They are growing into fine young wolves."

"Where are they?"

"Not far from here. Don't fret cub, you will be with them in a jiff, come on."

They were joined by Leaf and Moss who both made a fuss of Mistle. "My goodness me you all look so lean and fit. We could do with some strong able-bodied wolves about the place. Come on, I'll take you to Moon."

They picked their way through brambles to reach the den's entrance which was well concealed in a shallow bank behind a fallen oak. Moon had taken no chances. Swift hesitated, unable to believe he was home at last. His stomach churned with excitement.

Mistle turned to Leaf and Moss. "Let's take a walk shall we? I can bring you up to date on what's been happening." Swift stood at the entrance to the den, his heart pumping wildly. He felt as though a great weight had been lifted from his shoulders. His family were safe and in a moment he would be with them.

He walked to the den feeling as though he were floating. His voice trembled when he called her name. "Moon, I'm home. It's Swift."

Instantly she was there in front of him her eyes wide with disbelief. "Swift! My love!"

Two steps and they were together, licking each other's faces tenderly. Moon buried her face in the thick fur of his neck. For a moment they were silent, savouring each other's presence. Then Moon cried and he felt her sobs against his body.

He comforted her with gentle words. "It's alright my darling, I'm home. I'm home. I won't leave you again."

When her tears had subsided she looked into his eyes. "Swift, I've missed you so much."

"I love you," he said.

"If it weren't for the cubs I think I... The cubs, do you want to see them?"

He laughed. "Do I want to see them? Nothing could stop me."

She beckoned him into the den. In the half-light he could just make out their shapes. He wanted to lick them, to touch them and make up for the time he had lost. He wanted to feel their warmth as he'd felt the warmth of Beck's cubs. He wanted to tell them that they were safe, that he was home. He turned to Moon and she understood and nodded. He licked the nearest cub, then licked the others. He lay down next to them, licking and nuzzling their warm bodies. Each of them yawned and stretched and bleated for their mother's milk. Then he sensed their anxiety at his presence in the den.

Moon came closer. "It's alright my darlings, don't be afraid, your father has come home."

They eyed him warily and he spoke to them in a hushed voice. "Forgive me for leaving you." The nearest cub licked his nose and he felt relief more than anything.

Moon licked his ear. "Let's go into the daylight

where we can see them and I can introduce you to them properly." She went outside, followed closely by the cubs. The last one was smaller than the others and nervous of him. He followed them out into the sunlight where they lined up in a row next to Moon, the small female cub standing close to her. Moon looked towards the biggest of the three. He was predominantly silver-grey with darker facial markings. His shoulders were broad and he watched Swift with a penetrating stare. "This is Raven, he was the first born. This is Finch." Finch had much more tan fur in his coat and face than Raven and was leaner. "And this is Willow." He noticed her voice soften when she said Willow's name. She was silver-grey like Raven but had Moon's pure white underbelly and chest. His heart could have burst with pride.

He turned to Moon. "Thank you," he said. The next few days were idyllic for Swift. Leaf and Moss visited Hawthorn with Mistle to allow him to spend time alone with his family. At first the cubs were a bit reticent, displaying shyness and some resentment at their mother's attention towards another wolf even though it was their father. But they soon began to accept him when they realised how much he cared for them and their mother.

He understood their caution but was desperate to make up for lost time. It was obvious to him that Raven was the dominant of the three and set out to win his confidence. In no time they were play fighting in the ferns and Finch and Willow soon joined in. The two male cubs were rough and Swift treated them accordingly, but Willow just wanted him to chase her. He was constantly trying to protect her from her two boisterous brothers. She had won her father's heart from the moment he had seen her.

Eventually Moon stepped in to rescue him. "It's time you went out to find some food for your hungry family. You can't spend the rest of your life playing," she joked.

Swift widened his eyes in mock surprise. "You mean I've got to find energy for hunting as well?"

She shooed the cubs into the den for a rest. "Peace and quiet at last," she said, and sat down next to him.

"They're wonderful cubs, Moon."

"Yes and all ours. Swift, I am so happy." She looked longingly at him. "Is it all over now?"

"I wish I could say yes, my love, but whilst Talon is alpha wolf it will never be over."

"Can't we leave here and start a new life somewhere else?"

Swift wanted to say yes to please her but he couldn't lie to her. "Moon, too many wolves are relying on me. How can I desert them?"

"I worry so much about the cubs' future. If we stay here surely they are in danger."

"I won't let anything happen to them, Earthstar is with me now. If we put our faith in him we will survive."

"I don't just want to survive, I want to live. I want to be able to walk freely with my cubs, with you, wherever I please without being afraid."

"You shall my love, I promise. It's only a matter of time before Earthstar's influence will be felt and the ordinary wolf will rise against Talon."

"Oh Swift, I'm sorry to go on, we are back together. Let's forget it all and enjoy ourselves while we can."

"I'll go and find something to eat," he said.

He watched her disappear into the den and he was afraid. He wondered how effective Earthstar's power would be against Havnar. The ordinary wolf no longer believed in Earthstar. For Moon's sake he decided to shut all thoughts of Havnar and Talon from his mind and spend at least one more day thinking only of his family. This was their time and he wanted to enjoy being a father.

He set off on the trail leading to the north-east, knowing he had more chance of finding game away from the valley. Before long he found the tracks of a small herd of roe deer – it was good fortune he intended to capitalise on. Roe deer, being small, were fairly easy prey for a wolf hunting alone. The tracks were fresh and he soon picked up their scent. He ran at a canter, wanting to catch them before they were too far away for him to ferry the meat back to the den before nightfall. As the deer's scent grew stronger he proceeded more cautiously until he sighted them browsing on hazel saplings growing by the trail.

He stood still as though sculpted in wood, obscured by the trees. He watched the deer with rapt attention, deciding on the best approach. He crept forward, neck and tail extended, eyes fixed on the buck nearest him, his whole body tensed like a spring ready to uncoil. The deer were upwind and he got within fifteen yards before they sensed his presence.

For a fraction of a second they were mesmerised by his closeness. Then panic ensued and they bolted in all directions. Swift's concentration paid off, in a flash he closed down on the nearest buck, leaping into the bracken in pursuit. The unfortunate animal had been caught cold and Swift gripped a hind leg in his powerful jaws and dragged him to the ground where he despatched him swiftly with single bite to the neck.

He anticipated his family's pleasure at the first meal he had provided for them. Working quickly, he dismembered his kill and dragged a hind leg to one side before covering the remainder of the carcass with bracken to conceal it from the carrion eaters that would devour it given the chance. He gripped the leg in his jaws and carried it back to the den. Before the sun set he made four such journeys, bringing home more than enough venison for their needs. Moon licked his face profusely whilst the cubs ran around in circles before leaping onto the meat which they consumed hungrily. "They are very hungry," observed Swift, "haven't they been eating properly?"

"It has been very difficult to get enough food. I don't like to leave the cubs alone for too long and Mistle has been nursing Hawthorn."

"How bad is Hawthorn?"

"He's been very ill. It's his heart, Mistle found him collapsed. At first we thought it was too late to save him but he's been so determined to get well because of you, Swift. Waiting for you to come back has kept him alive. I'm sure of it."

"Moon, I must go and see him."

"I know my darling, I understand. This morning I

could only think of myself, you've been away so long but you must go to Hawthorn, he needs you. It is safe, Mistle has made the journey many times." Swift rubbed his head against hers and they said nothing more, content to be together, revelling in each other's closeness as the sun went down. When the light had gone they went into the security of the den.

CHAPTER 15

He woke to the sound of Moss' voice calling his name. He crawled out of the den whilst the others slept on. Immediately he was alerted by Moss' expression. "What is it, Moss?"

"It's Hawthorn."

"What's wrong?"

"I think he's dying."

"Can you take me to him?"

"We'd better hurry."

Swift went back into the den and woke Moon. "Moss is here. Things don't look too good for Hawthorn, I have to go."

"What's happened?"

"I don't know but he needs me."

She nodded. "Give him my love," she said. Swift licked the cubs tenderly then hurried from the den. The two wolves journeyed across the high ground north of the valley, through mixed woodland of ash, birch, maple, and oak. Moss explained to Swift what had happened as they went but Swift found himself refusing to believe it. He wouldn't accept that his old friend was dying just when he needed him most.

They covered the four miles in less than half an hour to where Hawthorn lay on his side flanked by Mistle and Leaf at the entrance to the den. Swift ran straight to him and called his name. Hawthorn could barely lift his head from the ground. Swift was shocked to see how frail he had become. He knelt on his forelegs to get close to Hawthorn's ear. "Hawthorn, is there anything I can do?" He could barely hear Hawthorn's reply, but it gave him hope.

"Swift, your being here is enough."

"There must be something we can get you? Tell me what herbs you need and I'll get them."

"I can feel your strength. Touch my paw." Swift gently laid his paw on Hawthorn's. Immediately he could see that the old wolf had received some sort of charge. His eyes became clearer and he was able to lift his head further from the ground. "There, what did I tell you? It is enough that you are here."

"Thank Earthstar I am not too late."

"Yes, we have a great deal to thank Earthstar for."

Swift felt Hawthorn's paw tense. "What is it?"

"Is Moondreamer still alive?"

"No Hawthorn, he is dead. But how could you know he was dying?"

"It came to me in a dream before you left. That was why it was so important that you went when you did."

"Why didn't you tell us?"

"There was no point, you were going anyway. If you had known there was a chance that Moondreamer would be dead when you arrived, you would have worried, and what good would that have been?"

"How did you know I'd found him?"

"I knew the moment your paw touched mine. You have a power you didn't possess before. A power which gives us all hope. Earthstar has an agent to match Havnar's. Nevertheless we should not underestimate Havnar. His evil is deeply rooted in the valley and he'll stop at nothing to achieve his ambitions. We'll have to plan a pretty good campaign to get rid of him. Even now he will be plotting against us."

"Where do we start?"

"Hawthorn you should rest now," interrupted Mistle.

"No, I'm alright. We should begin by restoring the ordinary wolf's faith in himself. Wolves believe that Talon is too powerful to be stopped because they've never seen anyone successfully oppose him. What they need is a victory."

Mistle interrupted again. "Swift, I really think Hawthorn should rest."

Swift stroked his paw. "Mistle is right, we'll talk some more when you are feeling stronger."

"I feel so much better already but I suppose some sleep would help."

Swift and Mistle strolled a short distance from the den. "How bad has he been?" asked Swift.

"I'm afraid he's been very unwell. It's his heart. But the transformation in him since you arrived is uncanny. Before you got here I would have said he was on his way any minute, but now I'm thinking about what I can get him to eat."

"I seem to have developed a knack of arriving just in time. I swear he is already planning our next move."

"Be careful not to tire him, Swift."

"I shouldn't rely on him so much. He's done his share of thinking for us over the years. It should be left to us younger wolves now."

"Well whilst you younger wolves do the thinking this older wolf is going to do some hunting."

Swift lay, head on paws, thinking over Hawthorn's words, and concluded that once again the wisewolf was right. A victory would demonstrate to the wolves of Tannon that Talon was not invincible. He wondered how he could convince them that working together, they could win.

Moss interrupted his thoughts. "Swift, it's astounding the change that came over Hawthorn. When I left him this morning I thought it would be the last time I saw him alive. How did you do it?"

"I didn't do anything apart from touch his paw and will him to get better. Earthstar did the rest."

"Well I've never seen anything like it."

"I believe Earthstar is channelling his power through me."

"Do you really think we have a chance against Talon?"

"I think we'll have a chance the moment we start believing in ourselves. When we do, we can begin to convince everyone else, that together, we can defeat this evil crippling the valley. What we need is a plan." He turned to Mistle. "Would you and Leaf go back to the den and tell Moon what's happened?"

"Will Hawthorn be alright?"

"I think so."

Mistle nodded. "We'll leave right away."

"Take care."

"Leaf will look after me."

He watched them depart, taking pleasure in the good news they were taking to Moon.

Hawthorn slept for two hours and woke up to find Moss and Swift lying by his side discussing the situation in the valley. "Ah, Swift, you've started making plans, that's good."

"How are you feeling, wisewolf?"

"Oh you don't need to worry about me for a while, put all your energy into defeating Havnar. What we have to do is fight force with force and we can win."

"You seem very confident, Hawthorn," said Moss.

"I am, and you should be too. Through Swift we have direct contact with Earthstar, and we will be able to channel the power of the spirits and provide Earthstar with all the help we can. Tomorrow we begin recruiting some help from the wolves in the valley."

CHAPTER 16

Talking fuelled their confidence and a plan began to take shape, but just as Swift thought they were beginning to get somewhere they were interrupted by Leaf looking hot and dishevelled. His expression made Swift's stomach turn. "Leaf what on earth's happened?"

"It's Willow. Talon has taken Willow."

Swift sat down, his heart thumping as if it would burst his chest. Fearful thoughts raced through his head as he tried to make sense of what Leaf had said. He'd only left them a matter of hours ago. Willow had been playing happily with her brothers. How could Talon have found them? He became aware that Leaf was speaking to him, something about Moon. Yes, Moon, is she alright? He must go to her. He stood up on shaking legs and pushed past Moss and ran as he'd never run before, a single thought in his mind. *Find Willow.*

He found Moon pacing to and fro, eyes red with tears and Mistle desperately trying to comfort her. When she saw him she stopped sobbing and stared at him, her eyes pleading with him to do something. He nuzzled into her and she sobbed uncontrollably. "Moon, I'm going to get Willow back, no one is going to harm her."

"What if it's too late?"

"Moon, it won't be, I'm going now, to the Beech Wood."

"Please bring her back safely," she pleaded.

Swift felt anger raging inside him, he was ready to face Talon and to repay him for all the anguish he'd caused his family. "I promise you my love, I will bring her back."

"Swift, why don't you wait for Moss and Leaf to come?" said Mistle.

"There's no time. I'm going now."

"But what can you do against the wolfrahm? Please wait for the others."

"No. I'm going to bring Willow back." He looked at Moon. "I give you my word I'll bring her home," he said, desperate to comfort her. Moon looked at him through glazed, defeated eyes and said nothing. He left the den site without another word, fighting to control the fury which raged inside him, threatening to destroy his chances of saving his cub. He needed to think clearly now more than at any other time in his life. He forced himself to calm down despite the anger and panic which fermented within him threatening to tear his composure to threads. He travelled at speed on the main trail, his desire to save Willow blinding him to danger.

He forced himself to slow to an even pace to conserve energy. When he reached the ford he encountered two wolfrahm sentries sitting talking by the river. He was on them before they realised what was happening. The nearest wolf, the smaller of the two, he grabbed by the neck and forced to the ground. The other one cowered in shock at the speed and ferocity of Swift's attack. Swift felt the wolf he was holding slump and he released him. The other sentry lowered his belly to the ground with tail between his legs, whimpering in complete submission.

Swift grabbed hold of his neck and forced him lower, placing a paw on his shoulder. Swift growled threateningly. "You are lucky. If you do as I ask, you will live. I have a message for you to take to your master. Tell him Swift is challenging him for the alpha position."

"Talon is not here."

"Where is he?"

"He's at the beaver meadows."

"What about the cub, Willow? Where is she?"

"The alpha wolf has taken her."

"What's happening there?"

"I don't know, some sort of gathering."

"What sort of gathering?"

"I'm not sure, a ceremony of some sort."

Swift was suddenly aware of other wolves coming down the track. He looked up to see Leaf and Moss racing towards him. They arrived, panting for breath. "Thank Earthstar we've caught you in time," said Moss, "it would be crazy to face Talon alone, on his own ground."

"He's not here. He's at the beaver meadows and he's taken Willow with him."

"What are you going to do?" asked Leaf.

"Challenge Talon for the alpha position."

"But Swift, he'll kill you. He's got the strength of a bear, no wolf has fought him and survived," said Moss.

"Moss, he's taken my cub and I'm going to kill him."

"What if you do defeat him? Will Stone and the others recognise you as the alpha?"

"It's the way of the wolf. If I defeat the alpha, then I command."

"What do that lot care about the way of the wolf? They spend most of their time trying to change it," said Leaf.

"That's a chance I've got to take."

"At least let us come with you."

"Alright, but we've got to move fast."

"What about him?" asked Leaf, indicating the wolfrahm sentry.

"He comes with us, I need him to take a message to Talon."

The riverbank at the ford was churned up where the wolfrahm had crossed. Leaf searched amongst the tracks for signs of Willow's tiny paw prints but without success.

"Blimey there must be hundreds of 'em. We won't have any problems following this lot."

They set out at speed for the beaver meadows. Swift glanced up at the sky.

"Leaf, do you think we'll make it before dark?"

"We will if we keep up this pace," replied Leaf.

Swift pushed on, conscious only of finding Willow, and they covered the two miles to the beaver meadows in less than half an hour, arriving just as the moon rose above the trees. The first meadow was deserted but Leaf found fresh wolf droppings and tracks, where the wolfrahm had passed through earlier that afternoon.

Swift left Leaf and Moss to wait for him with the prisoner whilst he went ahead to the next meadow. Moss managed to extract a promise from him not to do anything without consulting him and Leaf first. Swift hurried across the clearing and disappeared into the shadows of the wood, his senses keyed up for the slightest sign of wolfrahm sentries.

After he'd covered about three hundred yards he heard the sound of voices carried on the wind. They became louder as he moved closer and his movements became more cautious, afraid of snapping a twig and alerting a sentry. He worked his way stealthily to the edge of the next meadow. It was a clear night and the full moon had risen above the treetops to illuminate the clearing. Swift was shocked by the sheer number of wolves assembled there. Leaf had been right, the entire wolfrahm was assembled.

Wolves sat or lounged in groups chatting and whispering, most of them just dark shapes in the twilight but he could see the faces of those nearest him at the edge of the clearing. Many were wide-eyed, fearful with expectation. They chattered nervously, intent only on what Talon had in store for them.

He strained to catch a glimpse of Willow but there

must have been a hundred wolves in the meadow and he couldn't see clearly enough. The far side of the meadow was in shadow and the centre partly obscured by the huge boulder which dominated it. The longer he searched the more agitated he became. He began to wonder if the sentry had lied and the fury which had gripped him before returned. He was ready to tear the truth from him when the chatter in the meadow ceased abruptly. Talon had climbed onto the boulder. A pregnant silence fell across the meadow, broken only by an owl hooting its eerie call someway off in the distance. The scene was set for Talon's invocation of Havnar. Swift felt the hackles on his back rise.

Talon raised his muzzle to the moon. He gave out a piercing howl. Loach and Stone climbed up beside him, each raising his muzzle to the sky, to howl in the same high-pitched way. Every wolf in the meadow joined them until the noise was deafening. The cacophony reached all corners of Tannon Valley and beyond. Talon, head and shoulders above Loach and Stone, was a dark silhouette stark against a moon which seemed to be bigger and more brilliant than Swift had ever seen it before. The howl took on a lusting, hysterical note, losing any trace of melody it had, depriving it of any beauty and instilling it with an evil quality that stirred fear in Swift's stomach.

Swift witnessed Talon's absolute dominance of the wolfrahm, when every wolf ceased howling the instant the alpha wolf stopped. The silence which followed was uncanny. The light in the glade had increased, subtly illuminating Talon's features, and Swift saw a glint of triumph in his eyes. Assured of his subjects' rapt attention, he began his address.

"Wolves of Tannon Valley, tonight we are gathered here in an attempt to secure the future of the entire wolf species. We are under threat from human expansionism which will force the wolf from his traditional territories into the wastelands and deserts. There is only one spirit who will give us the power to resist and prevent this disaster and that is the spirit Havnar who is alpha of the universe. He has, through me, committed himself to the cause of the wolf. He will put at our disposal the negative powers of the universe if we bring him here incarnate tonight. You will put aside your personal fears and stand firm as we invoke his presence in Tannon Valley. If you pray with me from your hearts he will hear our appeal. You will repeat these words after me.

"Almighty Havnar, spirit of nature, you are the true spirit revered by all wolves. With your guidance the wolf nation will be victorious over all others. You have recognised the wolf as the prime species on earth and for this we are eternally in your debt. Give us a sign that you hear our appeal."

Talon threw his head back and sent another howl towards the stars. Loach raised his paw as a signal for the wolfrahm to assist the evocation. Again the air was filled with a cacophony of howling but this time more discordant and restrained. Five minutes elapsed before Talon was done and the unnatural silence restored.

Swift smelt the tension amongst the wolfrahm as they waited for Havnar's sign. He shivered, suddenly it was cold. The moon seemed to loom larger in the sky, spreading its silver light across the meadow. In its rays Swift saw the beginnings of a wispy mist appear as the air cooled rapidly. The mist crept inwards from the periphery of the meadow.

The shape of a huge wolf's head began to form in the mist which rose in the air beyond Talon, its density fluctuating from vapour to near solid. Its fluctuating form gave it life and the wolfrahm shrank back from it. Then there was a voice which had a distant quality, as though someone was calling from far away. At first the words were garbled and Swift could not make them out but gradually they became audible as the giant wolf's head solidified, causing gasps among the astonished wolfrahm.

"Talon, my servant, your lord Havnar is ready and willing to descend to Tannon Valley. Yet I am prevented. You have not shown me well enough that I am welcome. There are those among you who are not committed and one who defies me. They must be sought out and destroyed. Destroy all those who lack faith in my mission to make the wolf supreme and I shall come among you. How can I help you when I don't possess your mind and soul? This is the price of your survival. If you are not willing to pay then you are damned forever. What have you to say, alpha wolf?"

"As your servant on earth I have tried to prepare the way for you, almighty lord. I have always done as you have asked."

"Have you provided me with a body that I might enter? The body which I need must be young and without disease, made up of youthful cells. It must be the body of a cub. You have failed me, Talon. You have not prepared the way for me. There are doubters among you."

"Lord Havnar, I am your servant. I have done my utmost to prepare for your incarnation on earth. Tell me what more I should do."

"I have heard enough words. It is time to act. You must provide me with the blood of a newborn cub. This cub shall not have seen the cycle of three moons. I need the cells of his blood and his bones to bring about my transition to earthliness. It must be done now. My power is stretched to the limit, do as I ask and I can join you. Together we can rule. Fail me and the opportunity will be lost, and you will rue this day forever."

Swift's heart began pounding. He watched, stunned, as Stone exchanged words with Talon. He watched as Talon leapt from the rock and spoke to several wolves close by. Six wolves followed him from the glade. Swift suddenly realised that Willow was not in the beaver meadow. He forced himself to keep calm. If he kept his wits about him there may be one chance to save her. Swift could not believe his luck. Talon had taken so few wolves with him. He, Leaf, and Moss could take them by surprise and free Willow.

Talon went east from the beaver meadow at a fast trot. The farther they got from the glade the happier Swift felt. It would take time for reinforcements to reach Talon. Twenty minutes later he turned off the track and entered a thicket of silver birch, his retinue close behind. Swift led Leaf and Moss silently toward the thicket. A small clearing lay in the middle of the birches and Willow was there. Swift watched Talon pick Willow up in his huge jaws by the skin of her neck. He carried her across the glade. Swift prepared himself for an attack when the strangest thing happened.

Talon placed Willow on the ground and called to Swift. Momentarily, Swift did not know what to do. Talon called him again. "Swift, come and take your cub." Swift's mouth hung open in disbelief. He glanced at Moss and then Leaf, who shrugged, and looked mystified. "Swift, I know you are there. Come out and take your cub while there is still time."

Swift took a step forward but Leaf cautioned him. "Be careful, it could be a trap."

"How do I know this is not a trap?"

"You'll have to trust me. Our differences can wait until another time."

Swift stepped into the clearing, his eyes fixed on Talon. He moved slowly towards Willow, who wagged her tail excitedly when she saw him. Swift looked her over to make sure she hadn't been harmed then picked her up in the same way Talon had. Talon spoke again. "Take her and leave the valley or I will hunt you down as a traitor."

Despite the threat Swift felt grateful to Talon at that moment for sparing his daughter's life. He didn't feel safe in the clearing and wanted to get away quickly. He gripped Willow tightly between his teeth and turned away without a word, making his way through the silver birches to the main trail followed by Leaf and Moss. He went as fast as he could, trying not to make things to uncomfortable for Willow, his heart soaring as he relished the prospect of returning her to Moon, his feelings tempered only by the thought of what might have been.

CHAPTER 17

It was just before dawn, the moon had long since disappeared behind clouds borne by a north-westerly wind which had blown up suddenly. Birds sang their morning song and daylight slowly penetrated the forest's gloom. Talon had not slept, he had spent the night trying to come to terms with what he had done. Returning Willow to Swift had broken the spell in the beaver meadow and he had abandoned the ceremony and returned to the Beech Wood.

He sat on the brow of Beech Hill, the cold north-westerly ruffling his fur. He knew he had compromised his relationship with Havnar but was unsure of how much damage he had done. He regretted the whole incident, and cursed himself for not foreseeing it. He had taken Willow on Stone's advice to use as a hostage to lure the rebels to the Beech Wood. He had been enchanted by her the moment he had seen her and made sure she was not harmed or frightened. His liking for her was something which had surprised him. He was not normally around newborn cubs, by the time they reached the wolfrahm they were bigger and more independent.

He had not expected Havnar's request for a sacrifice, and until he reached Willow in the glade, he had not known that he would let her go. Havnar had tested the depth of his commitment, and he had failed. Perhaps all was not lost and he could redeem himself. Whatever happened he would not give up on the alpha position. There was no one else capable of holding the wolfrahm together and controlling the valley. Only he knew what must be done to stop the two-legged creatures from usurping their island.

He needed to find out where he stood with Havnar. He got up and shook himself to remove the leaves and twigs clinging to his fur. He trotted through the Beech Wood towards the giant yew, the husks of beech mast crunching under his paws. He noted where the earth had been turned over by a wild boar that had foraged for fallen beech mast during the night. Overhead, he heard the wing beat of a pigeon and looked up to see a sparrow hawk pursue it through the trees.

When it came into view he focused his attention on the giant yew growing in the centre of the Beech Wood, a complete contrast to the tall grey-barked beeches. The huge girth of its reddish-brown trunk accentuated its squat appearance. It appeared darker than usual against the copper-coloured leaves of the surrounding beech. As always, it made Talon feel uncomfortable.

He could not feel Havnar's presence, it was as if the spirit had never occupied the tree. He sensed a prayer would be wasted. He was undecided about what to do; he had become accustomed to Havnar's guidance. The act of praying was usually enough to get him what he wanted but he knew it would be futile this morning. His feeling that he could successfully patch things up was replaced by one that he was losing control. Whenever he felt like this he did something. Anything was better than believing his destiny was left to fate.

He looked up into the branches of the yew. It seemed somehow malevolent. The hackles rose on his neck and he took a step back, fear stirring in the depth of his stomach. Instinctively, he growled as wolves do when they are afraid. Fear was a feeling that he wasn't used to and he didn't like it.

He turned his back on the yew in defiance and trotted back towards Beech Hill to organise the wolfrahm. Swift must be hunted down and eliminated. It could be the only way to appease Havnar. He woke up Stone and ordered him to assemble the wolfrahm. Soon a hundred wolves awaited his orders beneath the beeches. He had Stone brief them and assemble them in patrols of six.

Stone and Talon took a patrol each. Talon ordered Loach to join him. He waited and watched Stone lead his wolves down the slope, wanting to make sure that every wolf left to take part in the hunt. He watched the black wolf and his patrol disappear through the holly bushes. When he was certain that every wolf had gone he led his patrol down the slope. The wind had dropped and the Beech Wood was still, the only sound the crunching of leaves and twigs beneath the paws of the patrol.

They passed through the holly bushes and through the short stretch of woodland to the ford. The river flowed lazily, carrying leaves which had fallen in the wind that morning. Talon was about to enter the water when he heard a twig snap. He swung round and looked back towards the holly bushes. Stone and his patrol were trotting down the path.

"Stone, what are you doing? Why haven't you crossed into the valley?"

"I have business to attend to here."

"I ordered every wolf to hunt for Swift and that includes you."

Stone grinned sardonically. "It would seem that I am no longer obeying your orders."

"You had better be jesting, Stone."

Stone dropped the smile. "It's no joke. In fact none of us will be obeying your orders in future."

Talon scanned their faces. "What's going on here? If this is mutiny you'll be sorry."

"It won't be us who will be sorry, alpha wolf."

Loach had lowered himself submissively, ears flattened, and was backing away along the river path. Two wolves blocked his retreat. He whimpered like a cub. Stone growled.

"Don't waste your energy on that." They stood back to let Loach through and he scuttled off down the river path with his tail between his legs.

Talon took advantage of the distraction and rushed Stone. Stone stood his ground and they tore into each other, biting viciously, tearing at each other's flesh. Talon forced the black wolf down. Snarling, they rolled over into the mud along the riverbank. Stone pulled himself free and the other wolves closed in on Talon. Stone shouted encouragement to them. He had chosen the patrols carefully and there were twelve wolves facing Talon. Talon flew at them furiously, killing the nearest with a spine-crushing bite to the neck. The others attacked him savagely, inflicting bites on his head, neck, and flanks. He turned this way and that, trying to fend them off. He sank his teeth in many times but was sustaining serious injury. Stone had chosen heavy, well-muscled wolves. Although none were the size of Talon the weight of numbers began to tell.

Stone stood back and watched Talon repel several attacks. The air was full of snarling and yelping and several of Stone's wolves lay bleeding in the mud. Thorn had survived two counter attacks but his luck ran out when Talon splintered his foreleg with a savage, crushing bite. The grey and tan wolf lay on the ground squealing. Unnerved by this, the other wolves backed off. Talon's blood poured from several wounds, matting his fur.

Stone attacked before Talon had a chance to draw breath but Talon was still faster, swerving away in time to avoid Stone's lunge for his throat, instead Stone bit into the top of Talon's foreleg. Talon fell, unable to support his own weight. The wolfrahm moved in to finish him. It was then that he conceded defeat.

He summoned the remainder of his strength and tore himself from Stone's grip. He scrambled towards the river's edge and threw himself in. The cold water revived him and he found fresh reserves of strength. He struck out for the far bank, the water around him stained red with his blood. He heard a splash as a wolf jumped in behind him.

The current forced him on a diagonal course in his attempt to reach the opposite bank. When he reached halfway his energy began to seep away with his blood and he drifted downstream. He was still making progress across the river but it was slow. He had to get out soon if he was to stem the flow of blood from his wounds.

He glanced back. A powerful-looking grey wolf, with a tan muzzle, was gaining on him rapidly. He kicked harder, gritting his teeth against the pain in his foreleg. He had to get across first. Eventually his paws touched the river bed. He winced as pain shot through his foreleg when he gained a foothold. He had drifted downstream some way past the ford and there was no convenient depression in the bank to help him exit the water. He put his forelegs on the bank and steadied himself, summoning the rest of his strength. He pulled himself up, dragging his hind legs onto the bank.

He lay on his side, panting, trying to steady his racing heart. His pursuer was less than five yards from the bank. If he let the wolf ashore he was finished. His only chance was to attack him when he tried to get a foothold on the bank. He climbed unsteadily to his feet. When he was sure of his balance he moved close to the riverbank, anticipating where the wolf would land. The wolf changed direction and swam downstream. Talon followed to block him again. The wolf tried to land but Talon was ready for him. As he put his forepaws on the bank, Talon bit him on the snout. The wolf recoiled and fell back into the water yelping. When he'd recovered sufficiently, he retreated downstream.

Talon could not afford to use energy in pursuit, so he turned away from the river. There was bracken on the far side of the river path; although browned and wilting it would still provide cover. He no longer worried about the trail of blood he was leaving, he just wanted to lie down and rest.

CHAPTER 18

Hawthorn heard the barking from as far away as the Bluebell Wood. It sounded like a pitched battle taking place. Afraid it might be friends in trouble, he took the path to the river. He'd gone about a half a mile when he heard a low moaning coming from the ferns growing nearest to the path. He approached cautiously and what he found stunned him. The mighty Talon lay scarcely breathing, bloody and torn in the ferns. When Hawthorn recovered his composure he turned back towards the path, but something stopped him from walking away. The barking became louder and for some reason he glanced back at Talon, who had opened one eye. Without knowing why, he went back to the alpha wolf.

He sat down beside him and spoke quietly. "Talon, can you move?" he asked. The alpha wolf nodded weakly. "You'd better find yourself a better hiding place."

Talon dragged himself to his feet. He wobbled unsteadily at first but managed to stay upright. He was bleeding profusely from a neck wound which would have killed most wolves. Hawthorn was anxious to get him away from the path to a hiding place he knew, not far from where they were. If he could get him there quickly, there was a chance he wouldn't be found.

Talon stopped every few steps to rest, and each time, Hawthorn thought he would topple over but he seemed to have strength in reserve. Eventually they reached a hollow concealed by bracken but Talon's wound had left a trail. Hawthorn did not hold out much hope until Earthstar intervened. It started to rain. First a few drops, then torrents to wash all traces of Talon's spilt blood into the earth. Talon was scarcely breathing now and Hawthorn knew that if he didn't act swiftly the alpha wolf would die. He still couldn't understand why he didn't leave him to his fate. He searched for a dock leaf to press on the wound but was hampered by the rain's ferocity.

It was imperative the flow of blood be stemmed because the alpha wolf would rapidly develop hypothermia as shock set in. He searched systematically round the hollow for something capable of staunching Talon's wound. He found a clump of dock leaves and tore several out with his teeth. It was still raining hard and water began to collect around Talon's body as it drained into the hollow. Talon's eyes were closed and his breathing shallow. Hawthorn placed the dock leaves over his wound and held them in place with his paw. He prepared himself for a long wait, making himself as comfortable as possible.

Despite heavy black clouds which appeared to touch the treetops, the rain stopped as abruptly as it had begun. He needed to collect various herbs that would assist the healing process after he had stemmed the flow of blood. If he failed to do that, then the herbs would not be needed. Half an hour passed before he managed to control the bleeding but it seemed like an eternity to Hawthorn who had become cramped, and stiff, in the damp and the cold of the hollow.

He released the pressure on the dock leaf and checked Talon's breathing – it was still shallow but less strained than before. Hawthorn tried to work out why he found it so important to save the alpha wolf's life. He felt like a traitor to Swift, and the others, but he could not walk away. It was as though he was under someone else's control.

The bleeding had stopped but there was a long way to go before the wound healed completely, and Hawthorn worried about it becoming infected. He decided to look for some fennel to counter any infection. He soon located some and carried it back in his teeth. Talon's condition was unchanged. For a second Hawthorn thought he was dead, so feeble was the movement of his chest.

He chewed the fennel thoroughly, mixing it with his own saliva, before smearing it on the wound with his tongue. Realising that darkness was only an hour away, he pulled up fronds of bracken which grew in the hollow and covered Talon's massive body to protect him from the cold. Fortunately the hollow drained well and the water from the morning's deluge had soaked away. With luck, if the temperature did not drop by too much his patient might survive.

The day's activities left him ravenous and he began searching for wood mice and voles which were abundant in that part of the forest. He caught two mice and a bank vole which was enough to take the edge off his hunger. He settled down close to Talon, pressing his body against the alpha wolf's to keep him warm. He did not sleep. The consequences of keeping Talon alive haunted him. He was sure Talon would not rest until Stone had been punished and he had restored himself to power. This would mean a bloody conflict in the valley. But how could he sit by and watch another wolf die when he had the knowledge to save him? After all, Talon had returned Willow to Swift unharmed, when he could have sacrificed her to Havnar.

Talon developed a fever and suffered bouts of delirium and the succeeding days were filled with constant hunting and nursing which tested Hawthorn's failing strength to the limit. He made many trips to the river to soak a hare's skin with water to squeeze on Talon's tongue. When possible he hunted, catching the odd mouse or vole which barely kept him going. The fennel seemed to be doing its job, so he made a fresh application each morning.

On the fourth day Talon's fever subsided about noon, and he opened his eyes. Hawthorn was about to devour a freshly caught wood mouse when he felt Talon's malevolent glare. For a moment they stared at each other.

Talon broke the silence. He spoke in a hoarse whisper. "Who asked you to interfere? You should have left me to die."

"I couldn't. You saved Willow."

"I saved the cub and now I am finished. You should have let me die."

"It's not Earthstar's will. Without his help I couldn't have saved you."

"What does Earthstar care for me? My allegiance is to Havnar."

"It's never too late to change. Where was Havnar when you needed him? I think he was using you for his own ends."

"I was using him to save the wolf from extermination, but you wouldn't understand that."

"It doesn't look as though you were succeeding. Wolves are starving to death because of your policy on hunting. There isn't enough game to go round."

"I never said it would be easy."

"You never said anything. You just took it all on yourself."

"No one would have listened, all too narrow minded and lazy. Let's live for today and forget tomorrow. Well that won't do anymore. Those days are over for the wolf. You've heard the stories about the two-legged creatures."

"There are no two-legged creatures in the island forests."

"Don't be so sure. Havnar has told me of how they are spreading everywhere, disrupting everything."

"But how would they get here? We are surrounded by water."

"And how do you know that?" Talon replied contemptuously.

"It is said in the wolflore."

"Pah! Mumbo jumbo. There is no room for the wolflore in the new order. The wolf has to learn to live without it, learn to do things differently."

"The wolflore has stood us in good stead for thousands of years. Didn't Tannon lead us to the valley because of its teachings?"

"Tannon led our forefathers here because of the drought and because he'd heard stories of the two-legged creatures, who even then were killing us with sticks and stones."

"The fact still remains that you are expecting wolves to live in a way which is totally alien to their nature, and I don't think it can work. You've destroyed the natural balance in the valley."

"Can't you get it through your thick skull? The natural balance of things is being destroyed wherever the two-legged creatures turn up. We must organise ourselves and resist them or we are doomed."

"You are obsessed with them, and Havnar has used your obsession to infiltrate your mind and blind you to everything else."

"It is Havnar who has warned me of the dangers which threaten us."

"Havnar has fed your obsession, because it suited him."

Anger flashed in Talon's eyes. "Ignore the warnings at your peril, you stupid old fool!" he shouted.

Hawthorn changed the subject. "What do you intend to do when you have recovered?"

"I don't know, I have a lot of thinking to do."

"If Stone has control of the wolfrahm then your life will be in danger."

"You let me worry about Stone."

"Stone is cunning, don't underestimate him."

"Stone is vermin and I will kill him for what he's done."

"You can't do it alone. Don't you realise that when you handed Willow back to Swift, Havnar dropped you, like a dead branch falling from a tree? The black wolf is alpha now."

Talon's eyes darkened; he turned away and stared into the distance. Hawthorn had never been so unsure of himself. Swift and the others had suffered so much, if he told them about Talon surely they'd want to kill him. He could only conclude that Earthstar wanted Talon alive, but whatever happened, Talon must never be allowed to take the alpha position again. He had been ousted once it would be unlikely to happen for a second time.

Hawthorn went in search of food, his thoughts flitting from one possibility to another, throwing his mind into turmoil. In desperation he whispered a prayer to Earthstar for guidance. Unable to clear his head he returned to the hollow to sleep on his problems, hoping Earthstar would provide the answers whilst he slept. He didn't wake Talon but left a meal of three wood mice beside him for when he woke up. He pulled up more bracken to protect his patient from the nightly drop in temperature then curled up next to him to keep him warm.

Try as he may, he could not sleep. He had noticed a subtle change in Talon's attitude over the last twenty-four hours – he seemed less depressed and more assertive. There were long periods of quiet when Hawthorn sensed he was planning rather than brooding. He was coming to terms with his decline, as his mind grew stronger and his body mended. Once Talon was on his feet he would not be able to restrain him. He had to contact Swift. He was certain that it was Earthstar's wish that Talon should live, but he still could not understand why. He thought over his conversations with the alpha wolf. Talon had talked about the wolf species as though he really cared about its future. Hawthorn found himself wondering whether some of the controls Talon had imposed might be necessary.

CHAPTER 19

Willow's reunion with her family had been a time of great joy and thanksgiving. Moon indulged her and she had not left her mother's side since she'd returned. Mistle occupied the two male cubs as best she could with hunting trips looking for mice and squirrels. Swift and the others hunted elk, red deer, and wild boar. They stayed within howling distance of the den and instructed Mistle to howl at the first sign of trouble. He had heard about Talon's overthrow and knew he should be taking advantage of the split in the wolfrahm, but would not contemplate leaving Moon and the cubs. He was determined not to return to the valley until he had moved his family further north. They had already moved to an abandoned badger's sett about a mile from the old den but they would not be safe if the wolfrahm mounted a thorough search for them.

He'd caught two hares which he was about to take back to the den when he saw Hawthorn trotting along the main trail nearby. This was one occasion when he wasn't pleased to see him; for a split second he considered ducking down out of sight into the bracken but his love for the wisewolf got the better of him. Besides, Hawthorn would have news of the valley which he would be foolish to ignore.

He called after the wisewolf as he turned away from the den. "Hawthorn, wait, it's me."

The wisewolf looked back over his shoulder, his relief evident when he saw Swift. The two friends rubbed muzzles and licked each other's faces.

"Swift, I'm so pleased to hear about Willow, it's a miracle."

"Earthstar smiled on me that day."

"How are you and Moon?"

"We're fine, come and see everyone."

"Alright, but before we go I've something important to discuss with you."

Swift sighed. "Is it about Talon?"

"Yes."

"I was afraid it would be."

"I know how you must feel, Swift. You deserve to be left alone with your family, but Talon is still alive."

Swift's voice was flat with resignation. "Where is he?"

"He's in the valley, badly injured, but he is making a good recovery."

"You know where he is?"

"Yes, I've been looking after him."

Swift's eyes flashed angrily. "You've been looking after him, after what he's done?"

"I'm sorry, Swift. I had to do it. Don't ask me why, my head said leave him, let him die, but I did what had to be done to save him."

Swift was still angry. "Hawthorn, your judgement is deserting you. Ridding ourselves of Talon is the first step towards getting back to normal."

"I don't think we can ever do that in Tannon Valley or anywhere else."

"I don't understand. Has Talon turned your head?"

"I believe its Earthstar's will for Talon to live."

"But why? Talon is his sworn enemy."

"Havnar has deserted him. He is alone."

"And that's exactly what he deserves."

"I understand how you feel but don't forget, Talon kept Willow from being harmed. He showed another side to himself and I believe Earthstar wants us to see this." Swift shook his head in disbelief. "Please Swift, think about what I've said."

Swift looked up towards the sky and shouted his anger. "Why doesn't he tell us what to do?"

"The spirits can't make decisions for us, they can only guide us, and I believe Earthstar is saying talk to Talon. Go back to Moon and talk it over with her."

Swift felt the weight which had lifted when he had found Willow return to his shoulders. He didn't want to bring the subject of Talon up in his den ever again; he dreaded mentioning his name to Moon.

He placed a hare at Moon's feet and tossed another to the cubs, who leapt on it and proceeded with a game of Tug O' War. He didn't eat but watched Moon and tried to think of how best to say what he had to say. He could tell she had noticed his change in mood. He hated himself for bringing more problems to her. "What's troubling you, my love?" she asked when she'd finished eating.

"It's Talon, he's still alive thanks to Hawthorn and now he wants me to speak to him."

"Perhaps that's not such a bad idea."

"After what he's done to us!"

"He handed Willow back to us unharmed."

"But don't forget he took her in the first place."

"What are you going to do? Kill him?"

"If I have to. Yes."

"What, in cold blood?"

"Moon, I will do what is best for Tannon Valley."

"At least talk to him."

"I'm not going anywhere for the moment."

"Let him come here, show him what we have, and tell him what we and the majority of the wolves in the valley want. Make him see sense."

"Bring him here!"

"Yes, talk to him. Make him see sense," she repeated.

"Alright, perhaps you are right, it's just that I don't want to spoil things for us."

"Nor do I Swift, but we can't cut ourselves off from what's been happening."

"Moon, I dream about the time when peace will be restored in the valley. I see the valley bathed in sunshine and wolves hunting and playing without fear. Parents teaching their cubs the wolflore, knowing it will stand them in good stead all their lives. It is something I am prepared to fight for, but I don't want to lose you in the process."

"You won't lose us, my darling. The cubs and I will go somewhere safe until you are ready to come for us. Talon's grip on the valley has been broken and Earthstar's power is with you."

"I hope I can repay your trust."

"We'll talk to Talon in the morning. Come on, let's get a good night's sleep."

Swift did not sleep well. His sleep was fitful, punctuated with bad dreams until he woke about an hour before sunrise. He snuggled in close to Moon, who was sleeping deeply. He had resigned himself to Talon coming to the den but could not relax. He kept checking the cubs to make sure they were alright. He wondered how Willow would react to seeing Talon again. He wondered at his own sanity; all he loved dearly lay in the den and he had invited a viper to visit. He would be ready though, one sign of physical aggression from Talon and he would kill him without hesitation.

*

At daybreak he was up, sitting at the entrance to the den. Every now and then he paced to and fro, looking out for signs of Talon's arrival. He took several deep breaths in an attempt to stay calm. Talon had become a monster who had haunted his life and now he was about to meet him on equal terms. He was close to calling the meeting off when he remembered the alpha wolf laying Willow at his feet. He hadn't forgiven him for Willow's abduction but he couldn't deny his gratitude for her safe return.

At last they came through the bracken, Hawthorn closely followed by the huge figure of Talon who dwarfed the wisewolf, standing head and shoulders above him. They walked slowly and he noticed Talon limped slightly on his right foreleg. He met the gaze of the alpha wolf, whose eyes still held a glint of pride. The two wolves stopped a yard from Swift, who could sense tension between them.

Hawthorn spoke first. "Talon has agreed to discuss the future of Tannon Valley with you, Swift." The two wolves looked at each other in silence. Hawthorn tried again. "If our differences are to be resolved we have to talk. It's the only way. Talon, have you any questions for Swift?"

"Yes, I have a question for him. I want to know why he has persistently opposed the forces of law and order in the valley."

Despite his rising anger, Swift kept control. "What I opposed was disorder and the use of force."

"I introduced the controls needed to bring the wolf into a position of strength."

"The wolf has always been strong. We had everything we needed in the valley. There was no reason for change."

Talon almost shouted his reply. "No reason to change! There is every reason to change. You know of the creatures who carry sticks and stones. They are close to our shores and their advance must be stopped at all costs."

"They can never reach us here, the wolflore says our forests are cut off by water."

"Pah! I have already had this argument with Hawthorn. I know what is happening. Havnar has told me but you won't listen. I've had to bring control and discipline to the valley."

"You are being used by Havnar."

Talon's hackles rose. "I have allowed Havnar to use me, as you put it. If we do not welcome him, he will go to the creatures who stand on two legs, and where would the wolf be then?"

Hawthorn interjected quickly. "Please, both of you sit down. I know you don't agree but at least you are hearing each other's point of view and that's a start. It has become obvious to me, that despite your differences you have one interest in common, the future of the wolf nation. I'm asking you to put your differences to one side and concentrate on improving things in the valley. Swift, I know the sacrifices you have made. Talon, what about you? Are you prepared to make sacrifices?"

"Where is the point? We don't see eye to eye on anything, how could we possibly work together?"

Swift scowled. "I could only agree to work with him if his attitude to the ordinary wolf changed, and the wolfrahm were disbanded."

"At the moment I'm not in a position to disband the wolfrahm. Anyway, I think a trained fighting force is essential to the defence of the valley."

"What you've spawned is a personal body-guard trained to oppress free thinking."

Hawthorn interjected again. "We may have to compromise. Why not have a fighting force of volunteer wolves?"

"It's no good waiting for volunteers," snarled Talon, "the wolfrahm have to be trained from cubhood."

"Perhaps we shouldn't make these decisions alone," said Hawthorn. "Every wolf should have a say."

Talon's face hardened. "That is heresy. I'll have no part in it."

"If you accept the supremacy of the alpha wolf you accept Stone as our leader and the fact that he makes our decisions for us," countered Hawthorn. Talon lapsed into stubborn silence.

"Swift, I think this would be a good moment for Talon to meet Moon and the cubs," Hawthorn suggested.

Swift glanced over his shoulder. Raven and Finch were standing at the entrance to the den. Moon rushed out and hustled them back inside. She stood blocking the entrance and Swift could see she was trying to judge the mood of his meeting with Talon.

"It's alright," he said, "we have been discussing some of our differences." He tried to conceal his contempt but was not sure he had. "Bring the cubs out and show him what a family looks like." Moon called Raven, Finch, and Willow, who were only too pleased to leave the confines of the den. Swift introduced Raven and Finch, then Willow.

Talon gave the hint of a smile. "Ah, how is the

little one?" Willow smiled shyly, showing no fear of Talon. "She is very pretty," he said to Moon.

Moon's eyes filled with tears. "Thank you for returning her safely to us."

"She was not taken on my orders," he said.

Swift was stunned by Talon's remark. He had assumed nothing was done by the wolfrahm without Talon's consent. He said nothing; Talon, as alpha wolf, must take responsibility.

"This is what is important in my life, my family. I want them to live like our forefathers, free from fear, hunger, and oppression. Is it wrong to want this?"

Talon continued to watch Willow as he replied. "The wolf cannot have these things indefinitely without organising himself, and exercising self-discipline. If we think only of this moment without planning for the future then what will become of Willow's children?"

"What makes you so sure our future is threatened?"

"The Lord Havnar has shown me. In my dreams he has transported me to far off places where I have seen the creatures he calls man. They live everywhere in greater numbers than the wolf. They carry sharp stones on sticks which travel through the air. They steal the wolf's food and murder his cubs."

"Why did Havnar choose to show you this?"

"To persuade me to enlist his help."

"But what does he care for the wolf?"

"Havnar acts because Earthstar does nothing. Yes,

he has a price, but surely we must be prepared to pay something for our supremacy."

"If what you say is true, I agree something has to be done, but Havnar's price is too high."

Hawthorn coughed. "If I may remind you, Talon, it would seem Havnar has deserted you in favour of Stone."

"I'll have my revenge. Stone will not remain alpha wolf for long."

"And you think Havnar will give you another chance?" asked Hawthorn.

"I am the only wolf who can bring about his incarnation. Stone is a fool."

"Havnar has already shown that you are dispensable, so why not face reality? If you really want to help the wolf, join forces with us and oust Stone, disband the wolfrahm, and set up a council of wolves to take its place." They waited for Talon's reply.

"You ask a lot. I need time to think," he said.

"We haven't much time if we're to spoil Havnar's plans."

"Alright, I suppose I haven't got much choice," he said.

Swift stared penetratingly at Talon. "You have every choice," he said. "Unless you show commitment and are prepared to work with us we are not interested in your decision. You think over what's been said and let Hawthorn know your decision. But remember we don't have much time."

Swift sat next to Moon, watching them depart.

Moon snuggled into him and he licked her ear. "Well, how did I do?" he asked.

"You were wonderful," she said.

"Do you think I convinced him?"

"Yes, I think he's a cunning wolf who knows where his best interests lie."

"It'll be a long time before I trust him."

"We'll have to see what happens," she said. He licked her face tenderly.

"In the meantime we'd better prepare to move the cubs, we've stayed here too long."

CHAPTER 20

Swift found a suitable spot for his headquarters and sent Leaf to fetch Hawthorn and Talon. When they arrived he gathered the pack together for its first council of war. They agreed all she-wolves with cubs were to evacuate the valley and all able-bodied wolves to join him on a full-scale assault on the Beech Wood.

In small groups families embarked on their exodus to the safety of the north-western forests. The male wolves stayed with their families until they were beyond the boundaries of Tannon Valley. There, Mistle and her pack of she-wolves who were without cubs took charge, providing them with food and if necessary, protection.

The males doubled back to the Bluebell Wood. It soon became clear as they arrived that there wasn't a clearing big enough to accommodate them all. Swift ordered the relocating of the headquarters to the Beaver Glades, where wolves gathered in groups, friends and relatives sticking together. Leaf counted them and excitedly pointed out to Swift that they now outnumbered the wolfrahm. One hundred and thirty wolves had assembled in the beaver meadows.

This greatly heartened Swift. With the wolfrahm outnumbered victory was possible. Although a trained elite, Swift believed they were no longer well led and well disciplined. He hoped this would be their downfall. He needed to brief his troops. It was essential that they knew what was expected of them.

He gathered Hawthorn, Talon, Leaf, and Moss together. They sat in a semicircle discussing the details of a plan intended to drive Stone and the wolfrahm out of the Beech Wood. Swift planned to split his forces into two groups. One led by him, would cross the river at the ford, for a frontal attack. The other led by Leaf, would cross upstream and engage the wolfrahm from the rear, the brief being to inflict as much damage on the enemy as possible. Swift reserved Stone for himself, hoping to take him out of the battle early, in the belief that wolfrahm resistance would crumble at the loss of its leader. He knew it wouldn't be easy. Stone would relish the terrors of combat.

Leaf's detachment left the clearing first, having farther to travel. Before Swift set off he sniffed at the air to check the weather and noticed something unfamiliar. Small black particles were floating in on the north-westerly wind. He eased his way through the ranks of waiting wolves, their chatter ceasing as attention focused on him. He faced the prevailing wind, ears cocked, and heard a distant roaring. He took two wolves with him and trotted towards the sound.

The roar became louder and a gust of wind blew down thick, grey smoke, engulfing them completely. Swift could barely see the others. Choking on his words, he shouted for them to follow him. He didn't turn back but tried to follow the track, hoping he would find his way through. The smoke stung his eyes and he squinted, trying to focus on the track beneath his paws. Suddenly he was clear of the smoke, but his relief was short lived. Towering flames, high enough to ignite the treetops, were advancing rapidly, consuming everything in their path. The canopy crackled above their heads and flaming branches fell, singeing their fur. Swift glanced back, looking for the others – he called them. Another sudden gust spread flames all around him. His eyes watered in the heat's intensity. He searched desperately for a gap in the crimson wall. When he saw it he didn't hesitate, he sprinted and the heat of the inferno singed his fur as he passed through. He looked back for the others but there was no one with him.

He didn't hesitate but ran back into the ring of flames to look for them. The flames touched him but he felt no pain. He called to his companions. Suddenly they appeared from the smoke, fur singed but alive. He led them to the ever-shrinking gap in the orange ring. He watched them pass through and watched the gap disappear.

A burning branch fell and glanced off his shoulder. It startled him but his fur was not burned. He felt the heat of the flames but he did not cower in fear. He walked slowly to where the others had passed through and entered the flames. He felt them lick at his body but there was no pain; they caressed him and he was not afraid.

He ran back towards the river, but thick, grey smoke reached the pack before he did. Some of the younger wolves who had not experienced fire trembled, hackles raised. He ordered them to retreat to the river and reassemble at the ford, his voice barely audible above the din of barking and the crackle of burning wood.

In the time it took to get to the ford they opened up a gap between themselves and the flames but the wind was gusting toward the river, driving the inferno before it. He looked across to the far bank and back towards the smoke. If they crossed too soon, before Leaf was ready, they would be outnumbered. Besides, his wolves had been badly spooked by the fire, he wasn't sure he could hold them together.

He decided to delay the crossing to the last minute, and hope by then Leaf's detachment would be in position. Several wolves demanded to know his intentions. To calm them, he spread the word that they would soon be crossing the river. The smoke became denser and they felt the fire's heat. He prayed to Earthstar for guidance; if the pack deserted him, the uprising would be lost in the ashes.

Suddenly the wind changed direction, blowing from the south-west, bringing with it clouds the colour of granite. There was a chill in the air and the smoke began to thin. The first drops of moisture fell as a brief warning then the heavens opened, letting lose their water in torrents. Within seconds the pack was drenched. Fur flattened, they bowed their heads under the force of the downpour. Swift felt a surge of hope. Earthstar was with them. If it rained long and hard enough the fire could not survive.

He lifted his muzzle towards the sky and let the rain pummel his face, cleansing and refreshing it. *This is an omen*, he thought. As the rain would defeat the fire and begin the forest's regeneration, his wolves would defeat the wolfrahm and regenerate the true way of the wolf.

The rain lashed down in sheets, turning the ground to water and swelling the river. Swift felt the rain against his skin as it soaked through his fur and chilled his body. When the downpour relented Swift surveyed his bedraggled pack. Some stood and shivered while others ran around celebrating the death of the fire. He wanted to focus their attention quickly and get them moving. He gave the order to cross the river. Although the crossing was hindered by swollen waters there were no casualties. Swift crossed first. He stood on the bank watching and listening for signs of the enemy until the last of his wolves left the river. They shook themselves, shedding the weight of the water from their coats, then Swift gave the order to advance. He led them forward at a canter, shouting encouragement to them. They reached the foot of Beech Hill unopposed and Swift stopped them to take stock.

It was then that the wolfrahm hit them. Charging from behind the trees and out of the hollows, striking on both flanks. It was as though the gates of Falhallen had opened and unleashed its demons of darkness. The rebels were outnumbered and trapped. Swift was knocked off his feet by the attack's ferocity and several of his wolves suffered severe wounds in the opening seconds of the assault. Swift regained his feet and fought savagely, inflicting fatal bites in the throats of two attackers in quick succession. His ferocity deterred other assailants and he was able to help his comrades defend themselves.

When they'd recovered from the initial shock of the attack they fought back bravely. Wolves barked and yelped with pain, fur flew and blood spilled.

Several of the rebels panicked and fled and the rest were losing ground. Swift glanced around but there was no sign of Leaf. A stocky grey wolf with a tan muzzle leapt at him from the side but only managed to grasp a mouthful of his thick mane. Swift wrested himself free and lunged at his startled opponent, who dropped his tail and scurried off through the melee. He caught sight of Stone at the edge of the battlefield making a frenzied attack on a tan wolf called Tooth. He tried to push his way through the fray. A small tan wolf who reminded him of Leaf was on his back, squealing with pain, a big grey wolf pinning him to the ground. Swift grabbed the grey wolf by the neck and dragged him away.

The rebels fought bravely but the odds were heavily against them. Then, salvation – Leaf and his detachment came over the rise of Beech Hill in full flight, barking their arrival. The fighting ceased momentarily as the combatants took in what was happening. On seeing Leaf, the rebels fought with renewed vigour and many of the wolfrahm gave up, cowering to the ground in submission. Others fled, tails between legs. Leaf and his detachment swept through the battlefield giving chase.

The wolfrahm were now outnumbered two to one. Leaf's wolves pursued them to the river where some fled along the river path and others leapt into the water. Still swollen from the rains it swept their battle-weary bodies downstream to death or safety as fortune would have it. Leaf ordered his wolves not to enter the water but to concentrate on catching those who had opted for the river path. Injured wolfrahm were caught and dealt with swiftly. When he could run no more he ordered his wolves to give up the chase. Swift arrived at his side, tail wagging and panting for breath. He licked Leaf's face then howled in triumph. The pack responded, howling in harmony to celebrate and to let the rest of the valley know of its victory.

Swift had mixed emotions, relief and elation at the victory and sadness at the loss of many comrades. He was bitterly disappointed at Stone escaping unscathed, total victory could not be claimed whilst the black wolf still lived. He blamed himself for failing to carry out his plan and allowing Stone to get away. He called his wolves together to organise a search party. When he saw them torn and bloody, his heart ached for them, yet he was filled with pride and admiration for what they had done.

"Wolves of Tannon, today you have won your freedom. Your families will be proud of you. You have fought with great courage and determination. Together we will restore the traditions of the wolf pack and make sure that no wolf can tyrannise the valley again." Exited chatter broke out and he could see that they were high on their success. He shouted above the noise. "I am afraid our victory is not yet complete. The killer Stone has escaped. Before we can rest and enjoy the fruits of victory he must be brought to justice. We will split up into groups and scour the valley until we find him. If he surrenders himself hold him until I can get to you. If you find him and he resists arrest, kill him."

Leaf pushed his way through the pack. "What is it, Leaf?"

"I've been thinking and I'm worried. Stone may try

to get at you through Moon."

Swift felt the hackles rise on his back. "By Earthstar, you could be right. I'm going to find her."

"Who do you want to go with you?"

"I'll travel ahead alone. You organise the pack into smaller groups and send the best after me."

"You'd better be careful. Stone is a cunning weasel."

"If he harms Moon he's a dead weasel."

CHAPTER 21

He crossed the river at the ford and saw the devastation which the fire had left on the northern side. Blackened trunks bereft of foliage had twisted hideously in the searing heat. Charred earth crunched under his feet when he climbed the riverbank and he wondered whether the forest would ever recover. He checked his thoughts, to focus his mind on reaching Moon before Stone did; even the loss of the valley didn't compare with losing her.

He cantered towards the Bluebell Wood through the smouldering remains of once magnificent trees. His lungs ached with exertion as he climbed the outer slopes of the valley. He didn't rest at the top of the slope but pushed on, panting for breath, desperately trying to lose heat. He kept expecting to find the pack around the next bend but it was as if they had disappeared off the face of the earth. He fought off the panic rising in his stomach until he saw the tracks of a large wolf in the mud. He knew the paw prints belonged to Stone and his heart thumped against his chest. He had a sickening feeling that he would be too late. The trail was straight and clear so he pushed himself on, an image of the black wolf etched on his mind.

He gulped deep breaths, desperate to spread oxygen through his aching limbs and quell the panic in his stomach. He sped through the forest, his eyes scanning everything for tell-tale signs that he was getting closer to his quarry. Along the way he passed many junctions which beckoned him but he was not tempted by them, something or someone was guiding him. This realisation encouraged him but he could not shake off the fear that he would be too late.

He heard faint sounds of cubs barking somewhere ahead. He saw a female called Beech where the track forked beneath an oak tree. He asked where Moon was. The she-wolf turned towards a cluster of silver birches a short distance along the left-hand fork. He saw Moon immediately. A movement beyond her caught his eye. In the dusk he could just make out the shape of a large predator inching towards her from the shadows of a juniper bush.

"Moon, look out!" he shouted, but it was too late. Stone had her by the throat, pulling her to the ground.

Swift charged through the birches and leapt at the black wolf, biting him hard behind the ear, forcing him to release Moon, with a squeal of pain. Yelping, he pulled himself free, leaving Swift with a mouthful of fur. Stone's speed and strength surprised him and he was unable to avoid a savage bite to the shoulder. He yelped and Stone attacked him again but Swift dodged sideways, catching Stone off balance with a quick counter attack that knocked him to the ground.

He bit hard, cracking Stone's muzzle. The black wolf scrambled to his feet, squealing in agony, his face swelling immediately. He fled and Swift sprinted after him. Stone twisted and turned, trying to shake him off, but Swift's superior agility rapidly closed the gap. He took several bites at Stone's hindquarters before pulling alongside him. He bit Stone's ear and hung on. Yelping, Stone tore himself free and his ear hung, ripped and bleeding. Swift bit at his jugular, but simultaneously Stone launched a counter attack. Their jaws locked together and they fought with a snarling frenzy. Swift forced him back until Stone lost his balance. As he hit the ground the black wolf's amber eyes were wide with fear but Swift felt no compassion.

He felt no pleasure in delivering the death bite, only satisfaction in knowing that justice had been done. Stone had paid the price for Stag and all the others. Swift wasn't elated by his victory, only relieved that it was all over. Suddenly he was tired, more tired than he had ever been. He wanted to lie down and sleep without fear but before he slept he had to see Moon and the cubs, to tell them everything was alright. Thanking Earthstar for his deliverance he looked down at Stone, then walked away leaving him to the flies.

He wanted to run but his legs were stiff from the chase. He saw Moon and the cubs ahead of him, along the track. When they saw him they broke into a run, shouting with delight. They ran circles around him, tails in the air, barking their delight. When they calmed down he licked each one of them and they walked back to the den together.

Near the den site, wolves lined the track shouting his name, cheering and barking to greet his arrival. He managed a smile but that was all he could muster. He entered Moon's den and lay on his side. Moon lay down beside him and the cubs leapt on him. Moon shooed them off.

"It's all over," he said.

Moon nodded. "Thank you."

"Perhaps at last we can be together," he said.

"Yes."

He rested his head, heavy with fatigue, on his forelegs and slept. He slept long and deeply. When eventually he woke he felt anxious until the events of the previous day filtered into his consciousness. He exhaled with relief and lay down again. The den was snug and he didn't want to leave it. Basking in the cosy solitude he stretched and yawned, and breathed in the scent of his loved ones. He had not lain in comfort like this for what seemed a lifetime.

He heard barking not far from the den, it sounded as though the whole valley was exercising their lungs. He rose reluctantly on stiff legs, and stretched his aching muscles. He peered out from the den's entrance. Every wolf in the valley had lined the edges of the clearing to watch a group of four wolves dragging the body of Stone into their midst. To barks and cheers of approval they dumped the black wolf in the centre of the clearing, his coat soiled with dust and leaves, his face swollen and barely recognisable. Several wolves unleashed frenzied attacks, biting viciously into the corpse.

Suddenly Swift was angry. He emerged from the den to a deafening chorus of barks and cheers. He was moved by the intensity of his reception and by the time he'd reached Stone's body his anger had subsided. The pack was giving vent to years of pent-up emotion and taking revenge for the loss of friends and loved ones. He stood next to the body of Stone and looked at them proudly. They had followed him and taken charge of their own destiny.

"Wolves of Tannon, by your own efforts you are free. In future let us share the leadership of the pack and its responsibilities. Let the decisions we make be considerate of all." He looked down at the mutilated body of Stone. "Let's not degrade ourselves to the level of the wolfrahm. Take Stone's body away and leave it for the scavengers. Let it be of some use at last."

Every wolf had come together in the beaver meadow to celebrate; united, they were unafraid of the leaderless wolfrahm. Leaf organised hunting. Soon there was enough food for everyone, elk, red deer, and even bison. The older wolves told stories of the days before Talon. Leaf told of their adventures in the north and the legend of Swift was born. Everyone called him alpha but Swift would have none of it and so formed a council of elders who would elect a new alpha wolf each year.

This brought him to the question of Talon. He had been valuable in the defeat of the wolfrahm but most wolves hated him. They blamed him for all the ills of the valley. Swift believed Talon had changed and now understood more about the problems ordinary wolves faced, but he wanted Talon's future to be decided collectively by the pack. He intended to allow Talon to speak in his own defence. Every wolf was given notice of this and Swift called an assembly on the morning of the seventh full moon. Wolves chatted vociferously, discussing the fate of the former alpha wolf, and the atmosphere was buzzing. When Talon arrived with Hawthorn the pack fell silent, leaving an air of expectancy. Talon sat next to Swift facing the semicircle of wolves.

Swift addressed the pack. "Wolves of Tannon, today Talon will speak in defence of his actions. I ask you to be tolerant and hear him out before making your judgement."

Talon stood up, his gaze intense. "You have heard of the creatures that carry sticks and stones. They are close to our shores and their advance must be stopped at all costs. I have seen them myself. Their numbers are increasing year by year as they colonise the world. This island is one of the few places left uninhabited by them. They hunt the game wolves hunt, and soon there won't be enough for them and us. I have seen what they can do with their pointed sticks and their fire. If Havnar goes to them with his power there will be no end to the havoc they will cause. One day the earth itself will be under threat of destruction and no creature will be safe. That is why I had to organise the wolf and invoke the spirit Havnar. I know wolves have had to suffer some hardships in my attempts to secure the long-term future, but we can't just live for today and let the future take care of itself. Mark my words, the humans will hunt us down and try to destroy us, pushing us to the far corners of the earth, if you let them. We must make a stand together, to make sure this does not happen."

There was silence save for the sound of a warbler chirping obliviously in the branches of a nearby ash tree. Swift tried to gauge the impact of Talon's words. Some wolves he judged were considering what Talon had said but others waited patiently, their decision already made. Swift asked them to give full consideration to everything Talon had said. An excited discussion broke out and he noted the irony of the situation, glancing at Talon who sat impassively waiting for the pack to make its decision. At length Swift called for silence.

When he had everyone's attention he explained what he wanted them to do. "Those who wish Talon to stay in the valley stay where you are, those who wish him to leave assemble over here."

Some wolves walked quickly past Talon, eyes cast down. Others ambled by, glaring their contempt at the fallen alpha wolf. It soon became apparent that the majority had had enough and wanted to see the back of him. The vote went ten to one in favour of his departure from the valley.

He glared at those who had exiled him. "You may live to regret this," he said. "Your only chance is to organise yourselves into an effective fighting force ready to defend our territory. If you don't..." He stopped speaking and shook his head. With a final glance in Swift's direction he walked dejectedly from the clearing.

Cheering broke out but Swift's expression was grim. He looked at the joyful faces of those around him. Some wolves ran around playfully in celebration like cubs on a first outing from the den. He understood their feelings but Talon's warning lingered.

Moon smiled reassuringly. "What is done is done," she said and licked his face. "Thanks to you."

"Thanks to Hawthorn and Earthstar," replied Swift.

"Where is Hawthorn?"

"He was standing by that beech over there listening to Talon. That's strange, I can't see him anywhere now."

"Perhaps he's gone home. It's something he hasn't been able to do for a long time."

"I'll see if there is anything he needs," said Swift.

He ambled to the wisewolf's den, enjoying the tranquillity. He called Hawthorn but there was no reply. He went in. Hawthorn lay on his side asleep, nursing Talon over the previous few weeks had taken its toll. Swift lay down beside him to keep him warm. Undisturbed in the darkness, his mind retraced the events of the previous twelve moons. Much of it was like a nightmare but he had achieved what he had set out to do, although the cost had been great. He had lost his friends Stag, Roe, and Shade, yet he had met Moon and fathered the cubs. He had been close to death many times but his faith in Earthstar had carried him onwards to final victory. But was it the final victory, he wondered, or the end of the first battle? He didn't want to speculate on this for the time being. He wanted to revel in the valley's freedom and get on with his life. He was tired of making plans and taking decisions. He wanted just to be alive.

Hawthorn stirred beside him. "Who's that?"

"It's only me, wisewolf."

"Swift?"

"I wondered if there is anything I can get you?"

"No. I won't be needing anything more now, thank you."

"What do you mean?"

"I have done all I can. It is time to move on, I am old and weak."

"But surely with some rest and quiet you'll feel better?"

"It's too late for me. It is time to leave things to you younger wolves."

Swift put his paw on Hawthorn's. "Wisewolf, we owe everything to you," he said.

"You did it, Swift. The journey, it was physically beyond me."

"Without your guidance I would never have succeeded." The wisewolf closed his eyes and Swift licked his muzzle. "Thank you wisewolf, may Earthstar honour you in the spirit world."

For a moment Swift lingered, feeling a mixture of admiration and sadness. He left the den knowing it would be the last time he would see Hawthorn alive, just as he had done with Moondreamer. He remembered his cubhood days spent in the wisewolf's company, they were some of the happiest of his life. He regretted bitterly that Hawthorn and all those who had lost their lives would not enjoy the valley's freedom. For this he felt profoundly sad.

The sound of barking interrupted his thoughts and he looked up to see Moon, Willow, Raven and Finch racing along the trail towards him, tails wagging. Here was his future. He had fought for them and they had survived. He would help them live their lives in happiness and contentment, for all those who had suffered for Tannon Valley's freedom.